The Valiant

A Reluctant Hero's Journey from
Tragedy to Triumph

Col. Lee Martin
Mystery Novel

Also by Col. Lee Martin

ETH THIRD MOON IS BLUE

STARLIGHT

THE SIX MILE INN

TEN MINUTES TILL MIDNIGHT

THE MCGOWAN COLLECTION SERIES

ISBN: 979-8-9902075-7-8 (pbk)

ISBN: 979-8-9902075-8-5 (ebk)

Available on bookshelves or through orders at booksellers and Amazon.com

See all McGowan Collection Series on
https://colonelleemartinbooks.com

The Valiant

Table of Content

CHAPTER 1

he color of the sky above Hill 452 had been a deep, rich blue only a half hour before, much like Angelo had remembered on that day when he and Jake had taken that day-long autumn hike along Winnisook in the Catskills. New York City boys they were, chums all through high school who played kickball with one another in the streets of Queens when they weren't hanging out at Gottuso's Deli that not only had the choicest salami in town, but showcased that marvelous Gelato in the store's bins.

Jacobo…Jake, as everyone called him, and Angelo should have been brothers. Folks from the neighborhood knew of course that they weren't. There was hardly a day in the past five years one was not at the other's house. And on any day that the boys may have ventured out of the borough, people who did not know them would speculate they were probably non-identical twins… same shiny raven hair and olive complexion, same black, dancing eyes and same wide, toothy grins.

Their parents, however, did not associate. After all, Jake Dumas' family was Puerto Rican, and Angelo's folks, the Carusos, were very Italian. And that blood did not mix. There had been a kind of cold war between the two ethnic factions in Queens for years, and even blood shed in the streets. Jake and Angelo had avoided the gang pitfall and in doing so, were ostracized by their own kind because of their friendship.

It was on May 30th, 1943, at seventeen and graduating from Woodrow Wilson, they enlisted in the Army. Not only was it the patriotic thing to do, considering the world

1

was now at war with Germany and Japan, but the boys had gotten into a bit of trouble in early May when they were caught by Sean O'Leary using street lamps for target practice. Not only did he confiscate their Daisys, slamming the weapons to pieces against the brick wall on 14th Street, but the legendary Sergeant O'Leary, a six-four giant among New York's finest, 'suggested' that upon graduation they should consider service to their country. "I don't wanna have to hand you over to the court system, boys. So, if you gotta shoot at something, go kill Krauts."

The recruiting sergeant had seen to it they would go through their Basic Training together at Camp Pickett, and then would receive assignments to the same unit. Such promises seldom panned out since recruits were simply 'numbers' and were assigned wherever for the good of the Army. Jake and Angelo had somehow not only stayed together those nine weeks of training, but had deployed together with B Company, 1st Battalion of the 142nd Regimental Combat Team. Now, scantly four months since their last day in class, the day they stuck spit wads fired from their metal peashooters onto the chalkboard only inches from old Mr. Beecher's white head, they faced the business end of three German machine guns positioned to fire at the first pop-up target on Hill 452.

*****

The Fifth Army which had landed on the beach at Salerno earlier in the month under the code name Operation Husky had encountered significant resistance from German elements engaging in a series of retrogrades or fall-back skirmishes. These strategies were primarily intended to draw the allied forces into heavy kill zones where they would be enveloped and massacred. Field Marshal Kesselring, the German commander in Italy, had dug in his forces, making the best use of the rugged mountainous terrain, and making General Mark Clark's Army work for every piece of real estate taken. The Germans had to hold their lines. The bridge on the south rim of the Town of Montevilla, four miles to the north of Hill 452, was key to the Nazi supply line, and the hill was to be defended at all cost. If the hill fell, the town was all but lost.

As Jake and Angelo lay with their backs against the muddy hillside in the shelter of a huge fallen oak, at first they said nothing to one another. They had just low- crawled over a hundred meters uphill and their parched throats had all but silenced their voices. Physically spent and emotionally drained from their rapid ascension half- way up the steep slope, t=hey breathed heavily, sucking in the pungent gray and white smoke from the last barrage of artillery fired by friendlies which had hopefully softened up the German defenders. The haze passing over their faces blotted out the sun and gave the early-September sky the look of winter.

"What...what are you...thinking?" Angelo finally said between pants.

Jake took a few of seconds to get his larynx working again and then spewed out his answer. "I'm thinking... what a couple of assholes we are for enlisting. That's what the hell I'm thinking."

"Well, it was either that or face juvy. Anyway, everybody else was signing up."

"Since when do we care what everyone else does?"

Angelo, lying as flat as he could against the hillside, turned his head and eyes toward Jake and replied, "I guess you'd rather be hanging back with the sick, lame and lazy, facing the scorn of Billy Patton, ol' Blood and Guts' cousin, or Mister Shaunessey, the barber, whose kid went down with the U.S.S West Virginia."

"Let me see...face the nasty looks and contempt from people in the neighborhood or those German pill boxes up there. Pardon me while I take time to weigh that."

Angelo laughed. But the laugh came out fatigued and rankled. He then rotated his tongue around his lips. "What I wouldn't give for an ice cold Ballentine right about now. I'd suck that thing down in about three seconds."

Jake sighed. "What I wouldn't give for about five minutes in the back seat of my old man's Pontiac with Maya Cortez out on Make-out Point."

"You're thinking about sex at a time like this?"

A smile then came over Jake's face. "Man, I'm always thinking about it. I wake up in the morning thinking about her and she's the last thing that's in my mind before I turn it off at night. Just the thought of pressing those enormous bazookas against me...man, I can't stand it." Jake widened his smile into a grin and shook his fists in the air.

"Better keep down, Jake," Angelo warned.

As the two life-long buddies lay still trying to catch their breaths, a heavier, more oppressive cloud of artillery smoke drifted over them, burning their eyes and already tortured lungs, prompting them to place the sleeves of their fatigue jackets over their faces. When the funk had dissipated somewhat, Jake then turned toward Angelo.

"Are we gonna make it through this hell, Ange?"

Angelo blinked his eyes, then stared a hole through what remained of the cloud. "I don't know. Could be our names are stamped on any one of those Gerry bullets up there. I'm just not worrying about it, that's all."

"You're not scared?"

"I didn't say that," Angelo snapped. "But if it happens, it happens."

As the rat-tat-tat of BARs continued off the west side of the slope, they became silent once again, allowing the reality of the impending attack to re-enter their brains. Finally, Jake said, "Promise me one thing, Ange. Promise me that if…you know…I don't make it back home and you do, that you'll tell my mom and dad that I love them."

"Don't talk that shit, Jake. You'll jinx yourself. You go back home and tell them yourself."

Jake's eyes were now intense, even demanding. "Just promise you'll do it!"

Angelo sighed. "All right, all right, I will, okay?"

Jake then turned his eyes back to the sky and took in a deep breath. "They might resent you, you know."

"Who?"

"Mom and Dad."

"How so?"

"That you made it and I didn't," Jake said.

"Yeah," Angelo replied in a near whisper.

"They like you, though; so it may not be all that bad."

"I didn't think they liked me hanging out with you."

"It's actually your wop of an old man they don't like."

"Well, it's your spic of an old man that my old man doesn't like." Angelo then laughed. "Two damn old bastards they are, mired down in their prejudice."

"Yeah. Two old sons-of-bitches."

Both of them, drained and weak with exhaustion, lay on the Italian soil and laughed, long and loud. More than anything, however, it was a laugh that reflected the insanity of it all.

Suddenly, from their right flank, they heard the booming voice of their platoon sergeant, Gary Burns. "Dumas! Caruso! What the hell you assholes laughin' at? You think all this is funny? Check your ammo and get your shit ready to move out! We're goin' up on yellow smoke!"

"God," said Jake. "My stomach feels like it's going to explode. Should have hit the woods back there."

"Then when we rush the hill, keep behind me in case your bowels let go."

"Don't make me laugh or I'll let go right now."

"All right, boys! Yellow smoke is popped!" screamed Burns. "Let's go!"

The artillery now lifted, Company B of the 142nd then sprang from concealed positions on the west side of the slope and charged forward. The atmosphere fiercely erupted with hundreds of deafening M1 pops fired simultaneously. As gunners laid down a base of fire with BARs, men flooded the hillside to converge on the three deadly positions.

Immediately, three, five, ten men near Jake and Angelo were cut down, falling like bricks face down in the mud. Steady streams of machine gun rounds spitting from two bunkers at the top of the hill streaked and tore through the air, whizzing by heads like mad bees, ricocheting into rocks or sadly finding their marks. Mortar rounds flashed and whumped, sending fragments of hot steel into American flesh, separating limbs from torsos, their hateful explosions bursting eardrums, creating insane ringings in the head.

Angelo, who had surged slightly ahead of Jake, did not know his friend had fallen. When he didn't see him advancing beside him, he turned to find Jake sprawled headfirst in the mud, his M1 laying in front of him and blood spurting from his leg.

"Jake!" yelled Angelo as he turned back to help his friend. A bullet then suddenly creased the top of Angelo's helmet, sending it flying off his head and spinning down the slope.

"Leave him be!" barked Burns. "Medics will tend to him! Now get moving!" The sergeant then pulled Angelo up by the harness and thrust him forward only a couple of seconds before a bullet went through Burns' throat with a thud.

Angelo screamed in horror as Burns keeled backward and fell hard onto a rocky surface. Another round of German artillery whistled in and impacted less than fifty feet away, knocking Angelo off his feet. His entire body hurt from the concussion. The stinging dirt and debris in his eyes began to impair his vision. His ears rang, muffling the cries of his comrades to his left who fell wounded and dying. He felt a crushing heaviness in his lungs from a combination of the concussion and the choking gunpowder that hung in the air

7

like wood smoke. The steady staccato of machine gun fire from the bunker on the right kept his face in the mud.

Firing what was left of his clip without looking at the bunker, Angelo sprang to his feet and began running at a crouch. The gunner, seeing Angelo, trained the weapon on him and fired two to three round bursts that sliced harmlessly through a high spot in the ground beneath Angelo's feet. Angelo dropped down behind a large boulder to his right and depressed the chamber spring to load in another clip. After sending several well-aimed shots through the opening of the bunker, Angelo rolled further to his right out of the gunner's sight and low-crawled to within ten yards of his target. Adrenaline pumped through his vessels in anticipation for the first time in his life of killing someone. Or perhaps he himself might be killed. But it didn't matter anymore. The whole thing was all too insane.

Pulling a grenade off his harness, Angelo yanked off the pin, and with his best change-up, tossed the grenade through the opening. The voices of panic he heard sounded like chickens being rousted from the hen house by a fox. The first of two German helmets appeared as the gunners began climbing over the machine gun to escape. But it was too late. A brilliant flash accompanying the earth-shaking blast propelled the men through the opening like rag dolls. Secondary explosions from ammunition and grenades finally blew the cover off the bunker, scattering pieces of the machine gun more than ten yards down the slope.

Angelo's platoon leader, Lieutenant Hyman, who had crawled up behind him, slapped him on the boot and said, "Good job, Caruso. You just knocked out the last of the bunkers."

He was right. The firing had ceased and Angelo saw scores of his comrades sweeping over the back side of the hilltop checking trenches and holes for wounded or escaping Germans. He then looked back down the slope to see if he could find Jake.

"Keep moving forward with your squad, Caruso. We have orders to reorganize and consolidate in the tree line just south of the bridge at Montevilla. Hey, you need a steel pot. Get that one off Tompkins over there. He doesn't need it anymore."

"But, Lieutenant, my friend Jake's back there. Jake Dumas. He got hit."

"We have to keep moving, Caruso. Never mind him. I know he's your friend. I'll send a medic down there to check on him. I'll also make sure you find out his condition. Now get the hell going! We have to be at the consolidation point by 1430."

Angelo moved on without rebuttal, saying a prayer for his friend as he trudged through the mud alongside what remained of his platoon. God would save Jake. He had to.

Taking the hill was to be the beginning of the battle for Montevilla.

CHAPTER 2

Forward of the 142nd Regiment's advance the Nazis were enjoying superior observation in all directions from the Salerno Plain as well as in and around the Town of Montevilla. Perched on the rooftops and cupolas of the town's structures enemy machine guns had commanding fields of fire with the exception of a few ravines on the eastern and southern quadrants less than half a mile from the city proper. This is where the 1st Battalion of the Regimental Combat Team punched in. The evening fog that had settled over the muddy landscape provided the same effect as a smoke screen. But after a while, what was left of the sun began to break slowly through. The haze, which gradually drifted out, soon dissipated like an ascending ghost.

As the bulk of the Nazi defense had been killed, captured or routed from Hill 452, Clark's Army encountered little further resistance. Two to three man outposts along the western entrance wall to Montevilla were quickly compromised, allowing the swift moving Rangers from the Pioneer Battalion to enter the town and engage the remainder of the retreating Germans. Bazookas took out three of perhaps five of the machine gun emplacements along the roof tops. Several skirmishes ensued along Montevilla's main street, forcing the Nazis deeper into the town. Regrettably, the advancing combat teams were forced to fire into several homes and businesses to kill what was left of the defending force. Bodies of civilians whose lives may have been ended by either army lay scattered about the streets.

The 1st Battalion, still moving on line toward the town along with the 3rd Battalion, found that the Germans had blown the Montevilla Bridge, impeding the advance of the entire right flank of the 3rd. As they were met suddenly by a hail of machine gun fire and a deafening artillery barrage, both battalions became pinned down. It had been a cleverly-executed ruse perpetrated by the retreating Nazis who had given the impression that their remaining numbers were small. Pouring out from well-camouflaged positions just shy of the town, more than two thousand Germans descended on the 142nd. Simultaneously, a well-hidden German strike team which had allowed the Rangers to enter the town only moments before waged a vicious assault that scattered the Rangers in all directions into houses and shops.

The commander of 1st Battalion then ordered his men to put their heads down as he radioed the supporting 155 battery to fire its pre-planned defcons. Artillery rounds screamed over the heads of the Americans, striking the German elements which had advanced to within as little as fifty meters of the stymied battalion. Earth-shaking whumps devastated the German line, flinging bodies about like matchsticks. As the 1st was ordered by its commander to spring from position and advance upon the now disorganized enemy force, he also radioed the battery to lift fire. But timing being everything, howling artillery rounds were still in the air. The concussion from the exploding shells created a wall of shock that knocked friendly combatants off their feet, unfortunately killing or wounding several. Within seconds, however, the last round impacted and the 1st Battalion slammed into the routed Nazis, killing most by rifle fire and bayonet in close combat.

Meanwhile, British artillery in support of the U.S. assault on Montevilla pounded the town. Roofs and mortar crumbled. Pieces of wood and concrete became shrapnel. Buildings fell on both the occupying Nazis and U.S. Rangers.

Within a few moments, however, the artillery was lifted and Company B was the first unit to enter the town. Smoke and dust that still hung in the air choked the lungs and stung the eyes. More than a dozen stores and homes had been leveled. Fortunately, many of Montevilla's citizens, anticipating the battle for their town, had left for neighboring burgs the day before. After the few remaining Germans consolidated into a platoon- sized element to stage a rather feeble counter-attack, Company B quickly bore down on them, killing all.

Montevilla now secured, intensive building searches began. Germans and civilians alike lay dead inside doorways, some crushed by fallen rubble and others the victims of direct fire weapons or shrapnel. Upon entering what once was a handsome villa along the main street, Sergeant Angelo Caruso found in the first room what appeared to be the bodies of three family members. A forty-something man lay cradling his wife and baby. Their bodies had been ripped apart by a hail of bullets. Black-red blood pooled beneath their torsos. The man's face reflected the horror of his last moment of life. The family had fallen victim to the merciless god of battle.

And then Angelo thought he heard a whimper coming from the adjacent room…high-pitched like that of a bird or a kitten. Leading with the muzzle of his M1, he moved slowly through the doorway into what was probably a bedroom. Rays from the setting sun streamed through the bare window opening and onto a waif-like figure sitting huddled in a corner. Her knees were drawn into her chin and her arms hugged her shins. Long, brown-black hair hung over most of her face; but Angelo could still make out her two beautiful but frightened eyes peering out from above her knees. Softly, she said something. Angelo had learned a few words of Italian from his parents. She then uttered the words more clearly, "Per favor. Non vtr mi." (Please don't kill me).

12

Angelo pointed his rifle down and shook his head. Then placing his hand over his heart, he replied, "Non preoccparti di." (You are safe). In English he added, while tapping his finger on his chest, "Don't worry. Americano."

The girl dropped her face back onto her knees and began to sob. Barefoot and dressed in a simple smock, she could have been his age, seventeen or eighteen. Maybe she was even older, he couldn't really say. Just a wisp of a girl not a hundred pounds. With her hair combed out and face free of dirt, she was probably beautiful. A face to go with the eyes.

Slowly, Angelo moved toward her. Still not very sure about him, the girl shied deeper into the corner like a frightened bird. He then sat down beside her with his back against the wall and said nothing, wanting her to know that he would not hurt her. He was an American… and American soldiers did not abuse civilians. From his pocket he took out a candy bar and unwrapped it. After breaking off a piece of the Hershey block, he bit into it, then held out the remainder to her. She shook her head quickly and re-buried her face in her knees.

Of course she didn't want it. What was he thinking? She had just seen her family and her home destroyed. And for the moment…her life. She could not enjoy anything. Even anything as trivial as a piece of candy.

Slowly, gingerly, he moved his arm along the wall behind her until his hand lay on her opposite shoulder. She flinched as though she had just been shot; but when he tenderly drew her into his chest, she threw her arms around his waist and let flow the bitterest of tears. Angelo held her for what seemed like hours until there was little light left in the room. She shook and he did not know whether it was from sorrow or if she was cold.

Angelo then righted her head and gave her a reassuring smile. She looked back with eyes that smiled, weakly, but now trustingly. And then she rose to look toward the room where her family lay. Slowly, in almost zombie fashion, she made her way to the threshold between the rooms and looked down at them in the waning light. Angelo followed and stood behind her. Placing her hand over her mouth, she began to shake again.

"My…father," she cried. "My mother. My brother… bambino." Her face was pale and she then moved her hand to her stomach as though she would be sick."

Angelo placed his hand on her shoulder. "Come away with me. You don't need to see this."

She nodded. "You are right." She then turned her head away from her family.

"You speak English," he said.

"A little. Only a few words."

"I'm sorry about your family." Angelo knew that she knew they could have been accidentally shot by Americans as well as Nazis. "We need to leave here. I will see to their burial. We have a special team that will take care of them."

"I am ashamed," she said, sobbing.

"Why?"

"It was when the German soldiers came to our house and ordered my family into the street, I hid in a closet. I saw through the door my father refuse to leave and… they shot him. My mother attacked the man who shot him, and then they killed her and my little brother, too. I should have died here with my family."

Angelo shook his head. "No. Your life would then have been wasted. You did the right thing."

"But I was afraid…and my parents were brave."

"It's not a sin to be afraid. We are all afraid sometimes. Fear makes us do things we don't like."

At that moment, small arms fire erupted just a block away. She jumped. Covering her face, she began to shake again.

Angelo placed his arm around her and said, "Come on. I want you to be safe."

He took her into the street after signaling to two other GIs who were nearby manning a hasty observation post. Further down the street a command post had been set up in the town hall. A handful of civilians had returned to the street to look for family and friends. An old woman dressed completely in black sat on the edge of a curb, rocking, mourning over the body of an old man. A small girl, perhaps five, tottered around with arms stretched out, crying for her 'mama.' An airborne sergeant from the 504th, the unit the Germans called the Devils in Baggy Pants, swept up the child in his arms. She didn't resist, but welcomed the comfort and safety he provided.

As they walked along the now dark ballast stone street, Angelo again offered the girl the Hershey bar. This time she took it. Tasting its rich sweetness, her eyes closed as though that one taste of ecstasy took away some of her pain. At least for a moment.

They seemed to be going nowhere. Just walking.

"What is your name?" he asked.

For a few seconds, she did not answer. But then she looked at him with her dark, lovely eyes and replied, "Allesandra." Her voice was soft. Like music.

"And...you?"

At that moment, Captain John Beckham, Angelo's company commander, approached. "Who is this, Sergeant?"

"Her family was shot dead in that house over there, sir. Can Graves Registration see to their remains?"

Then Allesandra spoke. "I...would prefer, sir, if our mortician can take them. If he still lives."

"Yes, of course," replied the captain. "I'll find out for you. Sergeant, return to your squad. Indications are that the Germans are preparing to counterattack. Panzers have been sighted by our aircraft moving in the town's direction. We also need to get the civilians off the street."

Angelo saluted. "Yes, sir."

In the faint light of the half moon, Angelo took a last look at Allesandra's glistening dark eyes and smiled. She did not smile back, but did say, "Will I see you again?"

He nodded. "If we're still here in the next few days, I'll be sure to see you again. Where will I be able to find you?"

"On the next street called Cantori. Halfway down is my uncle's bakery. I will be there. He has a room in the back." She then glanced back in the direction of her broken house. "I will go there to get my things...after my family is taken away." Tears formed again.

Captain Beckham who was still hanging close barked "Move out, Sergeant!" He then looked at Allesandra and touched the brim of his helmet. "Ma'am."

Elements of the 45th and 82nd Airborne Divisions officially began their occupation of the Town of Montevilla that evening, 10 September, 1943. The regimental motto of the 82nd's 504th became Strike Hold. Montevilla was a picturesque town…or at least it used to be. At the highest elevation the majestic steeple of Santa Maria still stood unscathed from the artillery, although its white stucco had suffered a number of bullet holes. Other structures constructed mostly of stone and colorful mortar lay split and crumbled. Some had completely fallen into unrecognizable heaps. But the shops and houses on Cantori appeared as though they had been plucked from the belly of the war zone and placed in some serene alpine setting in a country at peace with the world. What a difference there was just one street over.

Allesandra's uncle, who was set to grieving about his brother's death, took in his niece, giving her the often- rented room off the alley in the back of the store. She was good to stay there as long as they both lived. Her parents and little brother would be buried the next day along with over fifty other of Montevilla's citizens who had fallen victim to the battle.

While on urban patrol on the 12th, Angelo caught sight of Allesandra at the storefront, sweeping away dirt from the threshold. He almost didn't recognize her in her bright-colored peasant dress. Her hair was pulled back from her face and carefully coiffed with two tortoiseshell combs in place behind her ears. He slung his M1 over his right shoulder and stopped to greet her. A smile, warm as the morning sunshine, greeted him back.

"Would you come in for a baguette?" she posed. "They are fresh and still warm. It will be the last of our food, I am afraid, as my uncle's supplies are cut off."

Angelo looked toward his new platoon sergeant who in return nodded and winked. "Catch up to us later, Caruso," he said. A couple of members in his unit grinned and made comments about his getting a piece of action from one of the town beauties.

Angelo glared at them with menacing eyes, then turned his attention back to Allesandra. "I will. Thank you."

It would be the first of many sun kissed days and cool, sweet evenings that Angelo would spend with Allesandra during the ten days of American occupation. Whenever he was not out on patrol performing sweeps of the area around Montevilla or manning an observation post, he was at the bakery. Their relationship began at first with lingering looks into one another's eyes and pats on the hand. And then there was that long, moist and succulent kiss while gazing upon a full, silver moon in the alley at the rear door of the bakery before parting the night of the seventeenth. They learned everything there was to know about each other, although neither of their young lives before the beginning of September was particularly momentous. She was merely a peasant girl who enjoyed an uncomplicated life with her parents and more recently, her fourteen month old brother. She earned a few lira here and there helping out in the bakery, went to school and Mass, and strolled arm in arm with her girlfriends, singing and skipping along the streets. She had not seen her friends Carmen or Maria for days, believing they had evacuated with their parents before the battle, and hoping they had not been killed.

Angelo's life had been similar. New York boy, running the streets with his friend Jake, and stopping to smell the olfactory delights that filtered out of bakeries such as this very one. He told her there were Italians in his streets as well. And sometimes they went to war with the rival ethnic groups, some of which were Hispanic like Jake. He told her stories about him and the crazy things they did together. As he went on about his friend, it reminded him to speak with Lieutenant Hyman about where Jake had been taken. And if he had made it to the field hospital alive.

Angelo and Allesandra had much in common, even though they had grown up a half world apart. They were only grateful for the war in Italy for one reason...it had served to put them together as lovers.

As there was only one straight-back chair in her back room, they sat on the edge of her bed, talking and holding hands, telling stories about life in Italy and America. That evening after he had told her his unit may be pulling out within two days, she took from a frame on her nightstand a 5X7 photograph of herself, taken only six months before in the happy times.

"This will make you not forget me, Angelo. It is yours to keep."

He held the picture in both hands, studying it for a few moments, and then smiled. "I'll cherish it forever, Allesandra. But you know I would not forget you anyway."

Allesandra placed her arms around Angelo's waist tightly and pulled him close to her. She then reached for the decanter and poured her uncle's Chianti into a glass, putting the rim to his lips. After he sipped it, he kissed her. Her lips, warm and velvety, tasted of the wine.

In that small war-torn village of Montevilla, two teens from different worlds shared a tender love in a time of uncertainty and impending death. In the short time they had been together, they had gotten so deeply into one another that the reality of the war, especially during the momentary lull in action, was growing further from their minds.

"Tiadora," she said softly.

He smiled and stroked her hair with the tips of his fingers. "I want to marry you, Allesandra."

Almost immediately, she turned her face away from him. "You know that cannot be."

At first he was taken aback, but then, after a moment of contemplation, he understood why she said what she did. And then he tried to make light of the comment. "Why? Is there a boyfriend around here you've been seeing you haven't told me about?"

She turned her eyes back to him and smiled. "No. You are silly. It is that you and your army will soon be gone from here. This war will continue and maybe you or I will be killed."

Angelo touched her lips with his fingers as if to cut off the words. "Please, Allesandra, don't say that. We don't know that will happen. Our time is now. You and I are watched over by the same God and He will see us through all of this. The war will not last forever and just as soon as it is over, I promise I'll be back for you. And you can then go home with me."

Allesandra turned away again and buried a good portion of her face in the pillow. She was quiet for the longest time. Angelo knew she was right. The army would move on from the Salerno Plains. Maybe even storm Berlin. And he knew the war would not end anytime soon. He wouldn't press the idea of marriage any further. For now, he would just enjoy the time he had left with her.

It was still light at seven-thirty and they had almost fallen asleep after their love-making. Angelo rolled over and looked at his watch in the dim light of the room, thinking he could catch a few winks, which he needed, and still be able to meet up with his combat team at 2200 for the night patrol.

The first round of enemy artillery whistled over and hit somewhere in the town just after 1930 hours, rousting both from the bed. Jumping into his boots, he slapped up his M1 and said, "Stay here, Allesandra. Get down beside the bed." He kissed her quickly and ran from the room through the back door and into the alley behind the bakery. More rounds screamed over and exploded into buildings in the vicinity of Cantori Street.

Angelo's comrades spilled into the streets. As squad leaders yelled out commands, they took up positions behind concrete barricades in the center of town. It was an all-out counterattack by the Germans who had regained lost ground in the neighboring foothills. The 504th had beaten back the first assault less than fifteen kilometers to the northeast, but Nazi foot soldiers reinforced by Panzer teams had broken through the western corridor to the village, compelling the small number of U.S and British forces to the west to pull back and take up positions in the town.

Lieutenant Hyman's platoon, which had set up behind barricades at the intersection of Ragusa and Cantori, waited. Rangers positioned in doorways and upper windows of houses and businesses along the main arteries in the town signaled one another after hearing the beastly growl of a Panzer V tank, a Panther, moving through the west gate. As its main gun swiveled left and right like a steel tentacle sniffing and peering into alleyways, searching for its prey, the tank rumbled toward Cantori Street, shaking the earth beneath the feet of those who lay in wait.

Angelo was the first to see the barrel when it came into view past St. Mary's. To see the Panther's iron cross in the same visual frame as the stained-glass images of Christ and St. Paul on the outer walls of the church seemed an unholy paradox. Beside and behind the tank, a squad of Nazi foot soldiers ran at a crouch, scanning the buildings for urban defenders. Suddenly, a hail of machine gun fire erupted from a window in a two story house within twenty yards of Angelo's position. The Germans ducked for cover behind the tank and returned fire on the building just as the Panzer's turret swung its cannon toward the house. An eardrum-shattering boom sent a 75 mm round into the building, followed in a split second by the explosion that half-leveled the dwelling. Angelo cringed as he heard the painful screams of the wounded Rangers. Lieutenant Hyman then gave the order to open fire as his platoon poured a steady volley of rounds onto the advancing force. More Germans appeared seemingly from out of nowhere and although they knew they had entered an ambush, they were confident that with their numbers and the second of three Panthers that had joined the fray, they could easily take the town.

Suddenly, another round from the first tank's main gun exploded into Angelo's position, blowing away the makeshift barricade and half of his squad. And then yet a third round whizzed over the remainder of the unit's heads and impacted into a building at the end of Cantori Street. Angelo turned his head just in time to see the walls and roof collapse, setting off secondary explosions from within. The bakery was gone.

"Allesandra!" he cried out. "No!"

As ricocheting rounds from German small arms fire kicked up the dirt around his feet, Angelo ran toward the demolished building. Hyman yelled out, "Get back here, Caruso. No cowards in my unit!"

Private James Garvey, who knew about Angelo and Allesandra, tugged on the lieutenant's sleeve and said loudly, "He's not running away, sir! His girlfriend lives in that building!"

"I don't give a rat's ass! We need every gun we've got! Let's go, men! Here they come!"

Angelo watched helplessly as what was left of the bakery suddenly erupt in fire. In assessing the damage, he knew then that had the collapse of the building not crushed Allesandra, she could not survive the fire.

Blinded by his tears and smoke from the burning debris, Angelo somehow made his way back to his platoon. Hyman, Garvey and three others laid dead, their bodies riddled by Mauser bullets. As the lead tank with a squad of Nazis closed within ten yards, blasting away on what was left of the unit, Angelo grabbed a dead gunner's B.A.R. and opened fire on the Germans, killing more than a half dozen. After expending the entire belt of ammunition, his anger propelled him to his feet where from the hip he fired six more rounds from his M-1, taking out three more of the enemy. With empty rifle in hand, he began to run toward a two-story building in jack rabbit fashion, screaming something unintelligible until a bullet ripped through his right leg at the thigh. As his body fell, the two remaining Germans advanced upon him.

"Bastards! Come get me, you Kraut bastards!" he screamed madly.

As one of the Germans stood over him, pointing a Ruger at his head, Angelo thrust the bayonet on his rifle upward and into the soldier's abdomen. He then placed his M-1 across the fallen German's body and put a bead on the second soldier. The man stopped in his tracks and raised his hands. He did not know that Angelo was out of ammunition.

The death struggle of the German that Angelo had gutted was long and violent. He convulsed and seized where the gaping wound had allowed a large section of his intestine to protrude, appearing as a bloodied, glistening white snake. It sickened Angelo and he backed away from the dying soldier, still keeping a bead on the second man.

Reinforcements from 3rd and 4th platoons of Company B led by Captain Beckham, who had been advancing on Hyman's position, converged on the series of shattered concrete barricades. A rifleman saw the German standing with arms in the air and fired a round from his M-1 into his chest. Beckham was livid. Back-handing his soldier across the face, he yelled "He was surrendering, dammit! He was surrendering!"

The Panther gunner then swung the turret back in the direction of Beckham's company. "Take it out!" Beckham yelled to his bazooka gunner. Just as the gunner knelt to kill the tank, the Panther fired on him, not only ending his life but five others in Beckham's force. As the second tank pulled up behind the first, Angelo grabbed the dead German's Ruger. A hot bolt of debilitating pain drove through his leg where the bullet went through. Blood gushed from the entry wound.

Angelo then pulled himself to his feet by aid of his rifle and drug himself through the door of what appeared to be a cafe. Seeing a staircase that led to the upper floor, he grit his teeth and climbed the steps, using the rifle as a crutch. Once in the upper dining room, he hobbled through a door out from which extended a balcony with a small round table and two chairs. He then saw that the Panther had drawn even with the building and come to a temporary halt on the narrow street where the tank commander perched at the top of the turret was now in close proximity. He appeared to be assessing the small fortification that lay in the path of the tank at the end of the street.

As the tank's engine revved up again, Angelo lifted his bloodied leg over the balcony railing, which proceeded to get the tank commander's attention. The German grabbed his Mauser only seconds before the bullet fired from Angelo's pistol struck the man between the eyes. The tank stopped abruptly and then the gunner popped his head up out of the hatch to clear away the commander's body. Dumping it off the turret, the gunner swung his rifle in Angelo's direction. When he pulled the trigger, the gun apparently jammed. The gunner then slapped the bolt twice and ejected a round that was wedged in the chamber. Angelo then knew he had to act quickly.

With his last ounce of strength, ignoring not only the immense pain in his leg but faintness in his brain, Angelo sprang off the balcony and onto the turret, knocking the rifle from the gunner's hand. Taking his last grenade from his harness, Angelo then pulled the pin and dropped it down the hatch. The concussion from the explosion jarred the tank as though the very heart of the iron beast had been cut out. But it also blew Angelo off the turret, face down in the mud.

The second tank, now trapped behind the first, tried to back away from the dead Panther. But another of Beckham's bazooka gunners, who had managed to flank the tank, fired a rocket directly into its fuel cell. The tank erupted, sending pieces of steel into buildings on either side of the street and shattering mortar walls.

The 504th, which had earlier retreated to the northwest sector of Montevilla, moved back through the town and joined the 1st Battalion. The command element of the Nazis' 4th Mechanized Regiment, now seeing that the reinforced American forces had repelled their armor and was slowly choking off all corridors, began a retrograde operation to abandon the Town of Montevilla.

When Angelo regained consciousness in a field hospital, the surgeon who had operated on his leg was standing over him, smiling, relieved that he was now out of his coma. The pain in Angelo's leg was immense, but he looked down anyway to be sure it was still there. He had lost a lot of blood and was suddenly afraid that he might die. But the longer he laid there on the recovery cot, reflecting on his pain, and grieving for Allesandra, he was then afraid he *wouldn't*.

CHAPTER 3

The hard rain woke him. It beat wildly against the batten board panels on the west side of Jake Dumas' small, one-story rental. Maybe an early morning squall line. Occasional wind gusts caused the house to shudder a few times, giving off the warning that at any time, the nine hundred square foot structure could be lifted from its foundation.

He sighed and blinked open his eyes. The streetlight on the corner at Laurel and Carriage silhouetted the huge oak in Jake's front yard outside the living room window. Its branches slapped angrily against the pane as though the tree had turned into some kind of monster created by the storm. Mostly, such storms were brewed up by late afternoon summer suns, further fueled by the warm, moist air off the gulf. But yesterday, a low pressure had developed in the Florida panhandle and stalled out over Alabama. And so the weather continued.

Great. Just great, he thought. Not only had he finally passed out on the couch in front of the tube scarcely three hours before, it was time to get up. He eyed the half-empty bottle of Merlot and a wine glass on the coffee table by the couch. Jake didn't drink much, but sometimes, it helped him get to sleep. Unfortunately, it didn't work its magic last night.

He then squinted to see the clock on the kitchen wall. Six-fifteen. Had to get up. He had to be at the school to be sure everything was in good order before the kids began arriving around seven-thirty.

It seemed that the pain was always worse after longer days on his feet…after he had finished out at the school somewhere in the seven-o'clock range. Twelve hour days sometimes. Yesterday was one of them. He reached down below his boxers to rub his horribly-scarred thigh, working over it like some divine healer, praying for just this one time, the pain would not be as bad today. Yesterday had been a bad day, what with the rain. It had also been the last day of summer vacation for the kids, but his fifth day at work after being off three months. This was to be his second year at New Hope.

After doing his bathroom chores, he sat at the two-person wooden kitchen table holding his hot coffee mug against his chin with both hands, pulling the rich aroma of the Maxwell House into his nostrils as though he were making love to it. The rain and wind had finally subsided and it appeared the stalled-out storm was finally moving out. It would be Georgia's problem today.

The '63 school year would be different. Last year's Class AAA football champion, New Hope High, would be lucky to win half its games. Principal Horatio Sharpe had seen to that. Three of last year's standout juniors, whose passing and receiving combination broke every existing state record, had been suspended for the entire football season. Seems that two weeks ago, as the team was being bussed to a pre-season scrimmage game with Pell City, several of the players, including the three high school All-staters, mooned several passersby in Birmingham from the port side of the bus. Although their derrieres were not conclusively identified, the boys did own up to it, thinking no one would dare punish the three most popular jocks on campus. Anyway, it was a prank everyone could laugh about. And most everyone did...except Sharpe.

Jake carefully unfolded the soaked newspaper and pulled out the Sports section. The 'moon platoon,' as they were called, were the headliners. He shook his head. "Stupid, guys. You had everything going for you," he muttered. Two of the three were going to lose out on a football scholarship. They would probably end up losers anyway. But not Blaise Honeycutt.

The dry toast lay cold and half-eaten in the saucer. Jake didn't eat much. Hadn't in years. That was why he was six feet tall and weighed 165 pounds. It made him appear gaunt and perhaps seven to ten years older looking than thirty-nine. But he was still strong and well- developed, nonetheless. Mostly, he ate enough of a lunch to sustain himself all day…that is, when school was in session.

He tossed the toast in the garbage container and laid both his cup and saucer in the sink bowl. After brushing his teeth, he donned a rain jacket from the hall closet. Stopping to glance at the tired blue eyes that stared back at him in the mirror by the door, he slicked back his black hair with the finger tips of both hands, noticing several more premature gray strands at the temples. The face in the mirror, though still handsome, had been left furrowed by hardships, too many of which he had already endured in his young life.

Jake exited the back door without locking it. He never did. He had nothing of value in the house and only those few items he did value were locked in the shed at the back of the house. Steps away in the gravel driveway, the beat-up but sound '60 Valiant, his only real friend who had only let him down once, sat waiting for the two mile jaunt to the school. Jake smiled as the motor hit at the first turn of the key. The little slant six purred like a kitten.

The town of New Hope had a population back then at just over thirty-five hundred. A few nicer sub- divisions were being built on the out-skirts of town toward Waterford where a new fabric mill, a shopping center and a hospital had gone in. There was talk that a new high school was on the drawing board as well. For the most part, however, New Hope was an older burg with fifty plus year old houses, largely small frame and decrepit, much like Jake's. A few businesses along the town's main streets had begun to fail in the past couple of years, thanks to the new, more modern shopping area. Some of the folks around had even referred to the town as No Hope. Especially since the town's centerpiece, New Hope High, would likely be torn down soon. Waterford would be the place to live.

New Hope High was football. Jake wondered what the mood would be among the faculty and administration, especially the coaching staff. Coach Billy (Wild Bill) Conroy had already incited the parents and community supporters to protest the suspensions of Blaise Honeycutt and chums to the school board, and a couple of the alumni were talking up getting Dobie Barnhill and firm to file suit to have the boys reinstated on the squad.

Jake pulled the Valiant into one of the staff parking spots and killed the engine. A couple of spaces down, he saw two men leaning against a Ford pickup talking and gesturing in animated fashion with another man, Principal Sharpe. The two men apparently arguing with Sharpe were the rotund Billy Conroy and his assistant, Ronald Jarvis. Suddenly, Conroy jammed a finger into the principal's chest and Sharpe swatted at it with a meaty hand as though he were flicking off a mosquito. After a few seconds, they split up and Sharpe stomped off in the direction of the faculty entrance at the back of the building. After sitting another five minutes to enjoy the last swallows of coffee from his thermos, Jake checked his watch, seeing that it was now just after seven. He then shut the door to the Valiant and with the ever-present slight limp in his gait, walked slowly toward the back door.

No sooner had he opened the metal door, Horatio Sharpe stood in his path, hands pompously folded behind his back. Tall, big-boned and rather distinguished looking with his coarse, sandy hair, he was an imposing figure of pallid haughtiness. His protruding, square jaw was as usual elevated to a point where he could look down his nose at subordinates, the narcissistic bully that he was.

"Dumas! I don't know what you do around here or why we ever pay you. When you left yesterday, you also left an over-flowed commode in the upstairs boys' john. Now get up there and do whatever you do to unstop it." He then stepped aside and slowly swept an arm in the direction of the stairwell.

Jake, the school's janitor, knew all of the toilets were spic and span and in good working order when he left yesterday. No students would have been in the building for any reason, after that. Today was the first day any student would be on site and he would not open the front doors to the building until seven-thirty. Jake figured the clogged porcelain pony was probably the principal's own morning handiwork and he was too embarrassed to own up to it. Why else would a man of Sharpe's importance be going inside the toilet rooms to check out commodes? But Jake just nodded without word and walked away.

Sharpe eyed Jake as he made his way to the custodian room and with a sneer on his lips muttered, ""Dumb ass. No wonder the kids call you that."

And some of them did. Sometimes it was 'dummy,' which was also a play on his name; but although they never ridiculed him to his face, when he had passed by them in the hall, he occasionally heard 'dumb ass' behind his back. It was the kind of name you called a meek- mannered custodian who seldom spoke to anyone. And if you were a boy of sixteen trying to impress his girlfriend and chums, why not make fun of a low-life janitor. If he were anyone at all, he'd have a better job than a commode scrubber.

Jake unlocked the custodian room, grabbed up a plunger and mop and ascended the stairs to the upstairs boys' room. Throwing open each of the five stall doors, he found the last one to be the culprit. Nasty. Would the plunger do the trick or would he have to go back downstairs for the snake? But after a few pushes and sucks, the mess went right down. Mission accomplished.

After his first lovely job of the morning, Jake returned downstairs to unlock the front doors. Students were already standing outside, eager to get a start on the new school year. Most were girls, making their way in, maybe seniors, a few that he recognized from last year. Good students. Cradling their books beneath their breasts like they were made of precious minerals, a few smiled at him, but none actually spoke. He nodded back.

Moments later, they came in. The three of them. They would perhaps not be so popular this year. Football was history for them. They no longer had any reason to be as brash and cocky as they were last year. There was no gravy train this year and they all would have to buckle down, academically. No teacher would now just pass them on. They would no longer be making touchdowns for the New Hope Raiders.

"Well, there he is with his girlfriend," Paulie Echols said, grabbing up Jake's mop from his hand. "Looks like she needs a new hairdo." He then fluffed up the wet strands of the mop.

Jake snatched the mop out of the boy's hand. "I expect you have no idea where this mop has been this morning."

Paulie's face turned sour and he immediately wiped his hands on his jeans.

Gordon Cain, dressed in a white tee with sleeves rolled up to his armpits and hair slicked back in a greasy duck tail, felt compelled to take his shot as well. "Careful, Paulie. You're talkin' to Sir Dunce-a-lot here. That's his sword he's holdin', not his girlfriend. Press his button and you could end up with a face full of shit." Both boys then laughed.

But Blaise Honeycutt did not. "Come on, guys. Let him be."

Blaise was one of them, all right. Although a tough kid, in and out of trouble, he still didn't have the mouth that his friends had. And he was never disrespectful to Jake. Clearly, Cain was the worst of the lot, and he could be not only insensitive, but immensely cruel as well.

The school's record-breaking quarterback in his junior year, Blaise Honeycutt had passed for more yards than any quarterback not only in New Hope's history, but also enjoyed the Alabama state record. Paulie, long and lanky with sure hands, had caught more passes than any receiver in school history. And Gordo, at six feet and two hundred twenty pounds, a bruising fullback, was within ninety-seven yards of the school's rushing record. The Triple Threat, they were called. Last year they took the 12-0 Raiders to the state championship. This year they would be the 'triple nobodies.'

"Aw, man," replied Gordo.

"We're just havin' a little fun with ol' Dumb Ass here.

Blaise gave both of his buddies a stern look and said, "Let's go."

As Echols and Cain swaggered down the hallway, laughing, Blaise shook his head to Jake and then turned to follow them. Cain then punched one of the wall lockers and laughed even louder.

Jake stood watching the three clowns pushing one another playfully as they walked in the direction of the gymnasium. He suspected they would hang out with the coach before classes began and check to see whether the principal had had any change of heart.

Jake returned to the custodian room where he had also set up a small office…not that he ever had any paperwork. But there was an old desk in there and a nicely-padded chair where in his lunch hour he would have a sandwich and read. A carnivorous reader, he kept a number of books on the shelf above the desk. The same shelves that also contained large concentrates of soap and disinfectant…and roach powder. Lots of it. Bugs stayed year round in Southern Alabama. People even joked that it was the roach colonies and nests that actually held up the walls in the ageing building.

Some of the books were his own, but most were ones he had checked out from the school and town library. Rosie allowed Jake to patronize the library, even though he was neither a student nor member of the faculty. Rosie Green was sweet. And maybe a little saucy, too. Also in her upper thirties, divorced, blonde, and quite the looker, she was as colorful as her name. Rosie was flashy, not trashy; but her rounded and petite perfect size eight body made anything she wore look provocative. As she moved with cat-like grace, there was a genteel softness about her. The boys called her a blonde bombshell, built like a brick 'you know what.' It was no wonder that a great deal of their studying and homework was done in the library… and that parents pondered why their sons stayed so long each day after school.

Jake read all kinds of books, but mostly the classics and historical novels, both fiction and non-fiction. He was especially drawn to modern writers who sought to revive the ideals of European romanticism which had somehow been abandoned by early American novelists. It was in the works of Fitzgerald and Hemingway that he found a renewed passion for beauty, wonder and wisdom. He drank-in their words as though they were written especially for him. In fact, they were…and romanticists like him.

Lunch was time-out for him from his long days. Had he taken the time to break down his thirty-five hundred a year salary into hourly wage, he would be lucky to make fifty cents an hour. But although he was not on the clock, it was imperative that he be at school at least a half hour before the students arrived in the morning. Considering he had to scour the place top to bottom after the last of the students and faculty had departed, most days he would leave campus well after dark. Long after band practice and after-school programs like Drama and Cheerleading, there would be toilets to scrub, hallways to mop, trash bins to empty and garbage to take out from the cafeteria.

Twelve to one was his hour, and no one bothered him unless there was an emergency. During that hour he sailed the seas of Europe and Asia, stood on the field of battle with Robert E. Lee at Chancellorsville, and squired Daisy Buchanan at Jay Gatsby's party in 1922. But then the bell would ring, returning the students to their classrooms, which was also Jake's signal to return to duty.

Being the only custodian at the school created a hardship for Jake. Considering maintenance personnel from the county seldom responded to work orders whenever a mechanical or technical problem surfaced, Jake often sat studying manuals, learning how to replace a stuck float valve on the boiler or troubleshoot an electrical failure. He had replaced old man Zicafoos the year before, who had been in the system nearly forty years until his retirement. Occasionally, Sharpe called him back in when Jake became stymied over something beyond his capability. Ziggy, as they called him, knew how to do everything. He, too, had been the butt of jokes and scorn, but he would just laugh right along with the boys through the years, giving back as much as they gave him. "Hey, maybe if you study hard," he would say, "you could grow up and be as important as me."

But Jake merely glared back at his ridiculers, few that there were. Most of the students just ignored him. Others mistook his closed-off manner as mysterious, even bewildering, wondering if he were some kind of psychopath who could go off at any time. That didn't stop Gordo and Paulie, however. They were relentless last year and it appeared this year would be no different. Maybe worse. They wanted to see how long they could press his buttons before his rockets went off. And why not? The place needed a little excitement.

The conversations between Jake and Rosie were for the most part 'one way.' She would greet him in her sultry, almost velvet voice when he came in and say, "Hi, Jake. Where are you going today? Paris? Istanbul? Shanghai?" She would then smile with those full, red- painted lips. And Jake would smile back. She could make anyone smile. Any lusty-eyed sixteen year old boy, of course; but even the math teacher, Bernie Feingold, the old queen, whose face was fixed on most days in a frozen scowl. Rumors were that she was moonlighting down at the Lady and Lace joint just off the interstate. One kid said he actually saw her there twirling on a pole. But considering he was only fourteen and would never have gotten past the bouncer, his story was quickly dismissed as a fairy tale.

The bell that sounded more like a buzzer than something melodious rang sharply at eight. Jake leaned back in his chair and listened as the last of the students scurried and tromped overhead into the first period Chemistry class. The wooden floor cracked and vibrated and he thought again that someday the whole mess may come falling down on his head. But this building was not long for the grave. If a new school was built over toward Waterford, New Hope High would be razed in favor of a new shopping plaza like the one across town. He had seen them go up in Birmingham and Tuscaloosa. They were L-shaped and all the stores were connected by common walls. Like a small village of storefronts all in one location. The plazas were the very reason that the downtown areas of little towns such as New Hope were dying out. And it was convenient to be able to do one's shopping all in one place without having to circle the block for a parking space on a downtown street. Not that he ever shopped for anything in New Hope.

Jake pushed himself up from his chair and stood almost in the military position of attention. As had been the tradition of the school for nearly twenty years, Mrs. Williams, the school secretary, placed The Star Spangled Banner on the record player. One of New Hope High's principals, Hiram Parker, a Great War veteran, too old to serve in WW II, mandated that every student would hear the National Anthem each day before starting classes. The recitation of the Pledge of Allegiance would follow. In the early years, the students, only numbering two to three hundred, would assemble in the gym where the school band played the Anthem. And then the righteous Mr. Parker would follow the music with a chapel service complete with scripture reading and prayer. Over the years, somewhere around 1959, the gymnasium ritual ceased and the Anthem was then played on a 45 record over the intercom. Teachers still instructed the kids to rise from their chairs, but few now stood as straight and respectful as their predecessors. Some leaned slovenly against their desks. Others yawned, giggled or whispered to one another in bored contempt. But the faculty, and yes, Jake Dumas, still stood erectly upon hearing the Anthem's first notes, wherever they were. Occasionally, the music caught Jake in one of the rest rooms with mop or toilet brush in hand. But he never failed to respond the way he always had.

CHAPTER 4

After a sweep of the hallways to check for trash which may have been dropped or strewn about, Jake went to the library with two borrowed books in hand. Every librarian Jake had ever seen when he was growing up, whether in a school or public setting, was fifty-plus, plump with white or blue hair, and had a pair of reading glasses hanging from a chain that laid softly on her breasts. But Rosie Green was not a typical librarian. And moms, realizing that, were afraid that just her mere presence in the school could morally corrupt their sons. Even fathers believed she did not project the kind of image their daughters should emulate. Which some of them did. A few of the girls bleached their hair Marilyn Monroe blonde and came to school wearing Rosie's same luscious shade of red lipstick.

But the girls also enigmatically resented her as well. Rosie was known to flirt with and tease their beaus, spurring pangs of jealousy which in turn more so fueled the gossip mill, both within the school and community. But other than her naturally-sensual appearance and the innocent fun she had with the boys, there was never any real allegation of sexual impropriety by anyone.

"Hi ya, Jake. Where are you going today?" she said in her sultry, Carolinian brogue. "The romantic Riviera or ancient Greece?"

He handed her the two books and smiled when she patted his hand. "We'll see," he replied. He then turned heel and momentarily returned with a book on nebulae.

"Oh, so that's where you're going, huh? Blasting off to outer space."

There was a side to Rosie that Jake did not like. Sometimes she could be condescending, treating him like a child or someone who may have mental deficiencies. Perhaps it was because he seldom engaged in conversations with people, especially her, which gave off the impression that he was 'slow', not to mention being an unskilled floor mopper. However, she did treat him nicely otherwise as opposed to members of the faculty who basically ignored him. But with the distance he preferred to keep from everyone, he was as much to blame for that. And he did have his reasons.

Jake was back in his closet room just before the bell to second period rang and spent the remainder of the morning reading. It was not that he was short-sheeting the school system, because considering his ten to twelve hour days, he worked hard…especially after the students had left for the day. There was just a lot of down time during school hours, that is, unless some emergency occurred which would require his services. At the noon bell, the rumble of shoes sounding like buffalo hooves on the wooden floor above prompted him to close his book and pull from a poke a bologna and mustard sandwich. Pouring himself a coke from a can…he preferred drinking it warm…he settled back to enjoy lunch. Perhaps tomorrow he would venture to the cafeteria. They were having baked chicken, done just the way he liked it.

At the bell to end the final period of the day, the horde of students poured into the hallways and pushed out through the front double doors as though they were being released from a penal institution. If they did not hurry, the warden may change his mind. Principal Sharpe, as usual, wanted to get a look at every student he could, either coming or going.

Standing at the front doors, he might make such comments as, "Your hair is too long. Get a haircut before you come back tomorrow." He would also stop girls, take a ruler and measure the hemline to assure that the skirt was no higher than two inches below the knee. "Too short!" he would bark. "You know the standard."

Today he yelled, "Cain! Hold up there!" Approaching Gordo, he said, "You put a shirt with a collar on over that tee shirt and roll those sleeves down. Also cut that nasty hair. That duck tail crap doesn't get it in my school. If I see you tomorrow like this, you get detention."

Cain snarled his lip Elvis style and did not reply.

"You're on thin ice, anyway, showing your butt like you did. I'm here to tell you, things are going to be different if you want to stay in this school. Ya hear?"

Cain stood and glared at Sharpe and for a long moment there appeared to be a standoff to see who would blink. Finally, it was Sharpe who walked away after saying "You'd better hear me."

Gordo shot him a bird while his back was turned and a few of the students who had stopped to listen to the tête-à-tête began to laugh. "What a jerk," he said lowly. "Hey, Blaise. Speaking of jerks, where's Paulie?"

"Over there," he replied, pointing. "By the lockers."

"Did he bring it?"

"He says he did."

"Okay, then. We need a place to stash ourselves until everybody's out of here."

41

"I don't know, Gordo," said Blaise, chewing on his lower lip. "Maybe we should think about it. Are you sure we should be doing this?"

"Yeah! Hell yeah!"

"But there're still people in the building even after seven sometimes."

"You mean like Dumb Ass?"

"Shhh. Don't talk so loud. Sometimes Sharpe is still here as well."

"Yeah, but they shut the school office door about four and Sharpe's office is at the other end of the hall."

"Still, breaking and entering a school office is a probably a state or federal offense."

"Come on, Blaise-man. You're not backing out are you?"

Paulie then came up and whispered, "Hey, it's almost four. Where are we gonna go for an hour or so until old lady Williams leaves?"

"We can hang out at the field house. The team will be at practice until about six," said Gordo.

"We're banned from there, you know," replied Blaise. "What if someone sees us?"

"We can't play football. No one said we couldn't hang out around there."

Blaise shook his head and turned his back on them, hands on hips. "I don't know, guys. We still ought to think about this."

Cain cast a disparaging look in Echols' direction. "He's gonna bomb on us, Paulie. Look, man," he turned back to Blaise, "it's not like we're stealin' anything. It's a frickin' prank, that's all."

Blaise tightened his lips and took a deep breath. "All right, all right. I'm in, okay? But I'm not liking it."

Jake finished up with the toilets in the boys and girls bathrooms around five-thirty and returned his bucket- on-wheels, mop and cleaning cart to the custodian room. He would stick around another hour and check all classroom trash cans, straighten up desks and assure the doors to offices, the chemistry lab, library and band room were locked. He would also do the thing he hated the most last year and that was to swing by Sharpe's office at the end of the day and ask if there was anything else he wanted done.

Taking down from the shelf his copy of Baldwin's The Fire next Time, Jake began reading the first chapter. It was a book he intended to get to before the summer break, but there were in fact a number of works he had wanted to get to that had to stand in line.

Suddenly, he heard a noise from the office next door, like a cabinet door being shut. And then someone laughed. He knew Mrs. Williams had already gone for the day and had locked the door behind her. Could be that Sharpe had gone in there, but why would he be laughing unless someone were in there with him?

Jake pushed open his door just enough to peer out and then heard the click of the tumbler in the office door as it was being shut. The first of three figures began running past the custodian room. Recognizing Gordon Cain and then Paulie

43

Echols as they hot-footed it down the hall, he then caught the face of the third boy pulling up the rear. Blaise Honeycutt.

Jake pushed open his door to its widest position, then reached out and grabbed Blaise by the shirt, slamming him into the wall. Blaise yelled out which prompted the other two boys well down the hallway to stop and turn. Meanwhile, Jake's forearm, shoved into Blaise's neck, pinned the boy's head against the concrete wall. Blaise's friends, realizing their act had been discovered, and by the janitor of all people, panicked and ran.

His windpipe partially cut off by Jake's forearm, Blaise struggled to plead, "Let…me go."

Jake lessened the pressure against Blaise's neck, then grabbed him by his shirt, flinging him through the doorway into the custodian's room.

"Sit down!" Jake barked.

Blaise, now shaking uncontrollably, grabbed the arms of the desk chair and slowly lowered his body onto the seat. His eyes were wide and he appeared as a frightened cat.

"What were you boys doing in there, Blaise?"

"N…nothing, Jake. We didn't take anything. Honest."

"Then what did you do?"

Blaise diverted his eyes from Jake to the floor. "I can't tell you that."

"No, you will tell me or I will turn you boys in. Breaking and Entering inside a government institution is a felony. Now what were you all doing in that office?"

Blaise sighed and shuffled his body in the chair. "Okay. But if I do tell you, will you still promise not to turn us in? My old man will..." He stopped short and began picking at a hang nail. "We were just pulling a prank, that's all. We...took the record off the phonograph... you know, the Star Spangled Banner. We stand up every morning and..."

"I know about that," Jake said curtly. "I stand right along with you kids. Now, get on with it. What did you do with the record?"

"We replaced it with Louie, Louie."

"Louie, Louie," Jake repeated, trying not to smile.

"What the hell is that?" He had actually heard the song, but had no clue what the words meant.

"It's on the Hit Parade...real popular right now."

"Uh huh."

"We thought Mrs. Williams would not notice it on the player and all the kids would get a kick out of it."

"I see." Jake was actually enjoying seeing Blaise squirm. He then stood with one hand on the desk and gave Blaise a chastising glare. "All right, then. Pick your ass up and get the hell out of here. If I find you lied to me and that you boys actually took something, not only will Sharpe have your asses, but the cops as well."

"Believe me, Jake. You won't find that's the case. I'm telling you the truth."

"Just go."

"Thanks, Jake," Blaise said sheepishly.

Jake followed Blaise out of the room with his eyes. And then he did smile. "Louie, Louie, eh," he said to himself. If Blaise and the other two jerks did pull this off, he would give a week of his meager pay to see the principal's face light up when the song started.

Just after six-thirty, Jake locked the custodian room and then checked the doors on the rooms and offices that were supposed to be locked. At least the boys relocked the school office door. As he limped down the hallway, finding everything on the first floor in order, he tapped on the door to the principal's office and turned the knob. As it was unlocked, he knew Sharpe would still be in there. After passing the secretary's desk in the outer office, he rapped on Sharpe's door. He then asked the question he always did at the end of the day, which often generated some smart-ass or condescending response from the principal. "Mr. Sharpe, do you need anything done before I leave?"

There was no reply.

Jake pushed open the squeaky door which would then surely get Sharpe's attention. As he peered further into the room, he saw the principal sitting in his leather wingback facing the window, seemingly in deep thought.

"Mr. Sharpe?"

No answer or movement.

Jake, figuring the man was either asleep or ignoring him, started to leave; but then he sensed something was not right. The first thing he saw when he rounded Sharpe's desk was the bright red blood on the collar of the principal's white shirt. As Jake moved closer he then saw something gold metallic sticking out of the left side of Sharpe's neck at the carotid artery. The man's eyes were half closed and face an ashen white. Jake knew immediately that the principal was dead. Murdered. But just to be sure, Jake touched the right carotid anyway to check for a pulse. The skin was cool and there was no throbbing. It appeared to him that Sharpe had been dead for at least thirty minutes.

Jake's thoughts turned immediately to the three boys. No. They would not have done something like this.

Pranksters, yes. Murderers, no. He knew they despised Sharpe, as did most everyone else, but they would not take their hate to this extreme. As full of the devil as they were, they would not kill Horatio Sharpe over football. However, there had been no one else in the building...at least that he knew of. He peered out the window to look over the staff parking area. Only his and Sharpe's cars remained. Of course, he thought, the killer or killers would be long gone. Jake also looked toward the field house. Football practice was over and the coaches' cars were gone as well.

Careful not to touch anything else, he pulled a Kleenex from the box on Sharpe's desk and took the phone book from the credenza. Finding the number of the New Hope Police Department from the emergency list on the inside cover, he placed his index finger in the rotary dial. After two rings, a woman's smoky voice came on the line. "Police Department."

"This is Jake Dumas, custodian out at the high school. You need to send officers out here. Somebody has been killed."

"At the school? Who?"

"Just send the officers, ma'am. I'll meet them at the front double doors." He then hung up abruptly.

Even before he could make his way down the hall to the front doors, Jake heard the sirens. As he moved at his best speed to meet the officers, they were already banging on the door, noses at the glass and peering in. Jake pushed the bar forward and released the right door. He recognized one of the uniformed officers right away.

"You're the janitor...Jake. Right?" asked the sergeant.

"Yes. The office is this way." He then turned heel and motioned for them to follow.

"I'm Sergeant Foster, Jake." He held out his hand as they were walking. "What's goin' on here and who's dead?"

"Murdered, Sergeant Foster. Horatio Sharpe is sitting in his office deader than four o'clock with a letter opener stuck in his neck."

"What? God, man, you said the principal? Holy shit...that's unbelievable."

Jake said nothing more, but led on.

By six-thirty, the coroner had arrived along with two detectives from the Alabama State Police. Seeing the cop cars and coroner's wagon, a crowd of curious on-lookers had already begun congregating on the front lawn. The press was there as well, trying to get in the front door. The only person the police let in was a frantic Doris Sharpe who broke into an immediate wail upon seeing her husband lying under a sheet on the coroner's cot.

State Police Lieutenant Jerrod Wade, sporting a crew cut, black-rimmed glasses, a white shirt and black tie, used the secretary's office as the hasty interrogation room to question Jake. If need be, Wade would take him on to the precinct for a more thorough examination, that is, if he didn't like Jake's answers.

"Tell me about yourself, Mr. Dumas. How long you been workin' here?"

"Just over a year. I came to New Hope last summer."

"And before that, where were you?"

"California, Lieutenant. For about ten years."

"I see." Wade took a loose cigarette from his shirt pocket and flipped open a Zippo that had a Marine Corps seal on one side. After lighting the Winston, he lifted his head and blew a stream of blue-white smoke into the ceiling light. "I was speaking with Foster out there a while ago and he says he knows about you."

"What does he know about me?" replied Jake.

"That you're a loner and don't speak much. No friends.

No family. What are you...some kind of drifter?"

"I'm just a very private person, detective. I like keeping to myself and I like others to stay out of my business."

Wade took another drag and puffed it out noisily. "All right. I accept that. But you know what I think? The way you speak, you come across as somebody a hell of a lot more intelligent and better educated than janitors I've ever talked to. Why do I feel this way? Help me out here...Jake, if I may call you that. Just from the looks of you, I'd say you could be a lot of things besides a floor mopper."

Jake, unwavering in his eye contact, was silent for a moment, then replied, "Every job has value, Lieutenant. John Calvin said that. I believe that. If a person cannot humble himself in life to do even the most menial of tasks, where is his worth?"

Wade crushed out his cigarette, though half-smoked. "Ya see? That's what I'm talkin' about. Smart and a philosopher as well."

No answer.

"Okay, we'll get off this. So, you come in here and find the principal, just as we found him...slumped back in his chair and a letter opener sticking out of his neck."

Jake nodded.

"Have you always come in here to check on Mr.

Sharpe at the end of the day?"

"Almost every day, unless he seeks me out first. I'm always the last to leave and part of my job is to see there is no one else in the building."

"And was there?"

"Was there what?"

"Anyone else left in the building."

"When I came into this office, no one else was left in the building. To my knowledge, anyway."

"You checked to be sure."

50

"I did."

"Did you touch anything in here?"

"Only the doorknob. Nothing else."

"Did you like the principal, Jake?"

"Not especially."

"Why not?"

"I'd rather not say."

"No, you will say. What was it about him you did not like?"

"I don't speak ill of the dead, Lieutenant."

"Then let's pretend he's not dead. Answer my question."

Jake was uneasy with the question and for the first time in the interview, he diverted his eyes. "Let's just say he had a habit of demeaning people. Like he was above everyone." He paused. "He rather enjoyed his position of power."

"That can make for a ton of enemies."

"Yes."

"Enough to kill him, even."

"I wouldn't know about that. Obviously, somebody was his enemy," Jake said.

"Obviously."

Wade, who had been leaning against the secretary's desk, straightened up and drilled out Jake's eyes with his.

"And how about you, Jake? Did you dislike him enough to kill him?"

A half-smile appeared on Jake's lips. "I don't dislike *anyone* enough to take a life, Lieutenant."

The two men stared at each other without word for a moment and then Wade nodded.

"One more question, Jake. Did you see anyone else in the building a half-hour to an hour before you found the principal?"

Without hesitation, Jake replied, "No." It was a lie and he didn't tell lies. But he saw no value in giving up Blaise and his friends. They wouldn't have done the murder. At least he was sure of that at the moment.

"Did you see any of the faculty or perhaps Coach Conroy hanging around between say five and six?"

"No. They were all gone and I believe the coach was still out on the practice field or in the field house."

Wade nodded. "Okay then. I may have more questions for you at another time. You'll be stayin' in town, I assume."

"My home is here in New Hope and I have my job here. There's no other place for me to go."

"My card, Jake. If you can think of anything else, call me. By the way, Coach Conroy is out in the hall. When you go out, could you please ask the uniformed officer to send him in?"

CHAPTER 5

There were no classes that second day of school out of respect for Horatio Sharpe. Faculty and staff were instructed by the assistant principal, Audrey Tuckwiller, to stay away...and to especially stay away from the press. It was also a day of mourning for the town. But as many of the town folk had been angry and disappointed with Sharpe in kicking the Triple Threat off the team, ambivalence was the rule. The emotion that most people were feeling was one of shock and disbelief. Not only had this been the first murder ever in New Hope, but it was a murder of a prominent figure. The man who had been in charge of the town's children. A killer was also living among them. That was clear. And that made them very afraid.

A few faces were missing from school the next day. Parents were wary about sending their kids to a place where a murder had been committed...perhaps even by someone teaching or working at the school. It made them suspicious about everyone. But among the kids who did return, small groups concentrated here and there before classes to talk it all out, even speculating which one of the teachers had killed their principal. Then when the bell for the first period rang, the chatter and buzz continued until teachers were compelled to call order.

Two minutes later, a pop and crackle began over the intercom. Time for the National Anthem. What with the murder and all the associated hubbub over the last two days, Jake, standing at attention beside his chair, had all but forgotten about the prank Blaise and chums had pulled. So when the first bars of Louie, Louie hit the airways, he chuckled under his breath and smiled. And then he heard the laughter and cheering from every classroom throughout the building on both floors, followed by singing...almost chanting. "Louie, Louie, oh, baby, we gotta go..." Jake's smile broke into a grin and then he had to laugh. This was exactly what the school needed. Pandemonium and jocularity had replaced apprehension and fear.

Mrs. Williams could not get to the record fast enough and suddenly everyone heard an obnoxious rip where the phonograph needle slid across the vinyl, violating the airway. But even so, the students' voices continued on almost in defiance to the god of establishment. After the school-wide acappella had finished, order was finally restored. Today's class would go on without the sacred Anthem.

At twelve-fifteen, Jake was sitting in the custodian's room at his desk eating a potted meat sandwich, when he heard a light knock at the door. Sliding his chair on its wheels to his right, he reached out and turned the knob. He opened the door to find Blaise Honeycutt.

"Jake, can I come in?"

Jake studied him for a moment and then nodded. "Come to gloat about your prank? I see it went off as planned." he said, pulling up a straight-back chair. "Okay, have a seat. What do you want?"

Blaise sat down and leaned forward in the chair, elbows on knees and hands clasped. He was a good-looking kid at just over six-feet with Troy Donahue blonde hair and a Paul Newman face. He had too much going for him with his looks and talent on the gridiron to end up in trouble with the law. Jake knew Blaise had to separate himself from the likes of Cain and Echols. But Jake had also known in his own youth a dozen kids like Blaise who had exchanged opportunity for trouble.

Finally, Blaise spoke. "Why didn't you tell the cops that Gordo, Paulie and I broke into the office and did the prank?"

"You are assuming that I didn't, of course."

Blaise looked surprised at the comment. "I'm not stupid, you know. They would have been all over us if you had, especially since we did it about the same time Mr. Sharpe got iced. What are you doing…holding this over our heads so that if Gordo and Paulie start annoying you again, you'll spill the beans?"

Jake leaned into Blaise and locked eyes. "Look, son. If I thought you boys did 'ice' the principal, your names would have been the first words out of my mouth. And secondly, do you really think that what your punk friends say to me bothers me in the least? I've seen a hundred guys like them, Blaise. They amount to absolutely nothing. And lastly, I gave you my word that I wouldn't turn you in. Does my word mean anything to you?"

"I'm sorry, Jake. I really am. I didn't mean to question you. And I definitely don't go for the way Gordo and Paulie treat you. I admit it. They are punks. But they're my friends, too. I trust them and they never let me down…on the playing field and otherwise."

"Like the other day when they ran out on you, leaving you up against the wall."

Blaise tightened his lips and nodded. "They were just scared is all."

"You have promise, Blaise. Why are these guys your running buddies? Don't you know they can bring you down? When you lie down with dogs, you get up with fleas."

"So, you're calling my friends dogs?"

"It's an old proverb, Blaise. Now, answer my question."

Blaise shrugged. "I don't know. We've kind of always been together. Played on the same teams since junior high. And they're funny. They might be a little rowdy, sometimes, but really, they're not bad guys deep down."

"You're better than that, you know."

Blaise sat back in his chair and folded his arms. "So why should you care one way or the other? You're not one of my teachers or a counselor. And you're not my dad..." He stopped short after mentioning his dad again, then folded his hands and began pulling on his fingers.

"Like I said, Blaise, I've seen a lot of kids with the same potential as you go off in the wrong direction. You might not think it, but I'm in a position in this school where I hear things in the hallways, in the johns and the other sides of walls. Things teachers don't hear. You see, everybody ignores janitors. Like we're invisible. And they aren't careful what they say. They think guys like me are ignorant and don't pay attention to anything except sinks and commodes. But I care about kids, Blaise. And the thing I hate the most is to see someone throw his life away on nonsense just to score points with his friends. Your grades were junk last year, you know. Is that going to continue this year?"

Blaise stood up looking rather pissed. "I didn't come in here for a lecture, Jake. So, the bottom line is, you're not going to tell anyone we were even in the building when Mr. Sharpe died."

Jake sighed, appearing disgusted with where their conversation went. "I'm not telling anyone, Blaise. And there are no conditions involved. Now is that all you wanted?"

"I guess. Thanks," he replied. And then he left.

On Thursday of that week, Sergeant Foster from the New Hope P.D. sat outside the school building on Jackson Street in his patrol unit. The Chief had detailed one of his officers each day during classes to watch the school for any suspicious activity, although the expectations of such were nil. When it appeared the last of the students had departed, he entered the school through the gymnasium door. Jake was just finishing up, pushing a large broom back and forth across basketball court.

"Hey, there he is," called Foster. "You 'bout done for the day, Jake?"

"Yeah. The kids left a couple of balls on the bleachers and once I put them away, I'll lock the doors and get on back to my work in the main building.

"Okay, then. If you don't mind, I'll walk through with you."

After returning the basketballs to the cage and bagging some trash left in the locker room, Jake assured the gym doors were locked and both he and Foster entered through the breezeway into administration building. As they passed the large windows on the south side of the complex, they could see the Raiders still practicing on the field.

"So, Jake, I guess finding the principal had to be quite a shock, eh? Is that the first time you ever saw anybody dead like that?"

"Like that…you mean murdered? Then yes. What's the latest on the investigation?"

"I don't know much since the State is handlin' it. And since a crime like this was committed in a gov'ment institution, the FBI has got people on it. As far as I know, they's no suspects. Did anybody bring you to the precinct for futha discussion?"

"No. I've heard nothing else from anyone."

"They did bring in Coach Conroy ta grill him some more. Maybe I'm not 'sposed to be tellin' that, but it ain't nothin' he haint told around town. He's freely talkin' all about the third degree he got. Was pulled back in twice. It's like he's proud of bein' a suspect or somethin.' Of course, he's used to bein' in the limelight…whether it's good or bad."

"Are they speculating on any motives?"

Foster shrugged. "Just the fact that in general, people didn't like the bastard much, and a hell of a lot of people has been upset about not lettin' them all-star boys play this year."

"That's not motive enough to kill a man. Somebody had to have it in for him. Either that or he got the worst end of an argument."

"Yeah. And I think in the end, he got the other fella's point," Foster chuckled.

Friday night was the Raiders' first game of the season. Earlier in the day, Blaise and his friends approached the coach about being reinstated on the squad, now that Sharpe was no longer around to say otherwise. But Coach Conroy had already beaten them to the punch by bending Assistant Principal Tuckwiller's ear about that very thing.

"No, Billy. Mr. Sharpe made that decision and I can't reverse it. You know he was pressured by the school board to punish those kids. They said it gave the school and the Town of New Hope a black eye. They're not going to change their minds. You better tell the boys to forget it. And I'm sorry…personally, I'd like to see them play."

It was not pretty. Obviously, the Triple Threat was going to be missed. Last year's two and eight Barclay Red Devils made mincemeat of the Raiders, humiliating the 1962 State Champs by a score of 37-7. It was going to be a long season.

Blaise Honeycutt and chums had all but avoided Jake that first week. They knew that at any point, Jake could spill the beans about them breaking into the office to perpetrate their crime while another even greater one was being committed. The police would somehow drag them into the murder or at least make a circumstantial case that could actually put them in jail for a while. The boys owed Jake, and as they now knew he was no dummy, it appeared they might even be able to trust him. Rest assured, there would be no more ridicule.

On the Saturday after Horatio Sharpe's murder, the pews of the First Methodist Church of New Hope were filled to their capacity. Friends and acquaintances alike sat listening to the Reverend Randolph Dixon's eloquent eulogy reverberating with commanding authority throughout the church, thanks to the sounding board that hung over his head. It seemed nearly half the town had congregated for the funeral, but for different reasons. The Mayor and Chief of Police were there as well as a contingency of the Lions of which Sharpe was an active member. Mrs. Tuckwiller and most of the faculty sat behind the grieving widow and her two adult daughters, Delilah and Dixie.

Many of those in attendance were the same lot who only the week before had railed against the principal for taking the 'hope' out of New Hope High when he killed the school's chances for a repeat of their 1962 season. Year after year young and old alike looked forward to that winning season that always seemed to materialize. If they were not State Champs, the school still went to the playoffs. It was not only New Hope's legacy, but the one real thing that kept the town on the map in the great state of Alabama. Football was what brought the newness of life back into the town after a long, hot summer. It was like the New Hope Raiders was the town's own college or pro team.

Horatio Sharpe's coffin sat parked on the altar adorned with a spray of roses and a banner which read Loving Husband. Dr. Dixon read from the Good Book about the frailness of life and that we are only renters of our lives. He praised the man who for a full nine years had handed to many of the town's children their scrolls, but was careful not to mention how he managed to come to his untimely end. Tears began to form throughout.

Was Sharpe's sin against their beloved football program forgiven after all?

Noticeably missing from the sanctuary was Billy Conroy. After all, would it have been proper for the prime suspect of the principal's murder to sit hypocritically with the weeping faculty? As the coach had nearly as huge an ego as Sharpe, he didn't seem to mind the notoriety. But it was certainly a crime he adamantly denied doing. A handful of teachers were missing as well, who did not enjoy working for Sharpe and made it so known. They too would not be accused of being hypocrites. Rosie Green and Jake Dumas were not there, and neither was the entire varsity football squad.

Many of those who occupied the pews were merely curiosity seekers...the same lot that would pack up the family car to ride down the street to see a house that had burned down only an hour before or stand in the checkout line at the Winn Dixie reading the National Enquirer that aired Hollywood's dirty linen. They were the people who lived for drama and thrived on hearing the most spectacular of news, terrible as it was. And they would certainly not miss attending the funeral of a murdered high school principal.

After purchasing a package of 60 watt bulbs and a can opener, Jake stepped from the doorway of the Western Auto just in time to see Blaise Honeycutt passing by, riding shotgun in Paulie Echol's '58 Plymouth. Paulie was of course driving. And Jake could also see a hand resting on the run channel of the rear window with a cigarette stuck between two fingers. He paused a moment to take notice of the boys who he in turn saw had taken notice of him. Blaise threw up his hand, which Jake acknowledged with a nod. To Jake's surprise, the hand with the cigarette owned by Gordon Cain raised in greeting as well, though feeble as it was. The car then moved on, disappearing from view after a right turn onto Palmetto Street.

Since the funeral was still going on and the parking spaces for three blocks around the church were filled, Jake found he had to park the Valiant on Hartwell in front of Mable's Diner. As it was nearly two and he had forgotten to eat lunch, he reached into his jeans pocket to retrieve four bucks, more than enough for a Blue Plate Special at Mable's. That is if Mable was still serving. After tossing his Western

Auto bag onto the front seat, he locked the Valiant and entered the diner. He then slid his bottom onto one of the red vinyl and chrome stools at the counter. The waitress, a hefty girl in her upper teens, almost immediately slapped down in front of him a menu, a glass of water and the Birmingham Star.

Jake unfolded the newspaper, right away catching one of the headlines at the bottom of the first page:

"Murdered New Hope Principal Funeral Today."

He began reading:

"There are no clues as to who may have murdered New Hope Principal Horatio Sharpe, authorities say. Sharpe, who had recently come under fire for his decision to suspend three all-state football players from the New Hope Raiders' squad for a mooning incident, was on Tuesday, the opening day of school, found dead at his desk with a letter opener in his neck.

State Police Lieutenant Jerrod Wade told reporters that fingerprints found on the weapon were smudged beyond recognition. The investigation continues, said Wade, and more interviews are likely..."

Suddenly from a booth to his right, Jake heard a soft voice of a woman, "Jake Dumas, is that you?"

Spinning his stool around, he found the lovely face of Rosie Green. His smile was automatic.

"Why don't you join me," she said. "I haven't been served yet."

"Sure. Why not," he replied, leaving his stool, taking his menu and water with him.

"Hey, he talks," Rosie said. "I don't think you've said more than a dozen words to me over the last year. Didn't know whether you were just shy or the cat had gotten your tongue some time back."

Jake smiled. "Well, I've never been much for small talk."

"Hmmm. Not that you've really ever talked to me at all."

"You're not at the funeral," he commented.

"Well, obviously," she replied. "And neither are you."

"Obviously. You've been at the school nearly as long as he had. I thought you would've seen him off."

She smiled. "He wasn't a favorite of mine pretty much like the rest of the staff. But let's let the dead be dead and talk about the living, Jake."

"Okay." He sipped some water.

"Gosh, this feels so strange, seeing you here and not at the library in your tan work clothes, picking up or returning a book. And what's even more strange is that we're actually having a conversation. You're so quiet and business-like at the school."

"I guess the school is our business, Miss Green."

"Rosie, Jake. Call me Rosie like everyone else does."

"Is that your given name?"

"Well, actually it's Rosemary. When I was born I had the rosiest complexion imaginable. For the longest time, my parents thought I'd stay that way. My dad coined the nickname and it stuck all through childhood. If somebody happens to say 'Rosemary,' sometimes it's like I don't know who they're talking about."

"I've seen your name on the school roster as Anise Green. Is that really your name?"

She laughed. "Can you see me as an 'Anise?' That's my first name and because that's what's on people's driver's licenses and other public records, we get stuck with it. I've asked Mrs. Williams to change it in the school's system, but she never has. She does things her way. One- Track Williams, I call her."

Jake smiled and shook his head.

"So, what about you, Jake Dumas? Where did you come from and why are you just a custodian? You're smart and certainly well-read. And you don't look like a Ziggy. Actually, you're a very good-looking guy, looking all handsome and such in that starched white shirt and tight jeans."

Jake flushed a bit. She was getting a little too fresh for him.

But she continued. "If I saw you out and away from school, I'd think you were a man of means…maybe an outdoorsman just back from sailing your sloop on the lake. I don't think I've ever talked with anyone who knows the first thing about you. Why is that, Jake Dumas?"

He stared at her for a moment and then looked out the large plate-glass window at a delivery truck passing by. "I think…I prefer it if we don't go there, Rosie."

A frown formed between her eyes. "Okay, then. Suit yourself, Mr. Enigma."

Mable then came up to the table and asked how everything was.

"We don't know, yet, Mable. Neither of us has ordered," Rosie replied.

"Well, I'll take care of that right now." She then shouted over her shoulder, "Hey, Cinderella back there messin' around with Manuel! Get you big butt out here and take these folks' orders!"

"Oh, please, Mable, we don't want to get anyone in trouble," Rosie said sweetly.

"No big deal, dear. That's just my lazy daughter. If I don't yell at her like that, she thinks I'm mad at her."

In a few moments the plump waitress with the peroxided hair sashayed through the double swinging doors from the kitchen to take their orders. "Hi, I'm Doreen. What'll you have?"

Rosie ordered a chef salad and Jake, the Saturday special...meat loaf and red-eye gravy. After scribbling on her pad, Doreen then chomped on her gum a few times, gave Jake and Rosie a quick, fake smile and tottered back to the kitchen.

There was only one other couple and an elderly gentleman in the dining room. It was after two and everyone else had eaten and departed. A number of the usual patrons were in the funeral procession which was just then passing by the diner on the way to the cemetery. Both Jake and Rosie watched as the last car in the procession disappeared from view. Jake thought he caught a tear in the corner of Rosie's eye and guessed that whatever she may have felt about the man, just working for someone for almost eight years had to conjure up a bit of sentiment.

But she turned her head back to Jake and continued her inquisition. "So, I guess I will have to go a tad longer before learning anything at all about the mysterious Mr. Dumas…except that he chooses to experience life vicariously from what lies between the covers of books." Jake did not respond, which made the moment even more uncomfortable for the both of them. He knew she would not give up probing him for information. But he would continue making it clear…to her and everyone else…that his life was nobody's business.

Even though Jake had allowed himself that one unusually close moment to converse with another human being in a social setting, he would return to the school the next week to have only the most minimal of dialogue with the lovely Miss Green. She would give him the book he asked for and then a smile. That was pretty much it. She figured out very quickly the afternoon at Mable's that even if they could become friends, there was territory that he would never allow her to enter. He was obviously a man living in a house of secrets. And she could not let herself get too close to a man who would not let her inside.

CHAPTER 6

The Monday of the second week after the funeral, the County School Superintendent appointed a new principal, Cecil Meadows. Now there would be a new controversy about town for the people to chew on. Meadows was a Negro. Although the Howard University graduate had his doctorate, was scholarly and spoke with articulation, there was no way in the town's mind that this man was going to be New Hope's principal. There were long-term White educators in the county system who deserved the job ahead of this token Black, that is, according to the majority of New Hope's faculty, not to mention the patrons at Guy's Bar and grill.

Big John Honeycutt, town council member and regular at Guy's slammed his beer down on the bar with such force the handle separated from the glass. "First, they bring in these Nigras to teach school…there's three of 'em you know…and then they make someone we never heard of our school's principal. Before you know it, one will be headin' up the school board."

Heads began to lift up as Honeycutt continued his rave. His bar chum, Curtis Leahy, a retired mill worker and perpetual stool sitter who spent more of his day at Guy's than with his wife, had no brain of his own; and when any such wisdom was spouted from Honeycutt's mouth, Leahy's head nodded continuously like that little toy dog on the parcel shelf in the back window of Benny Seymour's taxi.

"We're all with you on this, Big John. Yes sir."

"Here's the deal," continued Honeycutt. "We got that Catholic in the White House and his Nigra-lovin' brother, who're seein' to it that even some of the important jobs in government that are always filled by our kind are now filled by that kind."

"Well, I didn't vote for the bastard," chimed in Leahy. "It's all them communists and Hollywood types that put him in. They ain't enough of us good Amer'cans left to see that the right people get into office...no sir, they ain't. Somebody oughta knock that JFK off."

Honeycutt laughed and slapped Leahy on the back. "You be talkin' like that, Curtis old man, and the Feds will be knockin' on your door."

"Let 'em come. I got somethin' waitin' on 'em."

"What I'm sayin' is, a bunch of us ought to demand a special session of the school board and get this blackbird recalled."

"Recalled? What's that?" asked Leahy.

"Removed. A fancy name for cancelled, Curtis. What kind of education do you think our kids will get now? I guess Booker T. Washington's picture will be replacin' George Washington's in the classrooms. The only thing the kids will learn about the War Between the States is that our ancestors owned slaves. I don't know which is worse...bringin' one of their kind in here or keepin' on with Horatio Sharpe, that sumbitch."

"Yeah. The bastard shore got what he deserved. Somebody did us a favor with that guy."

Honeycutt nodded, but didn't respond. Instead, he motioned to Guy Porterfield behind the bar to get him another glass and pour down another draft.

On his third day as principal, Cecil Meadows floated around a memorandum that contained a list of the fifty- seven faculty members and support staff and the days and times each was scheduled to have a 'get acquainted' meeting with him. The list was printed alphabetically, so Jake's pow wow was in the first batch on the first day of meetings. All interviews would be completed within four days.

There was considerable apprehension in the air as to what Meadows intended to accomplish in these discussions. Would he lay out new rules and procedures, make changes to suit him, terminate certain members of the faculty…or was it his ploy to determine from the chats just who New Hope High's bigots were? Some of the faculty even feared he was a 'plant' by Robert Kennedy, if they in fact listened to people like Coach Conroy and Councilman John Honeycutt. For sure, no good could come out of these meetings.

At precisely two-thirty, Jake rapped three times on the principal's door after which he was invited to "come in." Upon entering the room, a smallish man in rimless glasses with features resembling those of W.E.B. Dubois in a photo Jake had seen in a book, rose from behind the principal's desk and stretched out his hand.

"Ah, Mr. Dumas, correct?"

"Correct." Jake took Meadows' hand, finding the little guy to have a surprisingly strong grip. The principal then gestured for Jake to take a seat in the worn vinyl chair in front of the desk.

"May I get you a cup of coffee or some water?"

"No thank you, sir," replied Jake.

"Okay, then," Meadows said, returning to his chair. "Wow! The sun has reached this side of the building and I see it is in your eyes. Let me close the blind a bit." Which he did. "Well, I guess you're wondering why I have asked you and everyone else to come in to meet with me."

"The thought crossed my mind."

Meadows smiled and nodded. "Sounds like you're a straight talker. I've heard about you, Mr. Dumas…a man of few words, but honest as the day is long. You've… been here just over a year," he said, glancing down at Jake's personnel shield. "And I hear you basically keep to yourself."

"Well, I suppose since I am the only custodian in the place, I have no real commonality with anyone else."

"Okay. Very good answer. Well, my only real purpose of these one-on-ones is to just get acquainted with everyone…you know, talk out any concerns or apprehensions about me. I believe there may be some who are not too keen on a man of color occupying this chair."

Jake didn't respond and remained rather stoic.

Meadows continued. "Actually, there are a great many in this community who believe I should have your job. How do you feel about that, Mr. Dumas?"

Jake was a little uncomfortable with the question, but did not allow Meadows to realize it affected him in any way. He remained expressionless. "Let's just say I appreciate your candor, Dr. Meadows."

"And I appreciate the job that you do here, sir…may I call you Jake?"

"That's fine with me. Most everyone does. Even the students."

Meadows studied Jake a moment, not sure if he should explore his history. But he had asked everyone else to that point to provide a kind of verbal curriculum vitae.

"Well, Jake, I have to wonder about you. I certainly don't want to seem invasive, but I like to know about people whom I have in my charge. You appear as a relatively young-middle aged gentleman, well-groomed, well-spoken and having an intelligent glint in your eye. I can spot that. So, why a custodian? Why a job where you're mopping up after everyone" he paused. "No offense, of course."

"And none taken." Jake sat for a moment, locking eyes with the interesting Dr. Meadows. "But in case you were wondering, I'm not a drunk or a pedophile. I live a clean life. I don't smoke and have only an occasional glass of wine or a beer. I prefer hard work…work like this. Keeps me humble. I avoid people most of the time and don't do small talk. Anything more makes my life very complicated. I guess most people would call me uninteresting, but I don't mind it. I like being uninteresting."

Meadows grinned and shook his head. "I'm not going to find anything out about you today, am I Jake?"

"I just did tell you about me," Jake replied, smiling back.

Meadows folded his hands and peered at Jake over the top of his glasses. "Yes, I guess you did. But what you didn't tell me is who Jake Dumas really is."

"What you see is who I am, sir," Jake said dryly.

"I like you, Jake. Obviously, you're a very private person and I respect that. I also have the feeling I'm going to get along with you better than anyone else in the school. I'm going to take a lot of heat from this community because of my appointment. People don't like Colored educators coming into their White schools. Can I depend on you to be in my corner?"

"Dr. Meadows, you're speaking to a relatively unimportant member of your staff. I have no clout or influence. How could I ever be impactive as far as you're concerned?"

"You never know, Jake. And let me just tell you, I think your job is equally as important as anyone else in this school."

"Thank you," Jake replied. "I appreciate that."

Meadows then rose to shake hands. His grip was warm and earnest. And that was enough for Jake to realize that Cecil Meadows was indeed a good man.

Blaise Honeycutt, cruising with Paulie Echols on Main Street in the Fury, as they normally did on Saturday nights, waved to his steady, Janet Lullwater, as she was preparing to enter Mable's with her friend, Lori Lynn McIlhenney. The girls were the head and assistant cheerleaders for the Raiders, respectvely; however, they had little to cheer about, considering the team had not won a game the entire month of September.

Paulie, keeping his eyes on strawberry-blonde Lori Lynn, pulled too close to the curb and raked his right fender on a parking meter.

"Ouch!" Lori Lynn exclaimed. "Nasty scrape."

Paulie was immediately angry with himself as there had never been as much as a scratch put on the car. Now diverting his attention away from her, he bounded out of the Fury to inspect the damage. Blaise and Janet had to chuckle, watching him rubbing the sheet metal as though he could somehow buff the dent out with his fingers. But then, resigned that it was futile, he turned and leaned against the perpetrator parking meter.

Janet, a stunning seventeen year old with long dark hair and deep, beautiful, Liz Taylor eyes leaned into the window where Blaise still sat and quickly kissed him on the lips. "Hi, Dreamboat," she said.

"She's referrin' to me," Paulie said.

"In your dreams, Paul Parrot," Janet replied. That was Paulie's nickname around the school, coined because when he laughed heartily, he sometimes squawked like a parrot.

Blaise exited the car and held both of Janet's hands, soliciting another kiss. "What are your plans tonight?" he asked.

"I think we're going to hook up with Tammy Jo and Lorraine and go to a movie. They're showing that Hitchcock movie, The Birds. Wanna come?"

"Naw. My old man told me I had to be home by eight."

"Eight? On a Saturday night?"

"Yeah. It's a kind of punishment. I got an F on my History test and a D on a paper I wrote in Social Studies. I'm lucky to be out of the house at all."

Paulie, still eyeing Lori Lynn, said, "Aw, come on, Blaise. If you're in the shit house with your dad anyway, you might as well go for it all and have a little fun tonight.

How much more could he punish you than takin' away a Saturday night?"

Blaise bit his lip and looked down at the sidewalk. "You know damn well how bad he can make it on me."

Paulie didn't respond. He did know how bad it could be for Blaise. But this was his chance to hang out with Lori Lynn. Something he had never had the opportunity to do. And he didn't want to be the only guy in a group of girls. He pulled Blaise off to the side. "You sure you can't just call your dad and tell him my car broke down or something?"

"He'd just come out to get me. Forget it, Paulie." They walked back to the girls and Paulie shrugged.

"Guess we're not goin' with you."

"Well, can we just talk for a few minutes?" asked Janet.

Blaise checked his watch. Seven-fifteen. "I suppose we can go inside and have a coke or something."

The place smelled of fried hamburgers from the kitchen grill and brewing coffee. A few kids they knew from school occupied some of the booths off to the left side of the diner and two men in flannel shirts and caps with herbicide brands on them sat at the counter smoking cigarettes.

Paulie had hoped Lori Lynn and Janet would slide into the booth opposite one another, so that he could bump buns with Lori Lynn, but no such luck. The girls took seats on the same side. As Blaise and Janet immediately clasped hands across the table, that left Paulie opposite Lori Lynn… which was not at all a bad arrangement. It kind of made it seem like he and Lori Lynn were a couple.

Doreen, who knew the girls from school, although a couple of years ahead of them, came up to take the order.

"Hey, Lori Lynn, Janet. Where you all been? You haven't been in here in more than a month."

"Busy, I guess," replied Janet. "School…you remember what that was like. Cheerleading. Drama. Chorus. It never stops."

"Well, I sure weren't no cheerleader, but I get all the drama I want right here. So I know a little bit about it, I guess. What'll ya have?"

"Just cokes, I guess," said Blaise. "Unless you all want something to eat."

They all shook their heads.

"Well, I won't get much of a tip off cokes, but suit yourselves," replied Doreen, somewhat huffy. She then turned heel and waddled toward the fountain service.

"I think she was actually mad," observed Lori Lynn. Janet nodded and then changed the subject. "Hey, Blaise, I over-heard Dad and Mom talking at breakfast this morning. They said your dad got together with three of the school board members yesterday, trying to convince the rest of them to get rid of Mr. Meadows."

Blaise appeared puzzled. "I didn't know about that. As much as he cusses around the house about them putting Meadows in, I'd have thought that would have made the top ten over our breakfast table."

"Well, I like Mr. Meadows," Lori Lynn jumped in. "He speaks to everybody in the hallway and always has a smile on his face. That's a far cry from the way Principal Sharpe used to treat us. It was like he was a warden and we were his inmates. I guess if Mr. Meadows was a White man, nothing would ever be said. Why would your dad want to go that far to get him out?"

"Because he's an ass, that's why. Big John thinks he's Big Shit in this town. I think the reason most people in this town eat him up and go along with everything he says and does is that they're afraid of him."

Paulie and the girls shot glances at one another while Blaise turned his head to look out the picture window. They knew he was embarrassed about his father and any mention of him would set Blaise off.

For a long while, they said nothing. Then Blaise swung his legs out and stood. "I'd better go. Come on, Paulie."

"But our cokes aren't here yet."

Blaise threw a dollar on the table and said "Sorry, Janet. Enjoy your night. I'll catch up to you. Maybe tomorrow after church."

She nodded and forced a smile. "Okay, tomorrow then."

On the way out of town as Paulie drove toward the Honeycutt house, Blaise stared out of the passenger's side window and said nothing. He also saw nothing, except his father's pompous face branded in his mind. At the end of every day, there seemed to be just a little more to hate about him.

As they came upon the large, white Victorian, Paulie decelerated the Plymouth. It was a beautiful, majestic old home with double turrets and a large, wrap-around veranda supported by columns. The house sat stately under three massive oaks with root systems that sprawled above ground where the red earth had eroded away perhaps a hundred years before. Paulie had never been inside the house...not because Blaise had never asked him. But he too was one of those who were afraid of Big John Honeycutt, especially since it got back to Paulie that the man never approved of any of Blaise's buddies.

"Do me a favor, Paulie. Buzz on by the house. I'm not ready to go in just yet."

"Okay." The RPMs began to pick up and the 413 Hemi roared even louder. "Where we goin'?"

"Take a left onto Cabbagetown Road."

"What's down there?"

"That group of houses about a mile and a half down called Driftwood."

"All right, I give up; why we goin' there?"

"Just drop me off...there," Blaise pointed, "at the end of the road."

"And then what?"

"You leave...I walk."

"Walk where."

"Ultimately, home."

Paulie stopped his car and placed his left arm on the steering wheel. Turning to Blaise, he asked him, "What's going on, man?"

"I'll be running back from here."

"From here. Are you nuts?"

"We ran more than five miles in practice some days."

"Yeah, but…"

Blaise opened the door and stepped out. The oil-starved hinges creaked and popped as the door swung shut. "Better take care of that," he said. "Catch you later."

Paulie shook his head and then pulled from the gravel shoulder back onto Cabbagetown Road.

With all of the thoughts running through his head, Blaise actually didn't care what Big John Honeycutt would say or do to him when he failed to return home by eight. If he accomplished what he envisioned, in the long run any further punishment his old man would deal out would be inconsequential. He just needed help, that's all.

Outside of the subdivision, the skeleton hull of a burnt-out Fiat sat ten feet into a field where unharvested cotton lay rotting on the branch giving off the effect of a clinging snow in the fading light. The asphalt on the road running into the low rent community was rugged and filled with pot holes. There was only one main drag though the subdivision with three intersecting streets that ended in cul-de-sacs. If Blaise was fortunate, he would have no trouble locating the house. Not twenty feet past the crumbling brick entranceway, he saw it. Five houses down on the right on Carriage Lane, he recognized the car in the driveway.

Blaise hesitated for a moment at the mailbox to look at the house. An unpretentious ranch, it had a modest front porch with a blue and white awning hanging over it. Two barren-looking windows without shutters symmetrically pasted on either side of the door looked back at him. Thinking a second time whether being there was a good idea, he turned to walk away, only to stop himself. He was already there. It would be ridiculous not to go in.

After ascending the three porch steps, he rapped lightly on the door. He heard in response the rhythmic thuds of footsteps inside which caused the front door to shudder a bit. The door then opened and the two men, one very young and one older, stood looking at each other for a few seconds through the screen.

"Blaise Honeycutt," said Jake. "This is unexpected. Is something wrong?"

"No. Nothing's wrong. I…"

"You just happened to be in the neighborhood and stopped by to see how the riff-raff lives."

Before Blaise could respond, Jake recanted the comment. "Sorry, Blaise. I didn't mean that like it sounded. Is something on your mind? Like what happened at the school? If it is, that's history as far as I'm concerned."

"No," Blaise replied. "That's not it." He then jammed his finger tips into his jeans pockets and shuffled his feet.

Jake stepped back from the door and said, "Come on in. Want a coke or something?"

"Naw, I'm good. I just wanted to ask you something."

"You couldn't ask me at school?"

"No. I had this on my mind and thought we could discuss it before the weekend was over."

"Now you've piqued my curiosity. Have a seat." Jake gestured toward a worn and faded blue sofa chair that faced the couch.

At first, Blaise didn't say anything, but searched the room with his eyes, stopping on a large reproduction of a sailing ship on a swollen, storm-tossed sea hanging over the closed-off fireplace. On either side of the fireplace were books…no shelves, just books, stacked in rows about waist high. Blaise then took note of a peace plant with yellowed and brown leaves perched on the brick hearth dying from neglect.

"Horticulture has never been one of my strongest suits," Jake said, smiling. "Okay, now what's on your mind?"

"Well, I don't know quite how to say this, but I know you're pretty smart, Jake."

"You came all the way out here to tell me that?"

"No…no. It's like this. I've seen you getting books from the library and Miss Green says you read all the time…read everything. Books about science and history and what's going on in the world."

Jake nodded and then replied "Yes. And where's this going?"

Blaise dropped his eyes onto his hands. His fingers were interlaced and he bent them back nervously to crack all his knuckles. "I need help, Jake. I'm already flunking American History and Social Studies and here it is only October."

"Sorry to hear that."

"Well, I figure with all that you know, you could maybe…tutor me."

Jake burst into laughter. He hadn't laughed like that in eons, he thought. "Me? Tutor you? You come to the school janitor for tutoring?"

"Why not? You're as smart as any of my teachers."

"And you know that how?"

"Because, most of them are stupid… and don't give a shit."

Jake laughed again. "Okay then. That makes me just smarter than stupid."

"No. It's not that. I don't mean that. I saw all your books in the janitor room. They're intelligent books… about history and the world, about war and politics. If you know everything in those books, you can damn sure help somebody like me get through a couple of classes."

"Good grief, son. I don't know anything about tutoring. Why don't you just turn to your History and Social Studies teachers for some after-school tutoring?"

Blaise settled back in his chair, seemingly more comfortable now with their conversation. "Because my History teacher hates me. He hates all jocks. And my Social Studies teacher, Mr. Billingsly, is so damn boring, he puts everyone to sleep. But with History, it's all about events and dates. What good is that stuff? It's what's happening now that's important."

Jake nodded. "You're right in a way. These are exciting times we live in, but so were the times and events of our past. You have to understand where we all came from and value what we have learned from the experiences of history to appreciate the present and the future."

"See? That's what I'm talking about. Just telling me stuff like that lets me know you're passionate about history and the world, enough to make it interesting for me."

Jake shook his head. "Blaise, my man. I can't tutor you. Why if the school officials knew that, they'd probably fire me. I'm not qualified or even certified to be a tutor."

"Well, I'll go to the principal or the school board or somebody to get it approved. I need help, Jake. If I flunk out this year, my old man will…" He stopped short of completing his sentence. "Just think about it, okay? I work with Gordo over at the filling station some nights and Saturdays helping out with some of the mechanical work. I'll pay you. If we could do this a couple evenings a week, I know it will help me."

Jake saw the desperation in Blaise's eyes. How many kids ever came to the self-realization that they needed help and then set about on their own to do something about it? Jake had been a kid watcher for over a year now. He passed them in the halls, listened to them talk, and sat near them in the bleachers at sporting events. Most of them were transparent and self-absorbed. But there was something special about Blaise Honeycutt that Jake did not see in the others. He had vision which in his mind was the blueprint for success. Blaise was a natural leader on the gridiron as well as the basketball court. And he had not only a commanding personality, but a sense of presence. But if he failed in these two classes, it would impede his ability to get accepted in a number of colleges and universities…at least the good schools.

Jake leaned forward with his hands on his knees and stared into the blue eyes of the young man sitting across from him. "If I do this...and I'm not saying I will, mind you...I don't want your money. But the caveats are that you come back to the school at seven, after my work is done, on the evenings we agree upon, for one hour sessions. You tell no one about it. We'll try this until your interim report card comes out. If it's good, we'll continue on. If it's not, that means I'm not being effective. Then it's a waste of your and my time. One other thing...I'll have to tell Dr. Meadows what we're doing. I believe he'll support it and allow us to use one of the classrooms."

Blaise's eyes lit up. "Why can't I just come over here after you get home, Jake?"

"Look at me, Blaise. This is not the same world I grew up in when I was a kid your age. People, especially your father and mother, won't understand a young teenager spending evenings in a house alone with a man who has no wife and family. That's your first lesson in both History and Social Studies. Open your eyes and your mind to learn about the world around you, son. You will have to do that to be able to absorb the information I will give you that reinforces what you should be learning in the classroom. So, it'll be done at the school, if we do it at all."

Blaise stood up and extended his hand. "Thanks, Jake. I already feel better about myself. But I too have a caveat...whatever that is. Please don't let this get back to my father. There are probably a lot of reasons he would go ballistic. And you mentioned one of them. My mom wouldn't care. She doesn't say much about anything, anyway. She just mostly stays out of Dad's way and goes on. As long as she's got her martini, she's cool."

"Agreed. All right, get on out of here. I'll see you Monday. But remember, I have to speak with Meadows first." He then looked out the living room window. "Where's your car?"

"I don't have one. My old man won't allow it."

"You're going to walk home?"

"Jog, actually. I need to get back in shape and no better time to start than tonight."

"But, it's pitch black out there and starting to rain. Let me get my jacket. I'll drive you home."

"Thanks," replied Blaise. "Just drop me off on the highway a block or so from the house, if you don't mind."

CHAPTER 7

As though there had not been enough drama around the New Hope High campus in the past couple of months, on the second Monday in November the hallways and classrooms were all abuzz. With eyes wide and mouths agape, students shook their heads in disbelief to learn that the Alabama State Police had arrested their beloved Coach Billy Conroy for the murder of Horatio Sharpe. "Coach didn't do this," Gordo Cain told Blaise and Paulie as he lit up a cigarette behind a large poplar, well out of sight of any faculty. "If he had, he would have used a .38 to kill the bastard, not a damn letter opener."

It seems that Assistant Coach Ron Jarvis, having also been grilled by the police, divulged that Conroy admitted to him he had stormed Sharpe's office just after school hours the day of the murder and had "had it out with the principal. And I took care of business once and for all." But Conroy had denied all along that he had been in the administration building at any time that afternoon...that the last time he had spoken with Sharpe was in the parking lot "and that conversation was cordial." Although Jarvis admitted that the parking lot conversation was actually not that pleasant, the Coach had made no threats upon the principal. It was merely an exchange of opinions as to the three suspended players. Given the hearsay evidence and the discrepancies in the two coaches' stories, the State felt there was enough circumstantial evidence to indict Wild Bill for the murder.

At five minutes past eight, after the students had settled down, after the National Anthem had ceased echoing throughout the building, Mrs. Williams from the school office knocked on the door to the custodian's room. "Jake, there's a Lieutenant Wade here to see you. He's in the office."

Jake followed her into the school office where he was immediately greeted by the lieutenant. "Good mornin', Jake. How are you, today?"

"Feeling well...and you?"

"The same, I reckon. Won't do a body any good to complain." But then he got right down to business. "Say, is there a place where we can go to talk?"

Jake nodded. "I guess back to my room would be fine, if you don't mind the smell of Lysol."

He then led the officer out of the office and into the custodian room.

"Mind if I smoke?" Wade asked, pulling a pack of Winstons from his jacket pocket.

"Actually, I do. There are some industrial-strength cleaners in here and any spark could in fact start a flash fire."

"Okay, sorry. I wasn't thinkin.'"

"So, what's on your mind, Lieutenant?"

"I see you like getting' to the point."

"I'm a busy man."

"Yes. Well, okay, I guess you know by now we picked up Billy Conroy last night."

"That kind of news travels fast."

"Uh huh. Well, we hated to do that, knowin' what he means to this school and the community, but the evidence seems to be stackin' up against him."

"Circumstantial based on hearsay as I understand it," replied Jake.

"You obviously heard more than I thought."

"I hear a lot more than people think."

"I'm sure. Well, I want you to think back at exactly the time the coroner figures the principal was murdered... about five-thirty. Where were you again about that time?"

"I would have either been cleaning the rest rooms or back in here. I don't know exactly. I may also have been mopping the hallways, which is the last thing I do."

"Right. So you would have been in pretty good position to hear anybody comin' or goin'...maybe someone down the hall arguin' with the principal."

"It's possible."

"Now I asked you this before...are you sure you heard or saw no one in the buildin' anywhere during that time frame?"

Without batting an eyelash, Jake replied "No." He wondered if Wade had somehow found out about Blaise and the boys and their high jinks, and that he had caught them in the act. But as the police had already arrested the Coach, why would he be going in a different direction?

"If you're asking if I heard or saw Coach Conroy at that hour of the afternoon, I did not. But, if I'm at this end of the hall or upstairs flushing toilets and such, anyone could have slipped in and out without me hearing him."

Wade settled his eyes for a moment on Jake's, then said, "Look, I'm just tryin' to tie up loose ends on this arrest. Anything significant you could add would certainly help the case."

"I'll say this again. I neither saw nor heard Billy Conroy on the floor."

"And you saw or heard no one else."

Jake made sure he did not break eye contact when he said, "No, Lieutenant. I can tell you nothing. Now, if you don't mind, I have work to do."

Wade then jumped to his feet and extended his hand. "Okay, thanks, Jake. We're done here."

And Jake hoped for good.

On his lunch hour Jake quickly ate his tuna salad sandwich and washed it down with some juice. He had business down the hall.

"Yes, sir, come in," said Cecil Meadows, rising to greet Jake.

"I won't take up much of your time, Dr. Meadows. I just wanted to chat about one of your students."

"Which one?"

"Blaise Honeycutt."

"Ah, yes. The High School All-American with the golden arm, currently without a job. Are you here to plead his case to put him back on the team? This won't be the first conversation I…"

"No. That's not it. That's a school decision that I have no business discussing. I know this will sound a bit strange to you, but the boy wants me to tutor him in a couple of his courses. And I have basically agreed."

Meadows studied what Jake had told him for a moment with one reflective finger against his cheek.

"Well, I don't know it's all that strange. I have suspected since our first conversation that you are a learned man and would be quite capable to do so. I also have no doubt you possess the knowledge and ability to tutor anyone in anything, but why are you speaking to me about it? Special tutoring would not require my permission."

"I figured that since I'm a school employee and would be utilizing one of the classrooms a couple evenings a week, it would be your business. At least the school's business."

Meadows nodded. "I see what you're saying. Okay, then. You have my blessing. You're the last to lock up around here anyway. Are his parents okay with this?"

"I don't believe they know as yet, unless he told them. I would of course meet with him at the school and not at my house for propriety reasons."

"Of course," replied Meadows. "I do know about the man they call 'Big John' Honeycutt…the man who appears to be after my scalp."

"Seems that you keep your ear to the ground, Dr. Meadows."

"And like I said before...I hope you will do so as well."

"Then we are agreed."

"Yes," Meadows said, rising, and then they shook on it. "When do you start with the boy?"

"Today."

At ten minutes till seven, Jake pushed the squeaking bucket-on-wheels down the hallway with his mop and broom sitting on his shoulder. Outside of his doorway, his student stood with his back and cocked right foot against the wall. A text book was in his hand.

"Hi, Jake."

"Be with you in a moment as soon as I put these away and lock up. Go on down to Classroom Six."

After securing his tools of trade, Jake then joined Blaise in the classroom.

"Let me see your text."

Blaise handed him the History book which was entitled America Revisited: the Twentieth Century.

"Hmmm. By Jennings and McNaught. I've read other texts by these guys. Adequate at best. Where are you in the book?"

"I think we're into something called the Depression."

"You think?"

"Yeah, all that the teacher talks about is what happened and when. We just had a matching test. We had to match stuff like the NRA with the date. Hell, I thought the NRA was the National Rifle Association not the National 'something something'."

"National Recovery Act, Blaise. Look, I have an idea of how you're being taught, but we're going to approach history a little different. We're going to talk out things that happened back then and I want you to imagine that you're listening to a radio serial or watching a movie like From Here to Eternity, complete with characters, sound effects and dialogue. And when you see the material again on your exam, you will know all about it. I want you to envision scenarios like the Allies entering Auschwitz to free thousands of imprisoned Jews who were awaiting execution, because I will have told you this powerful story in living color. I will take you to Warm Springs, Georgia where President Roosevelt died in 1945 and back to Washington where Harry S. Truman was sworn in as the 33rd President. You will get to know these people as surely as you know your New Hope neighbors. But you will have to stay with me every step of the way."

Blaise was already hooked. He hoped that Jake would indeed be the teacher and mentor he had needed all of his school life. Someone passionate. Someone caring. Someone interested in Blaise Honeycutt. And he would not let Jake down.

Just as the emotions at New Hope were beginning to subside…just as the students had now absorbed and accepted that their former principal was murdered right there in their school and a new controversial Colored man had replaced him and just as the community was finally coming to grips that its coach had been arrested for the murder…on Friday the 22nd Dr, Meadows interrupted fourth period class with a message over the intercom.

"Attention, faculty and students. I will need everyone to come to the auditorium as quickly and orderly as you can. Teachers, please be sure all students have cleared the classroom."

What now? Was there a bomb scare or a fire? If so, everyone would be sent outside, not to the auditorium. Maybe the Soviet Union and Cuba finally fired the missiles that got everyone upset last year. As students exited their classrooms, questions such as these rattled throughout the hallways, creating a kind of unintelligible white noise. Once assembled and seated, Dr. Meadows climbed the steps to the stage and stood behind the podium. Once, twice, he tapped the microphone, finding it in working order. For an uncomfortable moment he looked down and said nothing. Then in broken voice he began.

"Some...of you have already heard; but today, this afternoon, our President, John F. Kennedy, who was riding in an open limousine in Dallas, Texas, was shot by an unknown assassin. The networks have reported... (Meadows began to sob)...that he may not have survived."

Audible gasps could be heard throughout the auditorium, followed by the sounds of weeping here and there. Several of the women and girls placed trembling hands on their chests as though their breaths had been taken away. Boys sat looking at one another in frozen shock, mouths agape, but saying nothing. No one had any words except Dr. Meadows.

"I ask that everyone bow your heads and in whatever way you choose, pray for the President and the Kennedy family. Pray also for our country in this terrible time."

Jake stood in the back of the auditorium with most of the faculty. Rosie Green was beside him sobbing uncontrollably into a handkerchief, leaning her head on Jake's shoulder. And that was what finally caused him to lose it as well.

The stillness during the time of prayer and meditation seemed to amplify the audible sobs that continued on. After a few moments Meadows spoke again.

"Now, I will ask that in orderly fashion and with silent respect that you file out of the auditorium. I am dismissing classes and have summoned the bus drivers to be here momentarily to take those of you who live beyond town limits to your homes. If you are usually picked up by your parents at three-thirty, I will ask you to wait here until we are able to contact them."

Without word and with a maturity that went well beyond their years, students began to leave their rows. It was as though they were filing out having just attended a funeral. When the majority of kids and faculty had left the auditorium, Rosie turned and threw her arms around Jake's neck. It surprised him a little, but he understood that she needed someone, anyone who could comfort her. Her wet cheek felt cool and clammy on his neck. "Oh, Jake," she sobbed. "This is so horrible. Our poor President."

Jake placed his hands on her back and let her continue weeping for another minute or so, not caring how it looked to those still in the room. And then, gently, he took her shoulders in his hands to push her body away. Any other time, this would have been a sensually-tender moment for him; but neither allowed such feelings to materialize. Neither thought of their embrace to be anything else except mutual consolation.

She smiled her sweet smile through the tears. Her mascara had smudged and run in places, but she was still beautiful, messy or not. Then without word she walked away. By three-fifteen everyone had left the school except Jake and Meadows. They both stood for a few moments outside the door to the principal's office, arms folded and heads down.

"I met Mr. Kennedy, you know," said Meadows. "I was at a CORE meeting in Washington where he spoke. Such a polished and charismatic man. I got to shake his hand. Don't know why I'm telling you his. I guess that's what people do at times like this. A way of connecting ourselves to the moment."

Jake nodded. He liked Meadows. He liked people who maintained a sense of humility… especially people who held esteemed offices. "We are all connected to this moment, Dr. Meadows. This is a man who holds the same office as the Father of our Country. As such, he epitomizes our country, and therein lies that connection."

"Well said, Jake. Why don't you go on home now/"

"No, you go home to be with your family, sir. I'll have to lock everything up."

"All right. Thanks."

Jake heard within the hour on his transistor radio that the President had indeed died. As on every other school day, he would lower the American Flag from the front mast, fold it and place it on the shelf in his room; this day he lowered it to half-staff where it remained over the weekend.

Schools all over the state were closed on Monday the 25th, the day President Kennedy was laid to rest at Arlington on the grounds at the foot of the Lee Mansion. It was also the National Day of Mourning. Since Jake had never owned a television, he sat most of the day listening to the commentary on his old Motorola.

CHAPTER 8

Classes resumed on Tuesday. Teachers took up most of their hours memorializing JFK by revisiting his life and presidency. Moods were somber and the faces of the students still reflected their shock.

Jake and Blaise resumed their after-school session on Wednesday. Neither spoke about Kennedy. Blaise did tell Jake that he and his father had a heated exchange of words after which Blaise was ordered out of the house. He was to stay out until he gave his father some respect. It seems that Big John 'once a Marine, always a Marine' Honeycutt made a comment about Oswald. "Well, it just goes to show you what damn fine shots Marines are." Blaise proceeded to call his Kennedy-hating father an 'asshole' and his mother risked life and limb by stepping in between them. As Big John stood with fist cocked ready to lay into Blaise, Debbie Honeycutt told her husband that if he was going to hit someone, let it be her.

That happened on Monday and Blaise had not been home since. "I've been staying with Gordo. Mom knows where I am, but Dad said he didn't care where I was, that I could fall into a sink hole and turn to shit."

Jake listened sympathetically for a while as Blaise poured out his contempt for his old man. He supposed Blaise's father had never forgiven him for the 'indiscretion' that got him kicked off the football team. Blaise had not only ruined his future, but his father no longer had bragging rights down at Guy's about his record-breaking son. This was the year Blaise could have been the most- recruited high school football player in the country.

"We need to get back to it, Blaise." The lesson that week in Social Studies was on the welfare system…how it evolved, who benefited and how it affected people's motivation to work. Blaise's teacher was as dry as the Arizona desert. The man whose voice droned in nasal monotone, affecting the students like fingernails down a chalkboard, merely read from the text and put most everyone to sleep. No wonder a normally bright and high-spirited kid like Blaise was failing the class. But the way Jake embellished the material with real-life human stories and illustrations planted seeds of genuine interest in Blaise's brain that made him want to know more about the government.

As their sessions continued into mid-December, Jake gave out homework assignments to read specific articles in Newsweek and political commentary in The Birmingham Star to reinforce and complement the subject matter. Blaise began to realize the value in Jake's one- on-one engagement. Personalized instruction without all the distractions, some of which of course were good distractions like the lovely Miss Janet Lullwater.

Blaise's father finally let him back in the door that weekend, but the boy had to grovel. Anyway, it just wouldn't do for one of the town's esteemed council members to be known as a man who kicked his own son out of the house…especially Blaise Honeycutt, the All- American boy. Besides, Christmas was a week away and how would that look?

The first semester done, report cards went out. Blaise's Social Studies grade came up to a C, but he scored a B in History. Considering that a month and a half before he was carrying an F, his History teacher, knowing such a rebound was impossible, pulled Blaise off to the side and accused him of cheating. "I don't know how you're doing it, but I'm going to find out. You'd do yourself good by confessing to me right now about it, and maybe I'll go easy on you."

"But I am not cheating, Mr. Connor. I've just been knuckling down, that's all." As Blaise was sworn to secrecy about his tutoring, this is all he could say.

But that was not good enough for Connor, so he set up a meeting with Blaise and Principal Meadows.

"There is no way a marginal student like Blaise Honeycutt could score A's on my History tests when he finished out the previous two months with a solid F. I say that somehow he has gotten copies of my exams and I want the boy investigated."

"Believe me, Mr. Meadows," rebutted Blaise. "I am not cheating. I've been studying my ass off…excuse me, sir. How could I be getting copies of his exams?"

Meadows sat with hands folded and fingertips touching his chin, eyeing both Blaise and Dirk Connor. 'So,' he thought. 'Jake Dumas' work with this boy is actually paying off.' "I'll tell you what's wrong here, gentlemen. I agree there has been a crime committed. Mr. Honeycutt, I'd like you to go sit outside on the hall bench while I speak with Mr. Connor."

Blaise hesitated, fearing what was coming.

"Go on, son."

Blaise stood, shook his head and gave both men a parting glare before he closed the door behind him. Connor nodded and half-smiled, waiting to hear what type of punishment Meadows would dole out. Detention? Even expulsion, considering Blaise was already in hot water over the mooning incident.

Meadows then stood and placed his hands on the desk. "How dare you dishonor this boy, not to mention the charge entrusted to you as his teacher! Blaise Honeycutt did not cheat on your exams. You have no damn proof that he did and you know it. You have embarrassed and defamed the boy by making false allegations against him. Does it not seem at all feasible to you that this bright kid could in fact wake up and set about turning himself around? You owe the boy an apology, Mr. Connor. As long as I sit in this chair, you will never again make such accusations against one of your students unless you have tangible, undisputed evidence of cheating."

Slowly, Connor rose from his chair, red-faced and fists clenched. "My colleagues were right about you, Mr. Meadows. You are neither competent nor otherwise capable of sitting in that chair. How dare you speak to me like that. I will do you a favor by letting you know that next Monday night there is a special session of the school board to determine your future at this school. Christmas will see you without a job. Happy Holidays, Principal." Connor then turned heel and left the room, slamming the door behind him. As he passed by Blaise, he turned his head away.

The county school board generally met the first Thursday of each new quarter and any of the meetings was open to the public. A special session of the board, however, was called by the superintendent for the 19th to address the divisiveness among the board members and prominent citizens of New Hope regarding his controversial appointment of Dr. Cecil Meadows as principal of their high school. As

Meadows, a New Yorker, had only moved into the county six months before, parents, some of the faculty and a number of community advocates still remained up in arms about the selection. At least that was their official premise. Why weren't other, more qualified people considered for the job? People like Dr. Maxwell Sanborn, a long-time educator who had retired from the system in '61, and Gwyneth Anne Carpenter, the popular Business teacher at New Hope High for fifteen years, both of whom had unimpeachable leadership skills.

It was Dr. Burt Peterson, school superintendent and prominent area pediatrician, who had recommended Meadows to the board, which in turn approved his selection five to four. Meadows, a polished and highly- sought educator, had taught at Seton Hall and had moved to the area to be near his critically-ailing mother in her waning years. He had had thoughts of joining the New Hope faculty whenever a position opened anyway. Peterson had met Meadows a couple of years back when he sat in on a Caring for Children seminar at Seton Hall where he heard the eloquent Education Department Chair speak. In reviewing Meadows' application for a teaching position, Peterson remembered him. And when

Principal Sharpe met his unexpected death, Meadows was the first person that came to Peterson's mind.

Normally, the board met in the Cannon Building conference room in town. Even considering there were only a dozen or so gallery seats opposite the conference table, seldom were they filled in any of the open forums. However, as more than two hundred interested parents, teachers, students and town folk had made known their intentions of attending this special session and to open a dialogue with the board, the meeting was moved to the Dabney R. Carter Courthouse jury selection room.

One of the first to arrive just before six-thirty was Big John Honeycutt, who took a seat on the first row. New Hope's mayor and two other members of the town council sat with him. Standing off to the side together were Police Chief Mervyn McCleary and County Sheriff Randy Owens. Other officers and deputies congregated on the steps outside of the courthouse. One would think from all the badges present there was a murder trial of some mob henchman taking place.

By seven, the room was completely full. Some had come to see to it that the new principal was removed, while others were there for curiosity sake…like when they went to the former principal's funeral. A number of on-lookers, mostly students, were there in support of Meadows, like old Miss Jarrett, the community social activist and staunch Democrat, and the Reverend Crutchfield, pastor of the First Presbyterian Church. Blaise was there with his two sidekicks about six rows back from Big John. Meadows had supported Blaise when butt hole Connors had accused him of cheating, and that was something Blaise would not forget. Anyway,

could be that a fight might break out, and the boys did not want to miss that.

Dr. Peterson brought the room to sudden silence with the rap of his coffee cup on the table at the front of the panel room where he and all nine of his board members sat. "The meeting will come to order. We are here tonight in special session at the request of members of this very board, as well as the New Hope town Council and other members of our community, to debate my decision on the appointment of the New Hope High School principal in September. There will be other business discussed as well, but I expect once the discussion about Dr. Meadows is over, this place will evacuate as though we were expecting a hurricane." There were a few chuckles at that, but Peterson was not smiling. The tone of his voice reflected his sarcasm.

He continued. "First of all, I'd like to make a statement. Christmas is upon us and I'd personally like to wish you and your families all the joy and peace of the season. May you have in your hearts the same love for our fellow man as exemplified by our Lord and Savior Jesus Christ. May this love be universal and unconditional. And it is in that same spirit that I ask you to ponder the issue before us this evening.

"Now with that said, I would like to open up a dialogue with this forum regarding Dr. Meadows and entertain any questions concerning his appointment as the Principal of New Hope High. Anyone may speak."

At first, there was nothing but silence; but within moments a mumbling ensued. Still no one spoke up. Finally a large-set man with white hair dressed in a suit sitting three rows back in the gallery stood and cleared his throat. Blaise elbowed Paulie and rolled his eyes.

Peterson acknowledged the man and said, "Yes, Mr. Connor."

"I think you all know me. I teach History at the school. I've taught many of you right here in this room. And as you know, I am a disciple of the Honor Code. I neither condone nonsense or frivolity. But above that, you know I specifically abhor cheating."

Blaise squirmed in his seat and shook his head, staring contemptuously at the back of Connor's head.

"I will not stand for cheating and will recommend the expulsion of any student I find breaking this cardinal rule."

Peterson frowned and interjected. "Yes, Mr. Connor. We understand that, but why is this relevant to this evening's agenda?"

"I'm getting to that," he replied sternly. "As such, I brought to the attention of Mr. Meadows a student's cheating, actually bringing the student before the principal. And what did Meadows do? He dismissed the offense as unfounded and proceeded to chastise me for insulting the boy. The principal actually believed him over me. I submit that we have a principal who not only refuses to uphold the Honor Code, but refuses to support his own faculty in such matters." Connor then sat back down.

John Honeycutt then rose from his chair. "If that's the case, Dr. Peterson, it tells me that the man you appointed has no respect for the honor system and would take the word of a dishonest student over one of our most respected faculty."

Connor stood up again. "Thank you, John. I failed to mention that the way he talked to me…like a dog…it was like I was the one lying, not the boy. He insinuated that if I accused a student again, I would be fired."

A few students in the gallery, to include Blaise and his friends, clapped and hooted at the idea. Peterson banged his coffee cup on the table like a gavel. "Let's have some order here, please."

Honeycutt continued. "So, the bottom line is, we want someone as principal who obviously does not practice the same standards of dishonor as Meadows did in New York, or wherever it was he came from. Maybe that's his culture. It's the kind of thing you'd expect from people like him."

Peterson glared at Honeycutt, too angry to say the words he was thinking. But then a voice from the back of the room resonated throughout the assembly clear and strong.

"Why don't you say what this is really about, Mr. Honeycutt?"

Big John turned around to see the man step from the shadows and into the glow of an overhead fluorescent light...a tall, thin man with neatly-combed salt and pepper hair, dressed in a gray sweater and black slacks. Every head in the room turned to see who would dare challenge one of the community's icons.

Dr. Peterson half-stood to see the man over the heads of people blocking his view. "And your name, sir?"

"My name is Jake Dumas, sir. I will restate my question if necessary."

Honeycutt broke into laughter. "It's the damn school janitor...the guy they call 'Dummy.' So what does a janitor know about stuff like this. As a matter of fact, why the hell is he even here?"

"I am both a citizen of this community and an employee working under the principal's supervision. I believe that answers why I am here. Now I ask you... what right do you have to railroad a man such as Dr. Meadows when it is not at all about his competency or the enforcement of the Honor Code. Admit it...it's about his color."

"What?" exclaimed Honeycutt. "I didn't say shit... excuse me ladies...anything about color. Why are you bringin' race into this?"

"Because, Mr. Honeycutt, it is exactly because of his race you want the man gone. You and this poor excuse for a teacher here. I happen to know for a fact that the boy in question was not cheating. He is an honorable young man who realized he was failing in a couple of classes and simply woke up."

"And how would you know that. Come on, tell us!"

"I know that he engaged a tutor to help him understand what two teachers in the school have failed to teach."

"I say again…you know that how?"

Jake hesitated, but then replied "I'd rather not divulge that."

A hush came over the room as eyes alternated between Jake and Honeycutt.

"Ha! Just as I thought. The dummy is makin' all this up just 'cause he supports this bird to continue on as the principal. I say this tutor don't exist and the boy cheated."

As the murmuring in the room began to escalate, Blaise slowly rose from his seat to everyone's surprise. He looked sternly at his father. "It was me, Dad. It was me that Mr. Connor accused of cheating. But I'm telling you and everyone here the truth when I say I did not cheat. I do have a tutor and he helped me bring my grades up in History and Social Studies. And I brought up the grades in spite of the crap these two teachers deal out."

Two, three and then perhaps twenty-five students rose to their feet, clapping and whistling. The coffee cup rapped several times on the table, but the uproar continued. Finally,

Sheriff Owens held out his hand and yelled out "All right, people, let's get order restored here! Sit down boys and girls!" And everyone did, except Blaise who suddenly found himself in a face-off with his father in front of two hundred or so people. Big John appeared embarrassed. His face was as red as the Christmas sweater he wore.

"Sit, down, Blaise!" Honeycutt barked. "We'll deal with this later. All right, Mr. Doom-ass, if you know so all-fired much about this, then who the hell is his tutor?"

Jake looked at Blaise who nodded a couple of times, then replied, "You're looking at him."

"You?" Honeycutt chuckled, appearing to choke and coughing it out. "A janitor teaching our boys?" He then turned around to face Peterson and held out his arms to dramatize his point. "You hear this, doctor? This is the kind of thing that goes on now at New Hope High. We have janitors who have become educators."

Blaise spoke up again. "And he's a damn better teacher than anyone else in this school."

"That's enough, boy," scolded Honeycutt. "Shut your mouth."

Dr. Peterson stood from behind the table and held up his hand like a traffic cop. "You both sit down. You're out of order and taking this meeting to a personal level. We're here to listen to tangible and compelling evidence that Dr. Meadows is not qualified to be the Principal at New Hope High School. So far, I've heard nothing which would cause the board to change its mind about his appointment. Does anyone else have anything specific to complain about with Dr. Meadows? From what I have heard, I'm inclined to agree with

Mr. Dumas as to why you disfavor the Principal." He then looked at the other board members at the table. "And if none of you has anything to say, I think we need to consider this matter closed. I see no reason for his dismissal. Anybody?" He looked around the room and no one else apparently had anything to say. "Then we will move on to other business."

Just as Peterson had speculated, there was a mass exodus. The first to leave because he was closest to the door was Jake. But when he turned, he came face-to-face with another figure standing in the room's shadows. Cecil Meadows. He had come not to plead his case or to see who would rant against him, but to experience first-hand what could have been his public ostracizing. He smiled at Jake and nodded. Jake nodded once in acknowledgement and then both men left quickly by different hallways.

The next day was the last day of school before the Christmas break. For the first time in nearly a year and a half, students passed Jake in the hallway, smiling and tossing him greetings such as "Good morning, Jake" or

"Hi, Mr. Dumas." Jake was not sure if it was because the students liked and accepted Dr. Meadows or despised Mr. Connor and goofball teachers just like him. But he was pretty sure that part of it was the fact that Blaise Honeycutt was the most popular guy in school and Jake was helping him get through.

At twelve forty-five, Jake heard a knock at his door.

It was Blaise.

"Can I come in?"

"Suit yourself."

"Are you sore at me for spilling the beans about being tutored?"

"No. Are you sore at me for telling them it was me who was tutoring you?"

Blaise shook his head. "I guess we both got caught up in the heat of the moment. But I couldn't let my old man keep whaling away at the principal. And I definitely wanted to make it clear that old Mr. Connor is nothing but an asshole who gets his jollies knocking us kids down."

"What did your father say to you last night?"

"Let's just say he didn't handle it very well. Don't worry about it. I'll be eighteen on January 24th and plan to be out of the house for good after graduation. I'll get a real job next summer, somewhere far away from here… like in Miami beach as a cabana boy bringing cocktails to rich, middle age broads wanting sunscreen rubbed on their backs."

Jake broke into a smile and then just as quickly it disappeared. "I assume you're thinking about college?"

"What for? I'm not bright enough to get into most good colleges and in finishing out my senior year without being scouted by college football coaches, there sure as hell won't be any scholarships dropped in my lap."

"Won't your sophomore and junior years with all those good stats count for anything?"

"Somebody may have been in the bleachers watching me play last year, but they've forgotten all about me by now."

"Don't give up on the idea of college, Blaise. I have a feeling somebody out there remembers you."

"Well, if I don't go to college, I might as well chuck it all anyway and get out of town. My old man will be all over my ass like a shitty diaper. He was sure depending on my football fame to put his name in the paper, like "Councilman John Honeycutt's son takes New Hope to back-to-back state championships." It's like he holds me responsible that he won't be an even bigger cheese than he already is. The past four months have been pure hell around our house."

"Like you said, you've got a short few months before you can get out and do what you want. But I wish you'd start applying for college."

"Yeah, but…"

"But what?"

"My grades are sure to drop again in Social Studies and History."

"And why is that?" Jake replied, looking a bit alarmed.

"Well…my old man put the squelch on any further tutoring."

"He what?"

"He said if I came to the school again to meet with you after classes, he'll kick the shit out of me and then have you fired."

"He actually said that."

Blaise nodded.

"So, in other words, he doesn't give a good damn if you pass your senior year or not."

"Oh, he said I'd pass, but you'd have nothing to do with it. He'd get with Mr. Connor and the Social Studies dude and make sure they pass me…and with a decent grade. Says he knows how to handle them. And then he said he'd have you arrested for fraternizing with a minor… right after he kicked the shit out of you."

Jake bit his lip and stared blankly at the wall. The bell then sounded for afternoon. "All right. Go on to your class. I'll give this all some thought over the Christmas break. We'll figure something out." He placed his hand on Blaise's shoulder and the boy flinched as though he had been shot.

"What's wrong," he asked.

"Nothing. I just banged up my shoulder in a pick- up touch football game." He shrugged it off and then opened the door to the hallway. "If I don't see you before Christmas, Jake, have a good one."

"Merry Christmas, Blaise."

After all of the students had returned to their classes, Jake went to the library to check out a couple of books to read over the Christmas holidays. Rosie, looking sweet and festive in her tight, red sweater and plaid skirt came to the desk to greet him.

"My goodness, Jake," she began. "I heard you were part of the fireworks at the courthouse last night. I shouldn't let you out of my sight."

Jake smiled, but didn't reply.

"Cat got your tongue today?"

"Aren't you supposed to be quiet in libraries?" he said.

"Well, I'm not telling you to yell or anything, just talk to me. You can even whisper sweet nothings in my ear if you'd like."

Jake squirmed a little from the obvious come-on and grinned sheepishly. He didn't know what to say after that.

"Well, anyway, now that you're here, I've got something for you." From her desk drawer she pulled out a package he estimated to be nine by five, wrapped in red and shiny gold paper. A fancy red bow finished it off beautifully. A book, he guessed.

"You can unwrap it at home or on Christmas Day, if you wish, or even open it now. Merry Christmas."

Jake smiled and stared at the package in his hands. "This makes me feel bad. I don't have anything for you. Wish you hadn't spent your money on me."

"Why not? All I have left to buy for is my mom who lives in Nebraska and I've already sent her present to her...another place setting for her Fostoria collection."

Well...thank you, Rosie. I believe I will wait till Christmas to open it."

"Will you be with anyone on Christmas Day? If not, why don't you come to my house for Christmas dinner?"

"That's very nice of you to offer. Are you sure you're not just taking pity on the poor school janitor to make sure he doesn't end up at the soup kitchen down at the YMCA?"

Rosie scrunched up her nose and shook her head. "I'm not sure how to take that, Jake Dumas. It is just a holiday invitation to a friend. One lonely single person asking another to share in the season."

"I didn't mean it like that. Sorry." He paused a moment and then nodded. "Okay, then, I'll take you up on it. It's very nice of you...thank you. But I'll need directions."

"You are such a gentleman...and so nice. It's the big yellow house on the corner of Poplar and Willow. Most everyone knows where I live."

"Yeah, I know the house. Nice. What time?"

"How about one o'clock?"

"I'll check my social calendar."

"Good. I'll look for you then."

Billy Conroy posted bond the next day. Had he not obtained the $50,000 from a bond agency in Birmingham, a hat would have been passed around the county to come up with the money. It would not only have been the Christmas thing to do, but the Coach would never skip out on his friends and fans. Anyway, there was no way their beloved icon had murdered Horatio Sharpe.

CHAPTER 9

Jake was actually looking forward to enjoying Christmas Day with the companionship of a woman, something he had not done in more than ten years. It was also the first Christmas he would actually be celebrating in as many years.

He owned only one sport coat, a blue blazer, which he had on with a pair of gray pleated dress slacks and a starched white oxford. The apparel was a far cry from the faded and worn work uniform in which people were used to seeing him. After splashing on some Old Spice, also something recently foreign to his freshly-shaven face, he ran his pocket comb one last time through his thick wavy hair and turned off the light by the mirror over the bathroom sink. He guessed he was presentable enough for the lovely Miss Green.

Jake pulled the Valiant to the curb directly across the street from Rosie's stately two-story. The house, appearing to have been built around the turn of the century, was in impeccable condition with fresh warm-yellow paint and what was obviously fairly new roofing. A drape of pine greenery accented with bright red bows hung from the banister on the wide veranda. For a few moments he hesitated opening the driver's door, wondering whether or not this was a good idea. He was socially out of practice and was sure to commit some kind of faux pas or say the wrong thing.

But with a poinsettia in one hand and a bottle of White Zinfandel in the other, he finally shoved open the door of the Valiant with his foot to get out. Then after using an elbow to slam it shut, he limped across the narrow street and entered the gate. At the door he paused to second-guess the wine. If

Rosie had prepared turkey or chicken, the wine would work. But what if she cooked beef? Should he turn around and go get something else? Of course nothing was open on Christmas Day, so picking up some table red somewhere would be impossible. The first faux pas perhaps?

His hands full, he rang the door bell with his elbow. A quick wipe of the tops of his loafers against the backs of his pant legs, it didn't really make a difference. There was no more of a shine than before.

Rosie came to the door wearing red again, which looked very sexy on her. The color definitely accentuated her candy apple red lipstick and bright blonde hair. Stunning in a floozy sort of way, she was obviously the most beautiful live Christmas ornament he had ever seen.

"Well come on in," she said. "Now don't you look handsome as a prince? And what a lovely poinsettia. Just set it over there. It'll look festive in the parlor window. Make yourself at home and we should be sitting down for din-din in about ten minutes."

After she had disappeared into the kitchen, Jake toured the living room on one side and then the parlor on the other. Both rooms were decorated tastefully in red and green for Christmas. Although it was a rather balmy fifty some degrees outside for December, she had prepared a fire in the fireplace. On the mantel was a large crystal vase flanked by a series of photographs in different sized wood and ornate metal frames. Several of the pictures were of Rosie and an older woman who Jake perceived was her mother. There were three or four of somebody's children and a couple of grinning adults posing for the camera on the steps of Rosie's veranda. On the wall near the entranceway was a framed newspaper clipping with the headline Anise Rosemary Green is Librarian of the Year.

Back in the living room he noticed that her drapes, couches and sofa chairs were done elegantly in vivid blues and lemon yellows, which seemed to complement her personality. Colorful yet classy. Then suddenly he felt very out of place. Everything about him was simple and unpretentious, not that Rosie was one to put on airs. But she was caviar and he was beans, and he knew there was no way in hell they could ever be a couple. He contemplated running out the front door just at the moment she called from the kitchen, "Soup's on!"

The dining table was an heirloom, she said, handed down through three generations, as were the silverware and lovely, bone china plates which held the pot roast and vegetables…which reminded him that he indeed brought the wrong wine.

She said a quick blessing…mentioning toward the end the reason for the season, which was the Christ child…at the conclusion of which she punctuated with an amen.

It was a delicious meal, home-cooked by someone else, something he had also not had in about ten years.

She smiled as they ate and he smiled back. He said very little during the dinner, mainly because he was a bit shy around her still and he was so hungry. Words would have just gotten in the way of his appetite.

"Did you open your present?" she asked.

"Yes, and thank you. A first edition of The Great Gatsby."

"I knew you liked Fitzgerald. I've kind of kept account of what books and literature you enjoy. Don't know why. Maybe I've just always thought you were an interesting man. An enigma...an intellectual with a mop. Which has always set me to wonder why that is...that you chose to work as a custodian."

"Does it bother you what I do?"

"I don't know. Maybe a little."

"So, you usually don't socialize with the likes of janitors, garbage men and window washers."

He could tell she was embarrassed. And it wasn't the white wine that was making her flush.

"I didn't mean it like that, you know."

"How did you mean it? That we could actually be an item if not for my profession?"

Slowly, she laid down her fork. Her face was not as inviting as it was just moments before.

"I wouldn't go so far as to say that, Jake. People don't quite consider what you do as a profession. But..."

"But you would not show up in church or at the New Hope Valentine's dance with a guy who wasn't a banker or a doctor. Maybe even a used car salesman before a janitor."

Her mouth fell open. How could their conversation have gone so sour in less than a minute? "What's the matter with you, Jake? Why are you so defensive about this? All I'm saying is that I believe you could be anything you want as smart as you are, yet you choose..."

Jake slapped his napkin down by his plate, which had stopped her in mid-sentence. Now obvious to them both, the atmosphere had deteriorated to a point where the spirit of Christmas Day had gone up the chimney with the last dying breath of the fire. Immediately, Jake was sorry he had acted 'so defensively,' as she put it. He was grateful for the invitation and for the superb meal Rosie had prepared. She had thought enough of him to spend this most special of all days with him. She was the kind of woman every other man in town would actually consider leaving their wives for. He knew, however, she was a woman who would be very selective with her choice of men. Her man had to be the whole package... handsome, near to her age and successful. And it was the latter requirement that would assure that would likely never be more than friends.

And then Jake did something that felt ancient and foreign to him...he made an affectionate gesture to a woman. Sliding his left hand across the table, he clasped and squeezed Rosie's right hand.

"I hope we're okay here," he said. "I really am grateful you chose to share your Christmas Day with the likes of me. I probably would have been sitting at home at this very time with a TV dinner and a book, feeling very sorry for myself. This is actually the nicest day I have had in years and I feel blessed to be spending it with you."

The life then came back into Rosie's face and so did her radiant smile. She squeezed back, but did not seem inclined to let go. It was like kissing...only with their hands, a sensual moment for them both. It signaled to them that talk about Jake's job was done for the day, not to be revisited anytime soon.

Jake offered to help her with the dishes, but Rosie said that in her family it was bad luck for a man to be in the kitchen for any other reason than eating. Dishes, especially valuable dishes, tended to get broken.

After everything was cleaned up, Rosie joined Jake in the parlor with two steaming cups of coffee in either hand. They talked a little shop, mostly about Dr. Meadows, and then there was that revelation about Jake tutoring Blaise Honeycutt.

"I just think it's great," she said. "Obviously you have reached this boy in some absolutely riveting way. For someone who is not a member of the faculty to take an interest in a kid to help bring up his grades…it's just admirable."

The conversation then turned to her mother…that over-bearing force to be reckoned with. It was just as well she was in Nebraska married to Rosie's new step-father. Hopefully, her mother would not drive this man to an early grave as she had done her dad. When her father passed some nine years back, Rosie moved away from the mid-West to live with her aunt in Atlanta. After her cousin, Marcie, took a position as a Civics teacher at New Hope, she wrote Rosie that the school librarian was retiring at the end of the academic year. As Rosie's degree was in Library Science, Marcie told her she would be a shoe-in at the school. And the rest was history. Rosie fell in love with and married a lawyer, but as he appeared to be more enamored with himself than with her, the marriage lasted less than two years.

After she had finished with her life story that took more than forty-five minutes, she turned to Jake for his. But she would get very little out of him in return. His life, he said, was very uninteresting to this point and doing what he did on a shoe-string salary, he was satisfied that it would probably continue being uninteresting. He did tell her that he was originally from New York, but never had the opportunity to return there after his stint in the Army. Both of his parents left the world in 1955. His mother died of cancer, and his father followed her three months later. He just withered away. Everyone said it was from a broken heart.

Jake said he had drifted around after that and found himself in Alabama last year. He was tired of traveling and New Hope was as good as any small town he had passed through. So why not look around for a job? So, he picked up the New Hope Register and found the open custodian position. It beat being a bus boy at Mable's, a position that was also open. So he took it. And that was all Jake said about himself.

Just after four, Jake said he should leave. Christmas day or not, he had laundry to do. Rosie offered him some leftovers that he could take home in a Tupperware container. He thanked her and said there were some leftovers of his own in his fridge that needed to be eaten. At the door she took his hand and leaned in to place a kiss on his lips. Her lips were warm and velvety which summoned a surge of passion running a course from his heart to his loins. That five seconds of tenderness took him back...years back. He had almost forgotten what it was like to experience the pleasure of a woman.

And so, that small bit of information was all Rosie would learn about the mysterious and evasive Jake Dumas. At least on Christmas Day, 1963. Perhaps next year as she got to know him better...and she definitely intended to...he would open up more. And then there was that thing about his job. He was better than that. She would try to do something about it.

*****

The Wednesday after New Years Day, the kids poured into the school building dragging their tails despondently, looking like the last rose of summer, all of them. The first semester behind them, they had five more months of school. An agonizingly long five months.

The Coach was still out on bail and hadn't gone any place. His pre-trial hearing was the sixteenth. To everyone's disappointment, the hapless Raiders had managed to win only three games. And it was not all about the loss of the Triple Threat. Some said that Billy Conroy was just too troubled and distracted to have his mind on the game. But no one held that against him. After all, he was one of the town's icons and had been falsely charged in a murder.

Dr. Meadows still had his job, although there was speculation he would resign at the end of the school year. But then again, it was only a rumor started by the handful of faculty and locals who still had problems with a Negro being at the helm of New Hope High.

Just before the first period of the day, Blaise stopped by the custodian's room to see Jake. He had all the intentions of getting up with his tutor, especially those days between Christmas and New Years, but he had put in a lot of hours at the garage with Paulie and Gordo to pay for the beautiful necklace he had gotten Janet. What time he was not up under cars changing oil he was spending with her. But he did have in his hand a small package wrapped poorly in shiny blue paper.

"You shouldn't be spending your money on me, Blaise, but thank you just the same."

"You can open now it if you like."

Jake proceeded to strip off the paper down to the box that read Buck. After opening the flap on one end, he allowed the pocket knife to slide out and into his hand. The handle was made of wood with shiny brass tips on either end. Digging his fingernail into the groove of the blade, he popped it open to its full extended position. He then took note of the small letters inscribed on the blade, Jake Dumas. Mentor and Friend. Blaise. He was deeply touched. For a moment he just sat in his chair fondling the knife without words. It was true. Jake had become as much his mentor, friend and defender as his tutor.

"This means a lot to me, Blaise. You know, I don't even own a pocket knife."

"Well, you do now."

"Thanks." Jake then closed it back up and laid it on his desk.

Blaise checked his watch and saw that he had about five minutes before class. "I still want to continue with the tutoring, Jake. I know my old man forbad it, but I don't care. We don't even have to continue sessions here at the school. It's probably the last thing you want to do in the evenings after you spend ten or twelve hours a day working. I could come by your place, like a couple hours on Saturday or Sunday. We could get in the sessions all at once."

Jake shook his head. "Blaise, it just wouldn't look right…a minor spending time in some single guy's house. We've talked about this."

"I'll be an adult in a couple of weeks and it won't matter at all, then."

"Still, you're a young man and if people around town get wind of it, tongues will wag all over. You don't want to hurt your mother."

"She'd be okay with it. She's pretty thick-skinned, you know, living all these years with my dad. And she likes you, Jake. When at the school board meeting everybody found out you were helping me bring up my grades, she was the first to say what a good guy you must be to do that. She knows you're not any kind of pervert. Anyway, we're only talking about a few months."

Jake wheeled his chair around and faced the blank wall behind him. He brought his fingertips up under his chin, prayer-like in deep contemplation. He didn't respond for a minute or so, but then wheeled back around. "All right. But we'll keep it on Mondays and Wednesdays after I get home from work. Your grades come up to A's in History and Social Studies and then we're done, regardless of where we are in the school year. Cappisch?"

"Yeah. That works for me."

"But, I think both your parents need to know about this, so you tell them. We begin on the first Monday after your birthday."

"I don't think I want my old man to know we're even continuing on, Jake. You don't know what a violent temper he has. I can just say I'm spending a couple of hours at the garage making some extra money."

"I don't want you to be deceiving either of your parents, Blaise. People need to be honest about things… always. Especially with their families. And be straight with yourself. Look in the mirror at the end of each day and say,

"Did I do right today?" If you can say 'yes', then you won't have any trouble facing yourself in that mirror tomorrow."

The bell suddenly rang and Blaise shook Jake's hand, then dashed off to his first period of class. In less than two minutes the familiar crackle came on the intercom followed by the drum roll…the prelude to the old national standard.

CHAPTER 10

At Billy Conroy's hearing, the judge dismissed the case for lack of evidence. It seemed that the argument in the parking lot before classes and Coach Jarvis' hearsay testimony that Conroy was the last person to visit Sharpe in his office were not strong enough to put on the prosecution's case. However, the D.A. informed the media that they still did not rule out Coach Conroy as their prime suspect.

Car-less and fully dependent on Paulie and Gordo for transportation around town, Blaise was dropped off at Jake's on the Monday and Wednesday evenings where the tutelage resumed in mid-January. As one of his friends always picked him up at the Honeycutt house around six, Big John would not suspect Blaise was doing anything else but working at the garage.

By the end of January, History class was well into World War II. As Jake told the stories of the Allied landings in Sicily and Salerno in 1943, the Normandy Invasion in June of '44, and the Summit at Malta where FDR, Stalin and Churchill met to strategize about bringing down Hitler and the Third Reich, Blaise listened intently. It was as though Jake had actually been there, he thought.

Blaise sat wide-eyed with mouth agape as though he were a five-year old perched at his grandfather's feet listening to colorful stories of mythical characters and of kings and knights in days of old. He dropped his eyes only to take notes or follow along in his text, which to him may as well have been a comic book or cliff notes. True to Jake's description of what teaching should entail, his tutor spouted out history as though he himself had lived it. Blaise wondered if Jake had read so much in his life that he knew a little something about everything or had he in fact even experienced a lot of it? Was Jake really an educated man who had fallen away from the world to become a simple, unassuming janitor, wanting no complications in his life, content to live out that life in obscurity? Jake was smarter than anyone he had ever met. But that wasn't saying much, considering the quality of teachers he had had over the years. Maybe old Mr. Bayless who taught Economics was as smart, but he was only smart where it came to his expertise. He didn't know much about anything else, and for sure everyone knew he didn't have enough common sense to pour piss out of a boot.

The more time Blaise spent with Jake, the more he wondered who this man really was.

Two months had come and gone. Blaise had elevated his History grade to a solid B and it infuriated Mr. Connor to give it to him. He knew Blaise was cheating and watched him like a hawk trying to get a bead on how he was doing it. And even though his Social Studies teacher Mr. Billingsly continued to spit out dates to match events with no embellishment of the material, Blaise managed to score A's on every test and quiz.

On the first Monday in March, Blaise showed for his tutoring with a shiner. His left eye was not just black and red, but his eyebrow had a cut on it as well.

"Hey, what happened to you?" Jake exclaimed.

Blaise hesitated a moment and then simply said "Gordo."

"You got into a fight with Gordon Cain?"

"No, no. We didn't fight. Last Saturday we were working down at Phillips' Garage. I asked him to toss me a wrench and he did all right. Popped me right in the eye. I guess that's why I never tried out for receiver. I can throw, but obviously I can't catch."

"Nasty cut over that eye."

"Yeah."

"Okay, you're wasting my time, young man, and we didn't finish Chapter 12 last week.. Let's get down to it." He slapped Blaise playfully on his back as he entered through the front door. Blaise immediately winced in pain.

"What's the matter? I didn't hit you that hard."

"Nothing. Nothing's the matter."

"I think there is. You flinched like I had hurt you."

"No I didn't," Blaise replied defensively.

Jake eyed him suspiciously, but said, "Okay, guess I read that wrong. Go ahead and sit down. I'll get you a Coke before we begin."

That Thursday evening Jake took the old Valiant to Phillips to have a new battery put in. He had been noticing that when he turned over the engine the past few days it seemed to grind slower and slower. Both Gordo and Paulie were there with old Mr. Phillips under the hood revving up Mrs. Crenshaw's white Bel Air. When Gordo saw Jake coming, he wiped the grease off his hands with a blue cloth and began walking toward him.

"Hey, Jake. How're ya doin', man?"

"Doing all right, I guess. I think I need a new battery, though."

"Well, you're in luck. Mr. Phillips has his three year batteries on sale for $15.95."

"Okay. That's beats the Western Auto's price. Can you get me one? I'll put it in tomorrow after work."

"Sure thing. I'll go get one. But I'll put it in now. No charge."

"Thanks. I appreciate that, but I like tinkering with the old bag of bones myself."

He began walking back toward the bay, but then stopped and turned around. "Say, um, Jake. Hey listen, man. I never talked to you after...you know, sayin' those teasin' things to you last year. I guess it's just part of bein' a stupid kid. I..."

"It's all right, Gordo. I know what you're trying to say. You were just trying to impress your friends. Look, just because a guy wears a custodian uniform and mops floors doesn't mean he's less of a person than anyone else."

"I know that now, Jake. And I'm real sorry. I don't treat people like that anymore. Anybody. You're actually a pretty cool guy tutorin' the Golden Boy and also for standin' up for Mr. Meadows like you did." He then looked down and shuffled his feet in the gravel. "And I know what you did for us three when you caught us comin' out of the school office. You could have turned us in and we could have gone to juvy."

Jake smiled at how a couple of lessons and a little humanity could wise a kid up. "I may change my mind if you don't keep your nose clean."

"I will, man. You can count on that. Well, let me get to the battery."

"Fine, but hand it to me. Don't toss it at me. I might end up looking worse than Blaise."

Gordo stopped. "What do you mean?'

"You know…where you tossed him the wrench and hit him in the eye."

"I didn't do nothin' like that. Who told you that?"

"Blaise himself. He ended up with the black eye and cut on his eyebrow."

For a moment Gordo just stood there looking at Jake; then he called Paulie over.

"Yeah, whadda ya want? Oh, hi Jake. Need somethin'?"

"Yes I do. The truth. How did Blaise get hit in the eye? If you didn't do it, then who did."

The boys looked at one another and then motioned Jake off to the side out of earshot of old Mr. Phillips… although his hearing was bad anyway.

"Look, Jake," began Gordo. "Blaise didn't get that black eye from a wrench. His old man did it."

"What do you mean…'did it?'"

"He's beat Blaise up several times. Last Saturday morning, Miss Lila Creasy who lives in your neighborhood saw Mr. Honeycutt in the Seven-Eleven and told him she's been seein' Blaise come and go from your house. He went home and got in Blaise's face and called him on it. Blaise said he was still goin' to you for help on his studies…and what of it. That's when his old man hauled off and busted him. He knocked Blaise so hard into the fridge he broke the handle on the door with his back."

Jake was sure the two boys would see the steam coming off his red face while clinching his fists. "He did that, huh?"

"Yeah," said Paulie. "Hits him a lot these days. When we were playin' ball and winnin' games, Blaise's old man was braggin' on him all the time and everything was hunky dory. But with all that's happened this past year, he's been like a ragin' bull half the time."

Gordo nodded in agreement. "I've actually seen him shove Blaise around in public…and I know he hits Mrs. Honeycutt. That's why you don't see her out much. She's always bruised up and tries to cover the marks he leaves on her with powder and rouge."

Jake bit his lip and moved some gravel around with the toe of his boot. "Bad deal. Thanks for telling me that."

"You won't tell Blaise we told you this, will you?" asked Gordo. "He'll be pretty sore at us. He said never to tell nobody. But what's goin' on just ain't right."

"I won't tell him anything; but this thing will get addressed. You can count on it."

As Gordo went inside to get the battery, Jake slumped against the fender of the Valiant. He was so angry, his knees were actually weak and hands shaking. Blaise was a good-sized kid, but no match for his father who stood six- four and weighed in at over two-fifty. Jake wondered why Blaise even stayed in the house. But then again, friends or other members of his family would have to take him in. He also figured Blaise had to remain at home to look out for his mother...who Jake had just found out was one of Big John's punching bags as well.

John Honeycutt had his routine on Saturdays. Errands in the mornings, yard work or college ball on the tube in the afternoons, and Guy's Bar and Grill by six for the taco spread, a half dozen steins of draft and raucous dialogue with his fellow drunks about the big eared bastard Lyndon Johnson, that troublesome Martin Luther King and whatever that escalating mess was in some place nobody ever heard of, Vietnam. "That sum- bitch Texan wants to send our boys in there to fight communists. I say the only way to take care of Russia, China and Cuba and any other commie country is to nuke 'em all. Light 'em up one by one."

"It would sure as hell save the lives of our boys all right," echoed Benny Tukes, the town barber. "Ain't one of our kid's lives worth that of a stinkin' gook."

Curt Leahy pointed an agreeing finger in Benny's direction. "Now you're talkin.' I say if Johnson is gonna send troops in, he oughta draft up all the niggar rebel rousers and ship them over. Maybe gettin' their asses shot off would make 'em appreciate this country. They want their civil rights? Make 'em pay for it."

Honeycutt shook his head. "And you really think that'll happen with the likes of Bobby Kennedy still in there? Fat chance. Somebody ought ta take care of him like they did his brother."

"Careful, Big John. One of J. Edgar's boys may be in here listenin'."

130

"And you think that sum-bitch likes Kennedy? I wouldn't be surprised if he had Bobby-boy wasted one day."

When they had universally agreed that all Washington bastards were a bunch of liars, hypocrites and whoremongers, and that somebody ought to run George Wallace for President, most of the regulars broke out and headed home, leaving Honeycutt alone at the bar with his fifth or sixth brew. He couldn't remember. At eight- thirty, when it was fully dark, he announced loudly to Guy and everyone else that he was leaving and he'd see them Monday night. Honeycutt was still not stumble- bum drunk, but not as steady as he was when he walked in. He prided himself on holding his beer and Johnny Walker Scotch, and had not had as much as a buzz in twenty years.

When he had passed by Bingham's Hardware he entered the alley where he always parked his Electra…in defiance of the town's ordinance. After all, he was on the town council and who the hell was going to say anything to him. Just as he reached for the door handle, a fist flew out of nowhere and caught him between the eyes. Instantaneously, a flash went through his sockets into the brain. Blood gushed from his nose.

"Son-of-a…" Before he could get the 'bitch' out, painful second and third thuds struck his left jaw and temple. Before his body went down, he felt a sickening shot to his abdomen and then another to his throat. Now lying face down on the cold asphalt, he tasted the metallic and salty mixture of blood that drained from his nose cavity into his mouth.

John Honeycutt awoke to the feel of cool, clean sheets, not fully realizing how he had ended up in bed. Had he at last gotten drunk, fallen and hurt himself? His eyes and nose felt like a two-by-four had been laid across them. Some type of bandage covered the left eye. He could now see that as he blinked open his right eye that he had obviously landed face-down squarely on his nose. The blurred figure of a man stood off in the distance at his two o'clock, and as he turned his head toward him, an excruciating shot of pain went through his neck. His vision gradually returning, he began to make out the face of Chief McCleary. What was the Chief doing in his bedroom? But then as he looked past him and further to his right, he began to realize he was not home at all, but in a hospital room.

"What…what the hell happened? How did I end up here?"

"Appears somebody beat you up, John," replied McCleary. "Your nose and two ribs are broken and your left eye is swollen shut."

"What?"

"Somebody cold-cocked you in the alley by your car. And whoever did it left this." He pulled from his pocket a hand-written note. "That somebody shoved this in your coat pocket."

Honeycutt struggled to read it with his one eye. "Here," he gave it back to the Chief. "You'll have to read it to me."

"You're not going to like it…and if there's anything to it, neither do I." He eyed Big John sternly and then began reading. 'Lay hands on your boy and wife again and next time it will be your neck that gets broken.' What's this about, John? You been beating on your family?"

"Well hell no. You're not gonna believe somethin' written on a piece of paper by some hood, are you, Mervyn?"

"I'm not sure what to believe. I saw Blaise the other day with a black eye. And my wife, Jane, noticed a bunch of bruises on Debbie's arms...finger marks, like somebody grabbed her. All this doesn't look good, John."

"I can't help what it looks like. All I know is, I'm lyin' here all banged up where some...criminal sucker- punched me and you're believin' somethin' written by him on a freakin' note. I love my family, Mervyn. Why would I want to hurt them?"

"You tell me."

"Well, obviously somebody's got it in for me. Look, Mervyn, you don't need to be concerned about somethin' that's not true. Trust me. This is just some work of some psychopath. Maybe somebody who just wanted to humiliate me."

"You're kind of an icon around here, John. I hope you're telling me the truth. If I find out different about this abuse thing, I'll not go easy on you. One thing I can't stand is a wife or child beater."

Honeycutt frowned and pain shot through his head. Now fully agitated, he took a couple of quick breaths and glared at McCleary. "Get this, Chief. I don't abuse my wife or my son. You're all over me about this stupid note and here I lay with my brains rattlin' around in my head. Now, why don't you get your ass out there and find out who did this?"

McCleary's eyes narrowed. Slowly, he folded up the note and put it in his jacket pocket. "I'll keep this for evidence." And then he left the room.

Honeycutt was not sure if the Chief meant 'evidence' against his assailant or him. He turned his head toward the window and lifted his fingers to touch the splint on his nose. The pain was bringing tears to his eyes. "Who the hell did this to me?" he whispered to himself.

CHAPTER 11

On Sunday afternoon, Jake was rousted from a deep, consuming nap in his sofa chair by a knock on the front door. When he groggily brought himself to his feet, the open pages of To Kill a Mockingbird fell from his lap to the floor. When he was immobile for a good while like he was today, his right leg stiffened and it always took a moment to steady himself. Today a little pain accompanied the stiffness. Recognizing the healthy head of blonde hair through the small window at the top of the door, he turned the knob.

"Hello, Jake. Can I come in?"

"Sure. Is it Monday already? I must've taken a hell of a nap."

"Sorry. I didn't mean to…"

"Don't worry about it. If I hadn't gotten up, I wouldn't sleep tonight. Come on in."

"You been cooking beans?"

"Yep. Pintos. Love 'em with cut up onions and cornbread on the side. I guess most people have fried chicken and mashed potatoes on Sundays after church, but beans are my tradition."

Blaise plopped down on the couch and scrunched up his nose. "Stinks. I'd rather have the chicken."

"Have you had dinner? I can fix you up a mess."

"Naw. I ate already. And you're right. We had fried chicken."

"Well, what brings you by today?"

Blaise locked his eyes on Jake's and rested his chin on his hand. "My old man came home today."

Jake shrugged. "He's been away?"

"You could say that. He was in the hospital overnight."

"Hmm. Was he ill?"

"Yeah. Big time ill. He got beat up outside of Guy's."

"He was in a bar fight?"

"No. He was mugged in the alley where he parks his car."

"That's too bad."

Blaise didn't respond immediately. He continued to search out Jake's eyes. "Yeah, too bad for him. But whoever did it, I'd like to tell him 'thanks.'"

"Why would you want to do that?"

Blaise squirmed. "He's had it coming for a long time."

"You're talking about your father here."

"I know. And no, I don't want to explain it."

"Is this the reason you came by? To tell me about your father?"

Blaise diverted his eyes and scratched his head. "No." he paused. "I'm going to need a place to stay, Jake. To finish out the school year. Is it possible…can I stay here?"

"Out of the question," Jake replied immediately.

"Why?"

"For all the reasons we spoke about when we first started up the tutoring. And anyway, I'm not sure the school would keep me on, knowing one of its students was habitating with an employee."

"I'll pay you rent. I'd be like a boarder. And I can cook and clean."

"Blaise, even if it were possible, I'm not equipped to have anyone else live here. I have a second bedroom, but it only has a twin bed in it and much of the room serves as a storage area. Boxes of books and junk are all over the place. Can't happen."

"I…have no place to go." "You're out of the house?"

"My old man gave me my marching orders. He thinks I had something to do with him getting beat up. In front of mom he actually accused me of getting some of my friends to do it."

"And why would he think that, Blaise?"

"Because all we've been doing is arguing. He says I'm a disobedient little shit. Says he's not having anybody live in his house who had something to do with his assault."

"He said that?"

"Yes."

Jake rubbed his sore knuckles. He definitely did not want Blaise to be thrown out of his house and never thought that John Honeycutt would correlate the beating he gave the man with his own son.

"What does your mom have to say about it?"

"She said if I go, she's leaving, too. Then Dad got furious. I thought he was going to hit her this morning, but then he stopped. Of course, he's in no condition to hit anyone. He looks like he got run over by a Mack truck."

"Had he hit your mom before?"

Blaise dropped his head and looked down at his weejuns. "Yeah, a couple of times."

"And you?"

"I...I'd rather not talk about this anymore, Jake." He paused and then looked Jake in the eyes again. "Will you let me stay here or not?"

Jake rubbed his forehead and closed his eyes. It was his fault the boy was standing before him, heart in hand. "Let me do this. I think I have a pretty good relationship with Dr. Meadows and really have to talk with him about this. It's not just about where you will go to live; it's also about whether the school has a policy against students staying at the homes of its employees. If your dad won't let you go back home, why don't you see if Paulie's parents will put you up for the night? But, if they can't take you, I'll see about it. I'll have an answer for you tomorrow."

Blaise nodded. "Fair enough. So, if the Principal says it's okay, then can I rent your other room?"

"We'll see."

"Explain to him I'm eighteen, and we're only talking about a couple of months."

"That will be on my agenda."

"Thanks, Jake. I won't be any bother. You won't hear me or maybe even see me half the time."

"Your mom won't like the arrangement."

"I think she'd be okay with it. She's been real grateful about you helping me with my studies. She said most of all, she wants me safe. But I'll be worried about her and where she might stay. Probably will go live with my aunt for a while over in Bessemer."

"She should be all right," assured Jake.

Blaise held out his hand and Jake shook it. "Will ten dollars a week be okay?"

"I haven't decided this will happen, Blaise. Don't get your hopes up."

"I understand," he replied. "I'll get my stuff from the house after school tomorrow and have Paulie haul me over here."

"Again, don't count on this happening. I've got to sleep on it."

"I know. But I'm an optimist," Blaise said, smiling. "It'll happen."

Dr. Meadows let out a heavy sigh. "Okay. Just try to keep this under the limbo stick, if you can. I don't like seeing a kid getting abused and then tossed out in the street. By the way, how do you know Blaise and his buddies didn't beat his father up? You may not want a boy in your house who'd do something like that."

"I'm very sure he had nothing to do with the assault."

Meadows placed his fingertips under his chin and nodded. "Hmm. I wonder how you're so positive about that, Jake."

Jake didn't respond to the question. Obviously, Meadows was fishing and he wasn't going to take the hook.

"Thanks for your support on this, sir. Now, I have to get back to work."

That evening just before eight, Paulie pulled his Fury into the driveway behind Jake's Valiant. Blaise sprang from the passenger's side of the car. Jake, hearing them outside, opened the front door.

"Jumping the gun a little, aren't you?" "You said today."

"I said I'd let you know after I spoke with Dr. Meadows."

"And I'm sure you did and he gave it his thumb's up."

"You're very presumptuous, Blaise."

"He did, didn't he?" Blaise replied, looking a bit alarmed and pausing before proceeding onto the porch.

"It was all about keeping my job, you know…not about you."

Blaise's eyes darted between Jake and Paulie. "Jake?" he said.

Jake held his stoic expression and then a smile appeared. "Get your crap out of the car and into your bedroom. I had a lot of rearranging to do, you know."

"Hoo-wee!" the boy exclaimed and then both he and Paulie began scurrying about dragging clothing out of the back seat.

"Hey. Before you drag your stuff in here, we need to talk about rules."

"Okay, then. Let's talk." Blaise laid an arm-load of shirts and slacks onto the trunk and leaned against the quarter panel, arms folded.

Jake saw that Paulie looked a bit impatient and said "All right. Go ahead and bring it all in. We'll talk later."

The three of them brought in a number of boxes, containing mainly textbooks, phonograph records and toiletries, folded and hanging clothes, and a record player. When it was all dumped in the spare bedroom, Paulie said he'd better run. "See you tomorrow, Blaise. You too, Jake."

When the rattle of tires on gravel died away and Paulie had gunned the car down the street, Jake motioned for Blaise to sit down. Blaise's face broadcasted his apprehension as to what Jake's rules would be.

"Okay," began Jake. "The first week will be a trial week. If by Saturday, neither one of us can stand the other, you're out of here."

Blaise nodded.

"Secondly, my rules govern. I like my space and my privacy. I'll let you know when I need it and then you disappear to your room or somewhere else. I don't care. You

140

hit the sack by eleven during the week and no girls in here. Tell pretty little Janet what's-her-name that goes especially for her. You'll also keep that stereo down. I don't like any of you kids' music these days."

Blaise continued to nod at each of Jake's rules without comment. "Okay, I'm good with all that. Do I call you 'Drill Sergeant' or 'Mom.'?"

Jake wanted to laugh, but he was making some stern points and intended to keep the conversation on a serious level.

"And another rule. You either have to eat my bad cooking or get something down at the Burger Barn. Of course, I always keep my main staple around… bologna."

Blaise chuckled. "I like bologna, and I'm sure I'll take to your grub just fine. But what about rent? Is ten a week all right?"

"I don't want your money, Blaise. If you want to make it an official rent arrangement, make it a dollar. Save your money for getting your own place after graduation. But, you can do some stuff to help out around here."

"You got it. Thanks, Jake."

"Okay. Let's talk about your parents. How did they react when you packed up this evening?"

"Well, my old man never said a word. I think he really didn't believe I'd leave, although he told me to. He just glared at me through those two black eyes and then walked out of the room. Mom cried a little and I said it would only be for a couple of months." He looked down at his clasped hands. "She

141

didn't leave like she said she would. I don't think she ever will."

Jake almost said 'too bad,' but then thought the better of it. Some things were better left unsaid.

It was then about a quarter till nine, still not bed time. "I guess we'll skip the History lesson tonight. Since you're now staying here, maybe we can pick back up tomorrow night."

"I'm supposed to work at the garage, but guess I can miss an evening until we get back on schedule."

"Have you eaten?" asked Jake. "No."

"Well, I have. But there is some left over fish that I fried earlier."

"Yeah, I thought so. It's still hanging in the air. I caught the first whiff of it when we turned the corner to enter the development. I reckon I won't, though. I will take a bologna sandwich, if you don't mind."

"Okay. It's in the fridge. Another rule I didn't mention. Nobody that lives here is helpless…so unless I'm cooking, you forage for yourself."

"Got it." He paused. "And Jake?"

"Yeah?"

"Thanks. I won't let you down."

"I'll make sure you don't," he replied.

The arrangement appeared to be working out that first week. And the second. Blaise tried to be as quiet as he could, respecting Jake's rules. Working as he did at the garage a couple of evenings a week and on Saturdays, he was not around much. And then he made sure he was back home by eleven, in his room and in the sack.

Sunday mornings his mom came by to pick him up for services at First Methodist after which she bought him dinner at Mable's. They almost looked out of place amongst the geezers and blue hairs decked out respectively in their seersucker suits and bright-colored flowered dresses, attacking their plates of fried chicken or Swiss steak with brown gravy. Then as Blaise normally did after Sunday dinner, he sat with Janet on the Lullwaters' back porch listening to records and making out whenever they were sure her parents were taking their ritualistic Sunday afternoon naps.

Janet would then return Jake to his new digs around five-thirty where a soup and sandwich supper scraped up by Jake awaited him. There would be some short talk over the table and then Blaise would help clean up the dishes.

On a warm Saturday morning in early April, Blaise found an old tire leaning against the shed in back of thehouse and some rope lying on a 55 gallon drum which Jake was using as a rain barrel. Tying one end of the rope to the tire and the other to a large limb on a thirty year old maple that over-shadowed the gravel driveway, he pulled on it to see that it was secure. After grabbing a football from a box in his room, he returned to the yard and set the tire in motion from side to side. Standing twenty yards deep in the yard, he threw the first of several bullets at the tire.

Jake watched from the kitchen window as the ball sailed better than two-thirds of the time through the opening. He had seen Blaise throw a number of passes, both short and downfield, in every home game in the '62 season with pinpoint accuracy; but considering Blaise had to estimate the range and deviation of the pendulum to zip the ball through the hole without touching the sides…well, that was just pure talent. Talent unlike he had ever seen. Blaise was a star whose brilliance would never be seen…unless he somehow caught a break. Perhaps after graduation he could walk on at some college or university, but there would be no opportunity for a scholarship. Coach Conroy was in no position to help him, considering the possibility he may lose his job…if not his freedom.

Jake slipped out the back door and stood leaning against the side of the house for a few minutes until Blaise caught his eye. Jake smiled and nodded, which prompted Blaise to cradle the football in his arm and walk toward him.

"Obviously, you haven't lost a thing, Blaise. Sharp as ever."

Blaise bent down, tore a few blades of grass from the ground and allowed them to fly from his hand in the light breeze. "No, you're wrong, Jake. I did lose something… my opportunity to play football for a major school like Alabama. I did something juvenile just to show off and didn't have a clue what it could cost me. I can't tell you how that's been eating away at me. Maybe my old man was right…I am a sorry-ass loser now. I guess I showed my ass in more ways than one."

"Don't beat yourself up over this, son. You made a mistake. And yes it did cost you; but you're not a loser. You can get that out of your head right now. If you were, I wouldn't be wasting my time with you. There are lots of ways you can get your football life back. You could walk on at a small college and after you break all their records, get noticed by a big school and nail down a scholarship. Or Billy Conroy can send copies of your films to a few schools and talk you up. Don't give up hope, Blaise. There are scores of influential people right here in this community who could become your emissaries."

"Well, if that's true, why isn't it happening? Why hasn't the coach been out there knocking on the doors of athletic departments?"

"I suppose Billy Conroy's been a little pre-occupied what with being charged for murder and suffering a humiliating season. I know what you're feeling, though. Somebody has to jump into your corner."

Blaise stood and nodded. "Yeah. But who...and how?"

That same Saturday night, Jake sat at the kitchen table, pen in hand, tapping the point on the laminated surface, reading and re-reading what he had just written.

Blaise had long since turned in, having returned an hour before from his date with Janet. Jake thought maybe one evening he would break his own rule and allow Janet to come by the house to be with Blaise. Maybe he would fix them a nice pasta dish such as Manicotti...like his mom used to make for him what seemed like a hundred years ago.

Just past midnight, he finally finished the letter:

"Coach Paul Bryant

The University of Alabama

Tuscaloosa, Ala

Dear Coach:

First, let me explain to you that I am not a coach. I do, however, enjoy the noble game of American football.

145

A young man whom I have been tutoring is simply the most outstanding quarterback I have ever seen play on the gridiron. In the fall of '62, he took the New Hope High Raiders to the State of Alabama AAA playoffs and won the state championship. Blaise Honeycutt, in his junior year, surpassed the state's passing record for yards and completions and was poised in his senior year to break even the standing national record for high school quarterbacks in those categories. Unfortunately, Blaise and two other players were dismissed from the squad for what most believe were minor indiscretions and for which he is deeply remorseful. Now, he has no opportunity to be scouted and as such, for a scholarship.

His heart's desire has always been to play for the University of Alabama. It is all anyone heard around the school campus since he was a freshman.

This letter may not even reach you; but given the chance that it might, I ask that you contact Coach Billy Conroy at New Hope High who will have game and practice films taken during Blaise's outstanding sophomore and junior years. Please find it in your heart to give this boy a chance.

I remain, respectfully,

Jacob Dumas

168 Carriage Ln

New Hope, Ala"

After folding and placing the letter in an envelope, Jake licked the five cent stamp and flap, then took it to the mailbox. The night was cool and the fingernail moon was just beginning to rise over the eastern horizon. He took a deep breath of the fresh night air and slapped the top of the mailbox. "Read it, Bear," he said aloud. "Give this kid a chance."

CHAPTER 12

No sooner had he crossed the threshold to the library, Rosie jumped on him. "Jake Dumas, are you avoiding me? You've hardly been in here or said a word to me since Christmas. A girl could get a complex."

"Well, I didn't mean to…"

"Didn't mean to what? Have anything more to do with me? I've been wondering if I may have said or done something wrong when you were at my house at Christmas. I thought maybe you'd call me and we'd go out some time. Do I have to hit you in the head with a two-by-four to get you to do that?"

Jake flushed. She was being a little forward; but of course that was her style.

"Well, I guess we could."

"Could what?"

"You know…go out."

"Well you don't have to act so excited about it," she said, hands on hips and head cocked back a little.

"So, if I were to ask you, where would you want to go?"

"You are definitely out of practice when it comes to this dating thing."

"That's an understatement."

"Okay, then...there's this dance place over in Sylacauga I go to every once in a while called the Sundowner. They're having something called a Country Spring Fling, a kind of Hullabaloo. Do you own a pair of boots? I know you have jeans."

"Yes. I'm not into country-western and square dancing, though."

"It's not like that," she said. "Have you ever heard of the Texas Two-step?"

"No. But I guess you'll be teaching me, huh?"

"It's fun, and I think once you get into it, you'll enjoy it."

"But I'm not much of a dancer."

"Don't worry about it. You'll do fine. None of these hay seeds can dance either. I've been stepped on so many times by big bubbas, it's a wonder my little toes aren't flat as dimes." She then looked Jake up and down. "You know, I'll bet you look smooth in jeans and boots. Have to watch you, though. The women will be all over you."

"Which wouldn't be a bad thing for me."

"Well, I'll tell you right now. If I take a guy into a place, I come out with him. I'm territorial, you know. Somebody makes a play for you, I scratch their eyes out."

"Does that mean they also have ladies' mud wrestling?"

"No, silly boy. But I have been in places like that. I think you'll like the Hullabaloo. It's this Saturday night. So, are we on?"

149

"I'll think about it; but it does sound like fun. And it's been a while since I've let my hair down."

"Then it's about time you did. Will that old car get us there?"

"The Valiant just keeps on cooking. I've been as far as Atlanta in it and it doesn't miss a beat. Never lets me down."

"Okay then. I'm counting on you not letting me down."

With that, she blew Jake a kiss, which was incidentally intercepted by Dr. Meadows who just happened through the door. Jake quickly dropped the book he was returning into the basket and then nodded to the Principal as he was leaving. Meadows gave him a coy smile and a wink, which told Jake that he had in fact taken note of the flying kiss. When Jake returned to his work station, he leaned back in his chair and interlocked his fingers at the back of his head. 'Why not,' he thought. It had been eons since he had gone out with a beautiful woman on his arm Saturday afternoon, Blaise came home from the garage about three, sweaty, grimy and in need of a hot bath. As Jake was in the only bathroom in the house, Blaise had to wait a few minutes. It was down-right boring living at Jake's place, considering there was no television and he had to tip-toe around so that Jake could enjoy his quietude. But the inconvenience of not having a bathroom of his own, like he had at home, was by far the most vexing part of their living arrangement. And of course, he couldn't blast the plaster off the walls with the likes of the Beach Boys and Jimmy Gilmer and the Fireballs, although his old man had jumped on him countless times about the racket.

But then Jake finally came out of the bathroom sporting a starched and pleated beige dress shirt, jeans and a pair of highly-shined western boots. Blaise lifted his nostrils and took in a whiff of a familiar scent...his English Leather.

"Hoo-wee, Jake! Hot date tonight?"

"None of your business, my boy," he replied.

"Okay, who is it? Do I know her?"

"Don't you have other things to do besides meddle in my affairs?"

"Come on. Give it up, Jake. Who is it?"

Jake faced off with Blaise and paused a moment before replying. "If you must know...and you'd better not spread this around...it's Rosie Green."

Blaise brought his hands together into a single clap and shook them. "Ah, man. You lucky dog. The kind of woman every guy dreams about. How did you..."

"You're wondering how a dumb-ass janitor like me gets a chance to go out with a looker like her."

"Well...not in so many words."

"I'll have you know, she asked me out."

"Ha, ha! Wait till the guys hear about this."

"The guys are not going to hear about this. Living under my roof requires an immense degree of confidentiality, boy. If it does get out...you're out."

"But what if somebody else sees you out? Then I get the blame."

"Little chance of that. After I pick her up, we're going to a dance hall halfway across the state."

Blaise grinned and shook his head. "Rosie Green and my friend Jake. Well now you be careful tonight and make sure you take some protection with you."

"What are you…my mother?"

"I'll be waiting up. You be home by eleven." He grinned again. "I've finally got something on you now."

It was going to be a lonely Saturday night for Blaise. Janet had gone with her parents to Birmingham for the weekend to see her sick grandmother. Paulie finally got a chance to go out with Luscious Lori Lynn, and Gordo would be working until late on Keith Brooks' hot rod down at the garage. Blaise had no TV, no companionship and no car. He was probably the only kid in town his age who had a driver's license but no car. But at least he had his stereo that he could play as loud as he wanted…and there was a box of Twinkies in the cupboard.

Jake parked the Valiant on the street in front of Rosie's big yellow house and was prepared to exit when he saw her already bounding down the sidewalk. Not giving him a chance to open the passenger's side door, she quickly slid onto the bench seat toward the middle as though she was a teeny-bopper out on a date with her high school sweetheart. Taken aback just a bit with the closeness, he inched his derriere a little to the left where his pelvic bone was touching the door pad.

"My but you look good. Smell good, too," she said.

"You clean up nice."

And she looked ravishing herself. Dressed in a beige lamb's wool blazer, a ruffled red blouse and jeans that accentuated every curve she had, she lit up buttons in Jake that hadn't been pressed in ten years. He smiled and flushed a little, then recranked the engine, checked his side mirror and pulled away from the curb.

For a few minutes, there was nothing but small talk…a couple of new books that came in to the library that may be of interest to him, and how unusually cool it was this evening for mid-April. But then she wanted to revisit an old topic.

"Okay, Jake Dumas, now that you're trapped in the car with me for an hour or so, I'm looking for some history on you. I've cornered you two or three times on the subject and somehow you escape. Come on, now; help me get to know you."

He knew if he didn't give her a few morsels about himself, she would be all over him like a shark following the blood trail of a wounded plankton.

"Well, like I said, Rosie, there's nothing interesting in my history that would be worth talking about. I grew up in New York, joined the Army, was discharged out in California, went back to school…and that's about it. Boring, huh?"

"You gotta do better than that. Were you ever married?"

That seemed to strike a nerve with Jake and he momentarily diverted his eyes to his left and into a field where a farmer worked over the soil in his John Deere.

"Yes," he replied quietly.

"What was she like?"

"Smallish. Sweet. Loving."

153

"Did you have any kids?"

Quickly, he turned his head and put his stern, even cold eyes on her. "What's with the twenty questions," he said almost hatefully.

The sudden change in his intonation and inflection actually startled her and he saw her freeze up. She looked hurt and he felt her edge away from him. "I'm sorry, Jake.

I...I didn't mean to get too personal. If you're sensitive about some kind of break-up, I won't go there again."

But Jake knew she meant to pry. She had been trying for six months, since their first conversation at the diner, to get him to open up about himself. And she couldn't help herself. It was her nature to be inquisitive about things. But he did his best to smooth out the moment by replying, "I didn't mean to bark at you, Rosie. Forgive me for that. It's just territory I never enter, that's all."

For the remainder of the trip to Sylacauga, neither said more than a half-dozen words. Rosie seemed to be sulking, looking out the passenger side window, and Jake stared straight ahead, concentrating on the road. Not a good start to an evening of fun.

Jake pulled the Valiant into the large parking lot at the Sundowner amidst what appeared to be more than fifty cars and pickups. The Hullabaloo had already started as they could hear the guitars and drums pulsating and spewing loudly beyond the doors and windows. Before Jake opened his door, he asked "Are we okay here?"

"I'm fine," she replied. "Just wondering about you?"

"Okay here, too. Shall we go in?"

She smiled sweetly and nodded. But Jake could tell she was not her usual perky self. Perhaps when he got her inside, her mood would pick back up. He would do his best to make it happen, two left feet and all.

Blaise had lain on the couch since about ten minutes after Jake left listening to the music that carried loudly from his record player into the living room. From his pocket he took a finger nail file to his cracked and tortured nails, scraping and digging out grease that he couldn't get out in his bath. After getting up to go to the bathroom and then again to fix himself an SLT (Spam, lettuce and tomato) sandwich, it did not take him long to start feeling sorry for himself. He had put on four LPs: the Beatles' Greatest Hits, Roy Orbison's latest, the Four Seasons, and the Animals. Then he turned them over and soon fell asleep. He must have been out for over three hours when suddenly, about half-way through We Gotta Get Out of the Place, the music died. Simultaneously, the lamp on the end table went out. It was the quiet that woke him up. Power failure. When he looked out of the living room window, he could see that lights were still on in the houses next door and across the street; so, it wasn't a neighborhood outage.

After fumbling through the dark and banging his shin on the coffee table, Blaise went to the kitchen to check the fuse box. Unfortunately, he could not tell whether one was needed or not. He figured he would just keep replacing fuses until he found the bad one. Then after checking the kitchen drawers and cabinets via a flashlight he found in one of the drawers, no fuses could be located. He also checked the bathroom medicine cabinet to no avail. Perhaps in the shed.

Knowing that Jake kept the shed locked, he shined the light onto a set of keys hanging on a nail by the door. There were four keys on the ring: what appeared to be a spare Valiant key with the familiar Chrysler emblem, a Schlage key that probably fit the front door, and two other keys, both of which he thought would fit padlocks. After following the beam out the back door to the shed, Blaise tucked the flashlight into his armpit, held the lock with his left fingers and inserted the larger key into the lock with his right. His assumption was correct as the lock popped open at the turn of the key.

When he opened the shed door and stepped in, he was greeted by a mouthful of cobwebs. "Blaat!" he sputtered, then spit several times. Brushing the silk strings from his face and lips, he wiped his hand on his jeans. There was no light switch in the shed; but even if there were, the power to the shed would likely have come from the house. Upon checking the shelves and still finding no box of fuses, he shined the beam of light onto the workbench and then under it where he found a large steamer trunk. It was also padlocked. After trying the smaller, serrated key, the lock clicked and dropped from the trunk.

Blaise pulled back the lid and allowed the beam to fall on a conglomeration of yellowed newspapers and other items, none of which were the fuses he was searching for. Beneath the stack of papers were some certificates and a framed photograph. The photo was of a beautiful young woman, perhaps eighteen or twenty, standing in the outer doorway of a building. She was smiling and a ray of sun highlighted her long, dark hair. He then picked up one of the framed certificates, finding a Department of the Army seal and the words The Congressional Medal of Honor under which was written in Old English script 'John Angelo Caruso.' Below the name was the citation:

"The Congressional Medal of Honor is awarded to Sergeant John Angelo Caruso for valor in a hostile

environment. Sergeant Caruso, facing intense enemy fire from a squad of advancing enemy soldiers and a Panzer element tank, single-handedly rose from his position to neutralize seven of the enemy combatants.

Although he had suffered a wound to his leg, he managed to advance on the tank, climb to the turret and place a grenade into the hatch, killing its occupants and stopping the armor advance.

While facing great odds, Sergeant Caruso distinguished himself by impeding the advance of a surging enemy which allowed his unit to hold the Town of Montevilla, Italy, until reinforcements arrived. His valiant and heroic actions reflect great credit upon himself, his unit and the United States Army."

Blaise wondered who the man was. Perhaps Jake's cousin or half-brother? Best friend? Fishing further into the trunk, he saw a small box which he opened to find four medals, three of which he recognized: the Silver Star, another medal where the star looked like copper or bronze, and the purple Heart. His uncle, who had also been in WW II, had showed him his. Further down in the trunk he then spotted a small case which he opened. There it was: The Medal Of Honor. Whoever John Caruso was…he was a for real hero.

Now even more curious, Blaise decided to leaf through some of the newspapers, soiled and fragile as they were. They were all printed by the Los Angeles Times, but had different dates: October 15, 1950; November 23, 1950; February 7, 1951, and so on. Eight neatly folded newspapers in all.

On the front page there were pictures of ancient men in ancient suits and hats, one of them President Truman. He was meeting with an Army general about the war going on in Korea, so the caption read. Blaise then carefully unfolded the paper, and still on the front page, read the bold caption, War Hero Avoids Death Penalty. He then ran his finger over the words beneath the caption:

"Former U.S. Army Sergeant John A. Caruso, Medal of Honor winner and a hero of the Salerno Campaign in World War II Italy, was found guilty for the premeditated murder of Joe "the Piranha" Romine. Romine, a reputed mob boss in the Los Angeles Gambino family, was on trial for the murder of rival mob henchman Carmen Morrelli, gunned down outside of a favorite L.A. restaurant last year on December 21st. Several innocent passersby were also killed, to include Caruso's wife and young son, John Angelo, Jr.

"As Romine was being escorted by Federal Marshals down the Los Angeles Courthouse steps, Caruso slipped through a crowd of reporters and fired two rounds from his Army .45 caliber pistol into Romine's heart.

"Found guilty by a jury of twelve, Judge Henry T. Thornton sentenced Caruso to twenty years in the State Penitentiary at Folsom.

"Pictured below is Caruso as he was taken from the same courthouse as his victim the afternoon Romine was shot. A crowd of more than five hundred Caruso supporters chanted "Caruso", some bearing placards calling for his release. Caruso had delivered a stirring testimony at his trial, proclaiming his innocence to the murder charge for reason of 'justifiable homicide.' He said that the California liberal court system would only give Romine 'life', and that it was his right to take that life. He owed that to his wife and son. But the jury saw Caruso's actions as premeditated murder. Caruso's lawyers have vowed to appeal the sentence."

Blaise then looked at the photo of the man in more detail and his heart skipped a beat, nearly taking his breath away. "Good God!" he exclaimed.

CHAPTER 13

Although fifteen years younger with jet-black hair, the man in the newspaper photo was unmistakably Jake Dumas. His hand now trembling, Blaise found it difficult to hold the flashlight steady enough to read on. Sitting cross-legged on the shed's floor, he laid the light onto his lap and pulled out two more newspapers. The earliest of the articles recounted the deaths of "*Emily Caruso and son, John, Jr., ages twenty-four and three, respectively. Another person also caught in the line of fire, Blaine Hopkins, suffered wounds in the shoulder and hip and is listed in stable condition. Mrs. Caruso, her husband, John, and young son were leaving Giovanni's, a popular Italian restaurant, when machine gun fire from a passing car opened up on Carmen Morrelli, a reputed mob kingpin. Morrelli was killed out- right. Emily Caruso and her son died in route to Parker General. Mr. Caruso was not hit.*"

For nearly an hour, Blaise sat digesting the articles, line by line, in seven newspapers, until the beam of light began to dim. Suddenly, he heard something snap outside of the shed. A twig, perhaps, under someone's foot. He shut off the flashlight and remained still, listening. It was now pitch black. His night vision would take a while to be restored. But the intruder had no trouble seeing Blaise as he charged the shed and lunged. The powerful assailant grabbed Blaise by the shoulders and flung him through the doorway into the yard. Blaise hit the ground hard and quickly the man was on top of him with a knee into the back of his neck, driving his face into the grass. The pungent smell of chlorophyll and dirt filled his nostrils.

"What the hell!" Blaise exclaimed.

Finally, the man released his knee and grabbed Blaise up by the shirt as though he were a rag doll.

"Do you know I could have snapped your neck, thinking you were a burglar?"

"Jake! You scared the hell out of me."

"Why are you going through my personal things, Blaise? I thought I could trust you."

"I…I didn't mean to…"

Jake cut Blaise off. "Get in the house, boy. I'll be in after I lock everything back up."

Blaise hobbled onto the back porch without reply, still feeling the effects of the fear that left his knees weak. He dreaded what Jake would say to him and figured before the night was over, he'd be out in the street.

The lights were still off in the house, but Blaise managed to grope his way through the kitchen and into the living room where he banged the same shin on the coffee table yet again. "Damn!" he yelled, wincing from the pain and plopping himself on the sofa.

In a couple of minutes Blaise heard Jake come in through the back door. Jake took the Bic from the counter top and struck the flint. Blaise then saw the flickering light move to the fuse box and momentarily the lights came back on. The record player once again started up and the singer's voice converted from a weird, garbled growl into something loud and opprobrious. Blaise quickly ran to the room to lift the arm, but in his haste, caused the needle to punish the LP as reflected by the ensuing ugly errrrrip. He then returned to the living room to find that Jake had already taken a seat in the sofa chair.

"Sit down, Blaise," Jake said sternly. His eyes seared with anger.

Blaise took his seat rather gingerly on the couch opposite Jake.

Jake then began in a quiet, more controlled tone of voice. "Why did you find it necessary to not only invade my privacy, but to betray our arrangement?"

Blaise opened his mouth, but nothing came out.

"Do you have no answer?"

"Jake…I'm sorry. The lights went out and I couldn't find a fuse in the kitchen, so I found your keys and went to the shed…"

"Never mind that. What were you doing going through my belongings?"

"I wasn't snooping, Jake…honest. While I was looking for a fuse in the shed, I found the trunk, thinking it had tools and such in it. When I opened it, that's when I found the newspapers and medals."

Jake's eyes remained steadfast on Blaise. "Okay, let's say I believe you. What are we going to do about it?"

"Do about what?"

"About what you may or may not have seen in the trunk."

Blaise stared back at Jake for a moment and then diverted his eyes to one of the andirons in front of the fireplace.

Jake pressed him again. "What did you see in the trunk?"

Blaise hesitated a moment. If he said 'nothing', he wondered if Jake would actually believe him, the perceptive person that he was. If he told him the truth, he figured for sure Jake would bounce him out of the house. Either way, Jake would wash his hands of him.

But then in a low voice he asked, "Who are you, Jake?"

Jake's eyes remained emotionless. "So...you know."

"I read the newspapers and saw your picture."

"And do you also know I went to jail for murder?"

"Yeah. But Jake, I know why. You were justified in what you did. Not to worry; I don't think bad of you."

"Badly."

"What?"

"You don't think badly of me."

"That's what I said."

"Okay, then. So you know my real name's not Jake Dumas."

Blaise nodded. "Do I now call you John?"

"Actually, I grew up with people calling me by my middle name...Angelo. But no. No you do not. I'm Jake

Dumas to you and everybody else in this town. I have taken great pains these last couple of years since my release to keep a low profile. And keeping that name allows me to do so. No one knows whatever happened to Angelo Caruso."

"That's all right. I don't think I could get used to calling you Angelo anyway. Where did the name 'Jake' come from?"

"Jake Dumas is the name of my best friend who was killed in Anzio. He had been hit in the same leg as me when we took a town from the Germans in 1943. He got better, but in the meantime I got shot. It took about three months for me to recuperate. The Army was going to send me home, but I pitched such a fit, they agreed to return me to my unit at the front. The very day before I rejoined my unit, Jake took a bullet to the gut. This time, he didn't make it."

"When did you come back home?"

"About two weeks after Germany surrendered."

"And then what?"

"I went to college out west and got married my senior year. And then we had a kid."

"And after that?"

"Before…before my family was killed, I was a school teacher out in California. And so was my wife. We loved California and decided to stay there after college. And after it happened, California was where I spent the next nine years of my life…as a guest of the state."

"'I knew you were a teacher. Somehow, I just knew it. So why didn't you take a teaching job after prison?"

"Well, it's like this, Blaise. A teacher has to come up with credentials…a college diploma, transcripts, references, and of course identification. The whole bit. No school system is going to hire a convict…a convicted murderer…to teach its kids. So, I had to take a name. And I'm honored to have taken the name of my friend.

"I have been taking a risk using Jake's Social Security Number. His card was among some of his personal effects that my commander gave to me. And I used it to establish myself. Fortunately, in the forties and fifties the

Social Security Administration was really screwed up. Its very infrastructure was flawed and they still had active records open on a lot of people who died in WW II and Korea. Apparently, there was a disconnect between them and the Veterans Administration. I'm not proud that I've had to use it. It goes against my grain. But although the government is taking money out of my check, I promise you I will never collect a dime at retirement age. I'm only using the number for the present, not for the future. Unfortunately, it's the only way I can get paid."

Blaise folded his arms and settled back, allowing all this to digest in his mind. "Your wife and little boy…they were killed. There was a picture of a woman and a boy on a beach in the trunk. Was that them?"

Jake bit his lower lip. "Yes," he replied softly.

"I'm sorry."

Jake laid his head back and fixed his eyes on the ceiling as though he were searching the Heavens for an answer to his twelve year old question that he had asked God every day. "A few years before, I went on to graduate with a degree in History and then both Emily and I became teachers at Bakersfield High. And the rest I suppose you read."

"I read that they died by accident on that street. Wrong place at the wrong time."

Jake's eyes flared with anger. "It was no accident!" He lunged forward and brought his fists down on the arms of the chair. "They were murdered…in cold blood. You can't call it anything else."

"Sorry, Jake. I didn't mean it like that."

Jake settled back down in the chair again. His eyes softened and Blaise could see tears forming. "I felt so helpless…like I could have done something. But all I could do is hold them in my arms until the ambulance came. And then in the back of that ambulance, Emily went first…and then Johnny." He turned his head away and dabbed at his wet cheeks with his sleeve.

A lump formed in Blaise's throat. Somehow he held back his own tears. "You didn't deserve prison for what you did, Jake. Why would they prosecute you for killing the guy?"

"I broke the law, Blaise. I committed premeditated murder on a man who had not even been convicted. It didn't matter to the court that the man was a killer of innocent people. He deserved a trial and was due whatever the jury decided. Not me. And there's your Social Studies lesson for the evening."

"Well, anyway, it doesn't seem fair."

"Not much in this life is, Blaise. And that's a lesson in Philosophy."

They were silent for a few moments and the only sound in the house was the deafening ticking of the mantle clock. Jake then leaned forward and rested his forearms on his knees. "You, Blaise, are the only one in this town…in this state…who knows the truth about me. I want you to promise that you will never tell another soul what you learned tonight."

Blaise nodded. "You'll never have to worry about me, Jake. Your secret's safe." A slight smile broke out. "It's like finding out that Clark Kent is really Superman. You are kind of a Superman, you know. A war hero. That's kind of one, you know."

Jake wiped his eyes again and laughed. "I'm not a hero, Blaise. And certainly no Superman. I'm simply Jake Dumas, school custodian. Remember that." Then he paused. "Now, I'll thank you to stay out of my things, boy."

Blaise grinned. "Changing the subject, did you have a good time tonight?"

"I actually did. It felt good after all these years to hold a woman."

"Ahh, you kissed her, then."

"I held her on the dance floor. And the kiss is none of your business."

Blaise shook his head. "What a dish. I can just imagine what it would be like to lock lips with her."

"Save it, Romeo. She's just a little younger than your mother, you know."

"Well, thanks a hell of a lot for that image."

"Just keep romancing the girl you've got. What's her name...Janet?"

"Yeah. I feel real good about her."

"Really, Blaise. You need to work on your adverbs."

"Yeah. By the way, Jake; back on the subject. How did you get from California all the way to here?"

The horse was already out of the barn. Jake had confided in his young friend things about his life that no one else in the State of Alabama knew. And the few people in California who would remember him and his act of vengeance had long since let it all slip from their minds. No one cared anymore. A few more bits of information would not matter. Somehow he knew he could trust Blaise.

"Well, it's like this. I was released on January 1st of 1962. A month before, on Christmas Day, President Kennedy issued me a pardon. My wife Emily's father had written the President about me and I was one of scores of pardons that he issued. I was supposed to serve twenty years without a chance for parole. So anyway, I was out early and not having to worry about parole or a probation officer. As the State of California frowns on ex-cons teaching school, education was out for me. But, you know, my heart wasn't in it anyway. I sort of became a lost soul for a while. I worked odd jobs, doing yard work and cleaning swimming pools for rich people, and stayed at the YMCA for a while. By April of that year I had saved up fifteen hundred dollars, bought the Valiant, and started driving. I drifted east, taking my time, stopping to wash a few dishes for gas money, and then by happenstance ended up here in Alabama. The alternator went on the Valiant outside of New Hope and old Mr. Phillips pulled me in. And here I stayed. I answered an ad in the paper for a custodian at the school and, well… you know the rest."

"You couldn't apply for a teaching job here?"

"Not as John Angelo Caruso. No. A criminal record follows a person anywhere. And Jake Dumas was not a college-educated teacher. So, I decided to live in anonymity."

"Where?"

"It's not a place, Blaise. It's a life-style. It means I had to change my name and live in obscurity. As people in small towns are inquisitive and nosy by nature, I really couldn't talk or act beyond what a custodian was expected to be. People would get suspicious. I have already raised a few eyebrows in the community by speaking up for Dr. Meadows and tutoring you in your school work."

"And that's why you've kept to yourself a lot."

"I've kind of gotten used to it the last couple of years. It's not a bad life, you know. I don't generally make any friends or establish relationships. No complications."

"Well, now you've got Rosie Green." Blaise grinned.

"I do not have her, as you say, Blaise. But I do find her interesting, even though we're worlds different. She's just someone to have some stimulating conversation with every once in a while. Nothing serious. Nothing will ever come of it."

"Too bad," said Blaise. "I like her."

"Yeah," Jake replied rather wistfully. "Maybe another time, another place." He paused and shuffled his position on the chair. "All right then, Blaise. I'll ask you once more. Will you respect me enough to keep all this in the strictest of confidence? Will you not let any of this slip out in casual conversation? And will you never again mention the name Angelo Caruso?"

Without hesitation, Blaise stood and held out his hand. "You can depend on me, Mr. Jake Dumas. I respect you more than any other person I have met, and I swear to you at this very moment that I will never tell your secret to another human being."

Jake stood as well and accepted his hand. "Thank you. I know that you will."

CHAPTER 14

The word came down on Monday. It was the word that teachers, students and parents alike had feared. The new Waterford High School would be completed by the end of July. New Hope's beloved old school, the school that had opened its doors in 1912, would close down at the end of the school year. The county had depended on a population growth spurt over the next couple of years, expecting that Ford Motor Company would build a new auto plant on the outskirts of New Hope and employ as many as two thousand people. Based on the manufacturer's intent, new housing would spring up and life would be restored to the New Hope downtown area.

But not only did Ford decide instead to expand its Atlanta plant, Katon Mills, the largest employer in the area, had filed for bankruptcy and closed its doors by the end of the year. More than five hundred men and women would have to find other jobs and probably relocate to do so. The Town of New Hope would likely draw its last breath in less than two years.

In the fall, New Hope High School's students would be bussed to the new Waterford Senior High fifteen miles away. Some of New Hope's faculty and staff would interview for and be placed into positions at the new school; however, as Waterford was also splitting territory with the over-burdened Warren G. Harding High outside of Birmingham, a few of their teachers had already accepted positions at Waterford. As a new principal, coaching staff and librarian had already been selected, Dr. Meadows, Billy Conroy and Rosie Green were out of jobs. Jake could apply for a custodian position, but would have to share responsibility with at least one other janitor in the larger school. And he wasn't sure he wanted to travel that distance.

Meadows would land on his feet by accepting a position on the faculty of Tuskegee Institute. As for Jake, there was always a job available somewhere for someone to clean up after people. But for Rosie Green and Billy Conroy, nothing immediately loomed on the horizon.

The last Saturday in April was already warm at 9:30 in the morning. Blaise had already left the house for work at the garage and Jake was just putting breakfast dishes away, preparing to cut the grass. The phone rang and Jake found Rosie on the other end.

"Hey, handsome, what are you doing today?"

"Yard work," he replied. "That's about it."

"Borrring. Hey, I'm putting together a picnic lunch. What say we go up to Crystal Lake?"

"I've heard about the lake. Where is it?"

"About twenty miles north of here in the high country."

"There are mountains around here?"

"Not mountains. Beautiful rolling hills and meadows. The azaleas are all out in bloom and it's a picture postcard day."

"I've got to get the grass cut and clean out the shed in back."

"You can do that tomorrow. Now put on some shorts and be over here to pick me up by eleven."

"You're a pushy gal, aren't you?"

"Just say you will, okay?"

Jake sighed, then said, "All right. Maybe I do need to get out for a little recreation. What do I need to bring?"

"Just your body…and a good attitude."

"Okay. Can do both. Be there in an hour or so."

In her basket were six pieces of fried chicken, potato salad, a bottle of German Riesling and long-stemmed glasses, paper plates and plastic wear, and a table cloth. After parking the car in the gravel lot that overlooked the lake, shimmering and still as it was, they each grabbed a handle on the basket and made their way along the well- tended path to where a half-dozen picnic tables sat under a grove of poplars and flowering pink dogwoods. Finding a table that still had a view of the water, Rosie busied herself by spreading out the gingham cloth and neatly setting the table with the contents of the basket. After working out the cork with the corkscrew, she allowed the wine to sit for a moment to breathe, then filled the glasses to about three-quarters full.

"To us," she toasted, clinking her glass to his. "To a long, enduring friendship."

"Ditto," Jake replied, then taking a swallow of the warm liquid.

Rosie scrunched up her nose. "I should have brought some ice to keep this chilled."

"It's okay. Warm or cold, it works for me."

"Have you found a job yet?" she asked.

"I really haven't thought about it. I guess I'm a last-minute kind of person. How about you?"

"Nothing yet, but I've already started making some phone calls."

"Well, you shouldn't have any trouble landing anything. Smart…beautiful, you're the perfect package."

She clasped her hands on his across the table and leaned in to plant a kiss on his lips. A good day already,

he thought.

"How are things going at your house with you and your border? Are you wild boys behaving yourselves?"

"We stay out of each other's way. Blaise has his school work, work at the garage and social life. We get our heads together a couple evenings a week to recultivate what's been planted in his head…or not…at school. And at other times, he keeps to himself while I read. Exciting, huh?"

She smiled. "You're a good man, Jake. How many people would take the time and effort to help out a kid these days? Everyone's so self-absorbed."

"I hate to see ability wasted."

Jake thought Rosie would seize the opportunity to again open up a dialogue about him…that he too had abilities that were being wasted on mopping floors and scrubbing toilets. Her eyes said that she thought about it, but then thought the better of it. She didn't want this day to end up contentious.

They finished their lunch, leaving two pieces of the chicken for the wildlife, and tossing the empty wine bottle in a garbage container. After returning the glasses and table cloth to the basket, she said, "Let's take a walk."

They deviated from the trail that led from the picnic area to the top of a hill that would give them a panoramic view of Crystal Lake by crossing a meadow. As they trudged through cardinal red and snow-white wildflowers, the warm sun and fresh breeze electrified their lungs. Halfway up, Rosie, noticing that Jake was limping a little more than usual, saw that as an opportunity to again be inquisitive.

"I've never asked you this, and hope you don't mind, but how did you hurt your leg? Were you in some kind of accident?"

"You could say that," he replied. "I didn't intend for someone to put a bullet through my leg."

"Somebody shot you?"

"It was a war wound, Rosie."

"Oh," she said. "Which war? WW II or Korea?"

"It was in Italy, just over twenty years ago."

"Is it something you can talk about?"

"Not easily."

"Then out of respect for that I won't ask about it anymore."

Jake smiled, switched the picnic basket to his right hand and took her hand with his left. "It's all right. If you really want to know about it all, we can talk about it."

She returned the smile and squeezed his hand. "Maybe someday. But today, we will talk about more pleasant things."

At the top of the hill they stopped and turned around. Fields of green and gold beyond the lake met the horizon perhaps ten miles away. The lake itself appeared as a beautiful mirror reflecting the deep blueness of the sky and white puffiness of cotton clouds, like the colors in a Van Gogh painting.

"Mmmm, so lovely," she said. She closed her eyes and smiled. The light breeze caught tuffs of her blonde hair, causing it to flick onto Jake's face. He wanted to take her at that moment, hold her, drop to the ground with her and allow himself to feel like a man again. But something held him back. Perhaps it was the openness of the hillside where anyone could walk upon them. But it was something more than that…something he just couldn't readily understand.

Rosie leaned down and took the table cloth from the basket, then spread it over a carpet of clover. She took Jake's hand and pulled him down beside her. Slowly, she guided both of their bodies into one another and then kissed him passionately. She stopped after a few seconds and grinned. "Nice," she said softly. They lay back until both were facing the sky, looking into the blue, looking into the very soul of Heaven, it seemed. But it caused Jake to think of another day…the day he lay beside his friend on Hill 452…the day when he was Angelo and his friend was Jake. He remembered the sky was that blue… but how it had quickly changed when the smoke from the artillery barrage engulfed the hillside, causing Heaven to take on the appearance of Hell. He raised up quickly, which startled Rosie.

"What's the matter?" she said, placing her hand on his bare thigh. It was then that she felt his scars. She looked down and saw that his Bermuda shorts had ridden up a little and had exposed the horribly deformed skin just above the knee.

Jake saw her horrified expression and quickly pulled the pant leg down. She looked as if she would cry at any moment. To disarm her distress, he winked at her and said, "It's why I haven't had shorts on for twenty years."

"I'm sorry," she replied.

"Naw, don't worry about it. We're up here to have a good time." And then he pointed. "Look. There's a flock of Canadian geese that just took flight, headed for the lake."

They watched as the geese formed their vee and flew gracefully further south until they disappeared over a tree line into the lake. It was enough to take her mind off of anything unpleasant, such as war and wounds, allowing her to focus on the beauty that lay before them. She again closed her eyes and lifted her face to the sun, taking first a deep breath and then sighing. "A perfect day," she remarked.

Jake studied her lovely, symmetrical face and smiled. "Yes," he said softly. "Perfect."

On the first Saturday in May, by 10:00 it was already hot. More like the 4th of July than the 4th of May. Jake had heard people around town say on hot, humid days, "it's hotter than the inside of Fireball Turner's car on a blistering Darlington race track."

Blaise stood positioned at the opposite end of a crosscut saw while Jake spit on his work gloves and grabbed the other. Lightning had struck a sixty-foot pine tree the month before, killing it out-right and stripping its bark, leaving it looking much like a barber pole. Its needles had already begun turning brown and it was a matter of time that insects would invade it, hastening its decay. Jake and Blaise had taken no more than three swipes into the tree when a black Lincoln pulled into the driveway. Momentarily, a portly man in a straw hat and a red sports coat stepped out of the car. Removing his hat, he reached into his pocket and pulled out a bandana, first dabbing at his forehead and then mopping his bald head. Returning the hat to his head, he then threw up his hand and let out a "Whew!" As he walked toward the lumberjacks, he said, "Man, it's like a sauna out here today. I hate to see what July and August have in store."

"Can I help you, sir?" asked Jake, expecting the man to be an encyclopedia salesman. But, driving a Lincoln? Britannica must be having a stellar year.

"Yes, sir, I hope so. I'm lookin' for a Mr. Dumas."

"You found me. So, what are you selling?"

The man laughed and waved off the question. "And are you Blaise Honeycutt?"

Blaise nodded, curiously. "Yes, sir."

"I stopped by your house, son. Your mom said I'd find you here."

Jake spoke up. "Well, you found the both of us. What is it you want?"

"Well, to answer your first question, Mr. Dumas, I am sellin' somethin.' The University of Alabama."

Blaise cocked his head, looking a bit confused. "The…"

178

"University of Alabama, son," restated the man. "My name's Yancey Taylor and I'm on the Bear's staff."

"The Bear?"

"Yes, my boy. He's inter'sted in givin' you a scholarship."

"A scholarship?" Blaise replied, thinking afterwards he sounded much like a parrot, repeating everything the man said.

"He's seen your game films, son, and likes very much what he saw. You're quite the talent, you know."

"How would he…"

"Know about you? Well, you see, son, his interest got piqued by readin' the letter Mr. Dumas here sent to him about you."

Blaise then looked at Jake. Jake nodded and then looked down at his boots.

"So, we got hold of your football coach…it wasn't easy to find him, though…somethin' about some kind of trouble he's havin.' Anyway, he sent us the films and I gotta tell ya, son, Bear says you have a hellava arm. Says you're a good'n."

Blaise didn't immediately respond, but stood mostly with his mouth open, waiting for someone to wake him from his dream.

"So, how 'bout it, son? You willin' to come to Tuscaloosa to take a look at us?"

"Y…Yes, I will, sir."

"Good, then. Well, we gotta take a look at you first. You gotta make them grades to be good enough for that scholarship. Here's my card. Call me any time, if you have any questions. The Bear and the Dean will make the decision right after you graduate. We're already done with spring practice, and this summer we'll be makin' selections for the freshman squad."

"I understand, sir."

"See ya, fellas." Taylor shook both Blaise's and Jake's hands and returned to his car. He stopped before getting in. "Is there a good res'trant in this town. Some place that's got some good sweet tea?"

"That would be Mable's. Just go down town and it's on the main drag on the right. Can't miss it."

"Thanks."

"No, thank you, Mr. Taylor," Blaise shot back.

The man replied, "Roll Tide." And then he laughed.

When Taylor had pulled away, Blaise turned to Jake and grinned. "You son-of-a-gun. I can't believe…"

"Forget it, Blaise. You don't have to say anything."

"But, I do, Jake. Why…why would you do this for me? My own dad didn't do shit for me after I screwed up this year. And then I'd have thought Coach Conroy would've helped get me a scholarship."

"The coach was pretty much consumed with his own troubles. And your father…I expect he's been dealing with a lot of frustrations, many of his own making."

"You're being too easy on him. He's nothing but a hateful, despicable man."

"I know how he's treated you and your mom, Blaise, and I can't say I blame you for how you feel. But seeing as how you've been living away from home for a while and school is coming to an end, perhaps it's time you went home to mend some fences."

"With him? Look, Jake, I haven't done anything to cause him to be the way he is. He's been like he is ever since I've known him. He drinks a lot and Mom says maybe it's the devil liquor that causes his meanness."

"I know. And booze doesn't give him license to be violent with you and your mom. I understand that. But he is nonetheless your father and maybe a frank face-to- face with him about how you feel…"

"I've tried talking with him, Jake, and at the same time staying out of his way; but he still finds a reason to smack me around."

Jake folded his work gloves and pressed them into his armpit. He then took a handkerchief from his pocket and wiped the rolling sweat from his face. "My father was a difficult man as well. I could do nothing to please him. And then I joined the Army, placing myself in harm's way until the war was over. For two years, my mom wrote me that Dad could not sleep. He would pace the floor at night and then sit down to try writing me himself. She said the words would not come. He was what they called the traditional father back then. Hard…even cold to me. It was his way. But when I came home from the war, I found him a changed man. He didn't throw his arms around me, mind you, but I could see it in his eyes. He was proud of me and loved me."

"Is he still alive?"

"No. He died while I was in prison. But before that… before I went back out to California to begin college and start a new life with Emily, we mended our fences, Blaise. And I can't tell you how glad I am that we did." Jake then took the handkerchief and wiped his eyes.

"But, I'll bet your father didn't hit you."

"No, he didn't. But he hit me several times with his eyes and his voice. I wouldn't have been able to tell the difference if he had hit me."

Blaise squatted down and leaned his back against the dead pine. The saw remained stuck in the tree above his head.

"Your father and mine were nothing alike, Jake. I hate my old man. I hate what he's done over the years to me and my mom. And I know you were the one to take him down a peg."

"You mean at the school board meeting? I was a bit out of line…"

"No, Jake. In the alley. I know it was you who put him in the hospital."

"You don't know that, Blaise."

"You're right. I don't know that for sure, but I'm pretty damn sure no one else did it. Don't you worry about me thinking ill of you, though."

Jake shook his head and held up his hand to Blaise. "Let's get off this. How did we get on the subject of your father, anyway? We're supposed to be celebrating your opportunity here."

Blaise stood back up. "You're right. Thanks again, Jake. I may not get the scholarship, but what you did…"

"Like I said…forget it. Now let's get this tree down."

The two men put their gloves back on, spit on them for grip and then continued pulling and pushing the blade across the seventy year old pine.

Graduation on the twenty-fourth was both a joyous and sad occasion. As this was the last hurrah for not only the senior class, but for New Hope High as well, the auditorium was standing-room-only. A great many of the attendees were older town-folk who had graduated years before and just needed to be there for nostalgic reasons. There were a couple of planned speeches, one at the beginning and then at the end, to reflect on the school and its history. Two congressmen and a U.S. Senator had graduated from New Hope. One of the keynote speakers was Alabama's Governor.

The valedictorian was Janet Lullwater, Head Cheerleader, Class President and girlfriend of last year's High School All-American quarterback. They had been the Ken and Barbie of the school. They were tight as a tick, but academically far apart. But Blaise did manage to finish out with Bs in History and Social Studies, giving him a 3.3 GPA for the year and a 2.8 in his overall high school experience. Would that be good enough along with his gridiron history to get him a scholarship? That was up to U of A. But nonetheless, he would walk across the stage. And miraculously, so would Paulie Echols and Gordon Cain who managed to eke out passing grades in the eleventh hour.

Cecil Meadows gave tribute to his predecessor, Horatio Sharpe, for his years of service, mentioning as well his untimely death. The response was mixed. When the

Principal was done, the majority of the graduates, a few of the parents and about half of the faculty stood and applauded. The others sat with arms folded, still in defiance of the decision to place a Black man in charge of the educational development of their children.

Jake, actually dressed in his one sport coat and tie, was standing at the rear of the auditorium with others who did not arrive early enough to find a seat. On the stage just to the left of the podium was Librarian Rosie Green, dressed in a pastel blue conservative two-piece suit, looking better than Marilyn ever did on her best day. Her eyes caught his and she smiled with those luscious red lips…lips the color of maraschino cherries. It caused him to think about that April day when she kissed him so passionately on the top of the hill.

The band, whose clarinets were as sour as ever, played Pomp and Circumstance incessantly while the names of two-hundred thirty-two students were announced. Each approached Dr. Meadows, shook his hand, received his or her diploma from the Assistant Principal, and then turned the tassel to the left side of the cap before exiting the stage. When Blaise's name was announced, the entire auditorium erupted in cheers and applause. Someone even yelled out "Golden Boy!" as he ascended the steps.

After the ceremony, Jake spotted Blaise in one of the aisles with his parents. His mother hugged him while the nicely-healed John Honeycutt, seeing much clearer than he was a few months before, snapped pictures with the Polaroid. Blaise then lifted his head and eyes throughout the room to search the auditorium for his friend and mentor. Finally spotting Jake at the back of the room, he broke away from his parents to seek him out. He would have hugged Jake had it not created a spectacle as a lot of eyes were still on him. Instead, he met Jake's out-stretched hand and pumped it with animation.

There were moist eyes all around. Some were tears of joy …parents for their children, and graduates who were happy to finally be out of school. But there were also tears of sorrow. Most of the kids knew they would go to different colleges and then move on in life never to see their friends of twelve years again. But then there would be tears for the old friend who had served the New Hope community for nearly fifty years. At the end of the day, Jake Dumas would close its doors to the community forever

CHAPTER 15

A letter arrived on June 2nd addressed to Blaise in-care-of Jake Dumas with the return address of the University of Alabama. Blaise was at the garage working until three. After tossing the envelope on the coffee table, Jake sat eyeing it like a child looking at a Christmas present. He wanted to open it, but since it belonged to Blaise, he would be breaking his own 'privacy' rule. Finally, after checking the mantle clock a dozen times in gnawing anticipation, Blaise finally came home just before three-thirty, grimy and sweaty, in need of a bath. Passing quickly by, he said "Hey, Jake," and then disappeared down the hallway into the bathroom. Jake had waited most of the afternoon to learn what was inside the letter. He guessed he could wait another fifteen minutes.

When he came out in a tee shirt and Bermudas, still toweling his blonde hair, Blaise's eyes went right to the envelope like radar. After seeing the university's address on the upper corner, he picked it up and held it as though it was made of crystal.

"Well, don't make love to it, boy. Open it."

Blaise shook his head and handed it to Jake. "Here. I can't take the suspense. You open it and read it to me. I believe I'll have a heart attack if I find out they rejected me. Break it to me gently."

Jake pulled out his pocket knife and cut through the flap. He then blew into the envelope and pulled out the letter. Stoically, he read the lines to himself and without word or expression, folded it and set it aside. Blaise's heart sank as he plopped onto the couch.

Jake continued with his blank expression, catching the look of rejection in Blaise's eyes. He cleared his throat and said, "Well, I've got just one thing to say about it." He paused another long moment. "Congratulations!"

Blaise lifted his head and allowed his mouth to fly open. "You're kidding. You're kidding!" he exclaimed. He then jumped up and grabbed the letter from the table and read it himself. "It says I'm to report to training camp on July 20th. And I got a full scholarship. A full damn scholarship! Jake," he grinned. "This is the best day of my life. And I owe it all to you."

"You did this yourself, you know. It was your athletic ability mostly; but it was also your tenacity to stay with your studies. I hope you read the words 'probationary basis,' which means you have to keep your grades up."

"And I will. You know I will."

"College is not high school, Blaise. You're going to find it a hell of a lot tougher, academically. And you think teachers at New Hope didn't care if you pass or fail? With sometimes a hundred or more students in a class, professors won't even be able to match your face with your name. That makes it easier for them to give you an F."

"You worked hard with me, Jake, and I won't disappoint you."

"Then I'd say this is a time for celebration. Let's go down to Guy's. I'll buy you a beer."

Suddenly, the joy on Blaise's face dissipated. "My old man will probably be in there."

"Well that's good. Then you can tell him the good news."

"I don't know about that. We haven't had more than a dozen words between us since I left the house. I thought he would choke on his tongue at my graduation when he said, "Well, you're finally done, boy. Congratulations." It was so plastic, you'd think I was just another kid who lived down the street from him."

Jake reflected on Blaise's reluctance. Inadvertently, Jake had partially facilitated the distance that existed between Blaise and his father. He had given the boy counsel, opportunity and a place to live. But then again he thought…what if he hadn't? Would Blaise have ended up under the hood of a car like Gordo and Paulie? Jake wondered if he was just being too hard on himself for being someone who actually gave a damn about the boy.

"Well, suck it up, anyway, and let's go have that beer."

The usual patrons were seated at their usual tables or stools, smoking and swilling their beers, talking the usual meaningless small talk about crop herbicides, the weather, politics and the Atlanta Braves, God bless 'em. Four or five stools at the bar were open and Jake and Blaise slid onto the two at the far end. Guy came over immediately with a damp towel across his shoulder that had soaked up an evening's worth of spilled beer. It was high time he had changed it. "What'll ya have, fellas?"

"What do you have on draft?" replied Jake.

"Got Schlitz, Budweiser and Falstaff."

"Schlitz will be fine."

"Same here," said Blaise.

Guy eyed them a moment, then said "Your first time in here, ain't it, Blaise? You old enough?"

"Eighteen now, sir. Graduated a week ago."

Guy laughed. "I'm just bustin' your chops, Golden Boy. I'll get your beer."

After their glasses arrived, Jake held his up and said "To Blaise Honeycutt. Job well done. Congratulations."

Blaise clinked glasses with him and then took a couple of gulps.

"I take it this is not your first brew."

Blaise laughed. "Hardly. Although I'm not much for beer. I guess we just suck these things down to be cool and fit in with the rest of the crowd."

"Now that's a pretty mature observation coming from a kid your age."

"Well, considering I'm no longer a kid…" At that moment, Blaise caught sight of the familiar lumbering figure coming through the door. He saw Blaise at the bar and plopped his large frame onto the stool next to him.

"Too good to have a beer with your old man?" Honeycutt said right out of the chute. He then looked around Blaise to see who was sitting on his right side. "I reckon this guy's your new daddy now. If you're gonna walk out on your family, seems to me you should take up with somebody better'n the school janitor. Oh, I forgot… he's your tu-tor."

The muscles tightened around Blaise's mouth as he locked eyes with Big John. "First of all, Dad, I didn't just leave. You kicked me out, remember?"

Honeycutt ignored the retort and motioned for Guy to bring him his usual double Scotch.

No one said anything else for a few moments and then Blaise coughed up the words from his throat, "If you're interested, I got offered a football scholarship from Alabama."

His father laughed. "Couldn't get into a real school, I reckon."

"What's that supposed to mean? It's the best football program in the country. Playing for the Bear…"

"What was wrong with Penn State? It was good enough for your old man."

"I've never even thought about any other school. Bama and Joe Namath are going to be National Champs this year. Why wouldn't I want to get into a football program like that?"

It was probably the most he had said to his father in months. Honeycutt turned full body on the stool toward Blaise. His eyes reflected something between anger and hurt. Blaise had excelled all right, but not from anything he had done for him. And he knew it. Blaise had excelled in spite of him. But pride being what it is, Honeycutt would not allow himself to admit it…especially not to Blaise.

"You know, boy, I don't give a good gawddam where you go to school. You as much put your pick in the ground when you divorced yourself from your mother and me. So go on. Go off to that cow campus and be another Joe Namath. I'm through with you. Been through."

Tears formed in Blaise's eyes and he bit his lower lip to keep from breaking completely down. Jake's fist tightened. It was all he could do to keep from punching the man squarely between the eyes...again. But that was the last thing Blaise needed to see. He turned up the remainder of his beer and then brought the glass down hard on the bar.

Blaise then regained his composure and said, "That's about how I would have expected you to respond, Dad. You're just mad because you didn't have a hand in helping me get this scholarship."

"Shut up, boy. You're talkin' to your father here. You show me some respect."

"And how could I ever do that? You never stuck up for me at that board meeting when old Mr. Connor was trying to get me expelled for something I didn't do. All you've done most of my life is berate me and embarrass me in front of people. Respect? I'd sooner respect Lee Harvey Oswald."

It was all the words Big John needed from his son. He cocked his arm to his left, posed to backhand Blaise, but Blaise pointed an accusing finger in his father's face. "Not anymore, Big John. You'll never hit me again."

Guy, who was positioned opposite Honeycutt prepared to pour him another double, saw the raised hand and broke in. "John, what are you doing? That's uncalled for, my man."

"Shut the hell up, Guy. This is a family matter."

By that time, with their escalating voices carrying further into the bar, several heads turned in their direction. Guy leaned over the bar and said in a lowered voice, "Maybe you'd better leave, John."

Big John downed the remainder of his Scotch and cracked the glass on the bar. "The hell with you, Guy... and you...and you..." he began pointing at not only Blaise and Jake, but others in the bar. "All of you...go to hell!"

The entire bar sat in stunned silence. Big John had finally gone off.

Looking around the room, Honeycutt seemed to dare anyone to say anything to him. He then planked two dollars on the bar and left amidst the silence without further word.

Blaise continued looking straight ahead at himself in the large mirror behind the counter. After a couple of minutes, he wheeled himself around as well and left the bar. Jake paid the tab and followed him out.

When Jake stepped into the parking lot, he saw Blaise leaning against the Valiant, arms folded and looking down. Big John had apparently already peeled out.

"Blaise..."

Blaise threw up his hand and turned his head away. "Save it, Jake. I told you we shouldn't have come here. Let's just go."

Jake knew this was not the time for any further dialogue and nodded. When Blaise opened the passenger side door to get in, Jake slid in on the driver's side.

Jake did not drive directly home. Instead, he pulled onto Fairview Road which became Route 111. Blaise, who had not said a word since they had left the bar, glanced over at Jake as if to inquire where they were going, but then turned his head away again. The sun which was now slipping over the tree line cast a soft orange hue over the landscape. It was setting on a day of paradoxical emotions.

It was amazing to Blaise how he could experience the best news of his life one moment only to spiral into a state of depression the next. His father could make that happen. And had done so, often.

After about fifteen miles of silence, Jake turned the Valiant into the lane that led to Crystal Lake. Within a few hundred feet, they were parked at water's edge.

"Why are we here, Jake?" Blaise finally said.

Jake didn't reply, but opened his door to get out. Finding a large boulder off to the left that overlooked the water, he climbed onto it and perched himself like a bird scanning the lake for supper. Blaise finally followed him and took an adjacent seat on the rock.

Jake lifted his head. "Do you hear that?"

"I'm not sure. What am I supposed to hear?" Blaise replied.

"A loon. Probably calling its mate. There. See it over there in the brush where the inlet begins?"

"Yeah. I see it. And there's another one," Blaise said, pointing.

"Ah, yes. He called. She came."

"That's the way it's supposed to be. Right?"

Jake smiled. "I used to come to places like this when I was a kid. There was a lake like this in upstate New York. My friend and I would take girls up there a lot during our senior year."

"Your friend, the real Jake?"

Jake nodded and continued on. "Sometimes the moon reflected like molten silver on the water, making it seem even colder in the winter. But it was a good cold... fresh, clean, not stinging." He stopped to listen for the loon again. "The creatures of the night will soon begin their chorus, and this place will sound like Grand Central Station. One by one, they will begin to break the silence of the evening.

"It is at moments such as this, you see, that anyone who ever doubted the existence of God Almighty will sense His presence. Sometimes you can't do that in the midst of human beings...especially the contentious ones. They won't let you. It's those human diseases called pride and bitterness that sends us to places like this for recovery...and a rejuvenation of the spirit. There's no one out here that can hurt your feelings or your body. There's a kind of healing you can get in a place like this. Insanity may send us here; but it is the peace that we experience here that, if we allow it, will purge the anger and hurts from our souls, and which sends us back to that other, bruising world to try once again.

"Breathe it in, Blaise. And when you exhale, spew out all your bitterness until there is no more left inside you. It's the best kind of therapy...and it doesn't cost you one red cent."

Jake paused and picked up a flat rock from the boulder, hurling it sidearm across the water. The skips temporarily broke up the shimmering calmness of the water, and then tranquility was restored once again. "You didn't go home the other day when I asked you to. Tomorrow, I want you to go home. Go home with a forgiving heart. Eat crow, if you must. Your mom needs you. And in his own way, your dad does, too. Although he may be temperamental and even violent sometimes, he's still your father. What you saw in the bar was how he deals with hurt. He knows he has not been the influence in your life this past year that got you your grades and the scholarship, and he's remorseful about it. He just doesn't express himself and react the way a father should when he gets hurt. What I'm saying, Blaise; just don't need to wake up one morning and find he's left this life without you doing your part to mend the fence. I'm glad I was able to reconcile with my father before he passed on. It would have haunted me the rest of my life if I hadn't."

Blaise also picked up a flat stone and skipped it four, five and six times across the near side of the lake. "I wouldn't know where to start, Jake. I don't think I have it in me to even set foot in the door. And then if I did, how do I rid myself of all the hard feelings?"

"I won't press you on this, Blaise. We'll go back to the house for the night; but I want you to sleep on it. Wake up with the words in your head to make this happen... and make it happen tomorrow. I'm kicking you out." Jake then jumped off the rock as agile as a cheetah. "You know, I just thought about something. We didn't eat. Let's grab a burger on the way back."

"Oh, my gosh! I just remembered. I was supposed to go over to Janet's tonight."

"Then how about us picking her up and we can make it a threesome?"

"You'd be in the way, considering what I've got planned."

Jake laughed. "I'm hearing you. Let's get a bite and then I'll drop you at her house. You gotta get yourself a car, boy. How can you romance a girl without wheels?"

CHAPTER 16

A skeleton staff was on hand for clean-up and close down of the school on that next Monday. Jake of course was there, and so were Dr. Meadows, Mrs. Williams and a crew from the county's school maintenance department. At the end of the work day, they would cut off the electricity and shut down the cooling system. Teachers had already cleared their classrooms the day before graduation. All pictures and posters in the rooms had been removed and the maintenance guys would be loading band instruments, library books and athletic equipment into the moving van in the parking lot for storage in the county's warehouse. The new school in Waterford would receive some of the items, especially the library books; but for the most part, it would get all new stuff.

Jake had already boxed his books and other personal items and loaded them in the trunk of the Valiant. As he made his final sweep of classrooms and toilets just after two, he found the Principal in the assembly hall seated alone in one of the chairs on stage.

"Dr. Meadows," he called.

Meadows, seeing him enter, smiled and motioned for Jake to come on stage and take a chair beside him.

"Is anything wrong?" Jake asked.

"No, no, Jake. Everything's fine."

The two sat in their chairs for a few seconds looking out over the auditorium, and then Meadows began what amounted to a reflective soliloquy. "You know, I was only here these few months; but yet, through all the emotions, discord, sadness and even prejudice against me, I still felt I belonged here. I think eventually we would have all been good together, had we ironed out our differences and gotten to know and respect one another. But we would have needed to change, all of us, just as our country is changing.

"But I'm glad we had this year, Jake. We can all take what we learned from our experiences here and make it a part of what we have yet to learn about ourselves. And how we all fit into this complicated world of ours. When you look out over this auditorium, what do you see?"

Jake looked down the rows of empty seats and listened. The silence was almost deafening. "I think I see the same thing you see…history. The mature development of this town's children for many generations began here. If you listen closely, you can still hear their voices…talking, laughing, echoing throughout. But there are ghosts here, as well. Ghosts of those who sat here in the early part of the Twentieth Century who are no longer with us."

Meadows nodded. "Exactly, Jake. Neither of us knew these people, but yet, just the same, I feel a kinship with them. It's quiet now…a sad quiet. It's like we are sitting here at the funeral of an old institutional friend."

Suddenly, he slapped Jake on the knee. "I'm glad we met, Jake. Of all the people I served with in this school, I will miss you the most. I do hope to meet up with you again, my friend."

"Maybe we will, Dr. Meadows. I thank you for the respect you've always shown me, given my position here at the school. And thank you for not only your leadership, but also your example."

"Then let's quit acting like a couple of teary-eyed old war veterans and look forward to our futures. By the way, where do you go from here?"

"I don't know, yet," replied Jake "People are always looking for someone to clean up after them. I'll survive."

As they now stood by the podium, Meadows' brow narrowed into a frown. "I don't know your history, Jake, but I do know you have it in you to be a fine educator. You're intelligent. I could see that in your eyes the day we met. And you are committed to people…all people. I don't know if I ever thanked you for coming to my defense at the December board meeting last year. In doing so, I know that you gained the respect of many a student at this school and perhaps half the faculty as well. And as for the others? Well, God bless 'em. Anyway, whether you are an educated man or not, you would be impactive in any capacity that allows you to educate, counsel and otherwise administer to people. Think about separating yourself from that mop and doing it, Jake." He then shook Jake's hand.

And then from the rear of the auditorium a voice suddenly called out. "Hello!" A man dressed in a suit and carrying a briefcase cupped his hand over his brow to see who it was standing on the stage. Momentarily, Jake recognized Lieutenant Wade from the State Police. The murder of Horatio Sharpe had been all but forgotten by many of the people in the county, but it was still on Wade's radar screen…especially considering the D.A. had dropped the charges against Billy Conroy.

"Is that you, Mr. Dumas?"

"It is. Can I help you?"

"I'm sorry to bother you again, but may I have a few moments?"

Meadows nodded to Wade and then excused himself from the stage. Jake descended the steps and met Wade halfway down one of the aisles. They shook hands and the Lieutenant then asked Jake to sit in a seat on the aisle. Wade continued to stand. There was something about maintaining the high ground when one is interrogating another.

"Have you dug up something on the murder?" Jake asked, shooting first.

"Well, it's been nine months since your principal was murdered and given the fact that charges were dismissed against the coach, we're no further toward solvin' this mystery than we were last fall."

"You came here to tell me that? What more do you need from me?"

Wade pulled from his pocket a pack of Winstons, but then remembering where he was, he slipped them back in. "You can tell me who them three boys were that were in the buildin' at the time Mr. Sharpe had a letter opener jammed into his neck."

Jake wasn't ready for the question and felt like he must have flushed; but his eyes were careful not to give away what was going through his brain. "Would you like to explain that, Lieutenant?"

"Well, let's just say, word got around about the 'Louie, Louie' prank. One of the kids who did it must've been proud of it and told another, and another, and… well, you get the picture. And part of that story was that you caught 'em."

"Wait a minute, Lieutenant. I assume this is all rumor mill, and you're having trouble tracing the story back to the actual kid who spilled the beans. Otherwise, you wouldn't be here fishing."

"Well, we interviewed a kid named Bobby Dietz, and he said he heard it from somebody named Karen. I interviewed her and she says she can't remember who told her."

"And with all this solid information, somehow my name came up."

"That's what Karen what's-her-name said."

"Lieutenant, I thought we went over this. At the time

Mr. Sharpe was killed, I was either in the custodian room or cleaning some toilet down the hall. And I'm supposed to be chasing down kids."

"Maybe since the custodian room is next door to that office, you heard somethin.'"

"I can't help you on this, Lieutenant. You know yourself how stories start out and spread like wildfire. Like that 'gossip' game we used to play as kids. Before the story stops, Governor Wallace himself could have slipped in here and killed Mr. Sharpe."

"I'm not really likin' that example, him bein' my boss and all."

"Well, it just goes to show you how things can spread around out of proportion," Jake replied.

"And you don't know nothin' about these boys."

"Like I said, Lieutenant, I told you all I can tell you."

Wade placed his hand on his revolver and sighed. "All right, then. Officially, we still have nothin' but smudged fingerprints and smudged stories." He shook his head. "It's all very puzzlin' how some guy in broad daylight can walk into an office, kill a man, and nobody hears or sees him." He paused to look around the auditorium. "Heard this place is 'history.'"

"And that's no rumor, Lieutenant. There's a great deal of history here. Nearly fifty years. But in a couple of hours, all doors will be chained and padlocked. They'll doze the place next month."

"You have another job?"

"Not yet, but something will come along."

"As I said before, Jake; you come across as a very smart man. Ever think of becomin' a police officer?"

"Not on a bet, Lieutenant. I'm far from being cut out for that."

Wade then shook hands with Jake. "Good luck to ya, Jake." Wade's lengthy, pressurized grip on Jake's hand and his steely-eyed penetration said, 'I'm not done with you yet, Jake Dumas.'

"And good luck in catching your killer, Lieutenant."

Jake checked his old closet room again to be sure everything of his was out. One of his mops hung from the rack on the wall, the strands looking much like the hair of an old crone. He had to smile, remembering Gordo's snide comment about it being his girlfriend or something to that effect, a remark which Jake had long since forgiven. He thought to himself, there was no way he would give Lieutenant Wade the names of the three boys who had pulled the prank. They didn't kill Sharpe and nothing good would come out of him snitching on them. And he would never say anything which would keep Blaise from that scholarship. For Blaise to be tagged as a suspect in a murder, tied down by the police for weeks on end fielding a battery of questions, and then risking his show date at the Tide training camp…well, Jake just was not going to go there.

Blaise did go home the next morning, but did not take any of his belongings with him. After all, he would be leaving for football camp in a few days. And he wasn't sure his father would even let him in the door. At seven that same evening, he showed back up at Jake's place. He had run all the way from his house, partly because he wanted to convince himself he was still in top condition, but mainly because he didn't have wheels. He'd have to do something about that second thing…even if he had to buy a clunker.

"So, you're back. How did it go?" quizzed Jake.

Blaise shrugged. "All right, I guess. When I walked in, he said something like, 'What do you want?' Like I was a beggar at his door. I told him I just wanted to talk…that it was about time we cleared the air. He said I might as well come in, but what was there to talk about? And then I said it wasn't right that a father and his son had such hard feelings between them. I told him I always wanted him to be proud of me. He didn't say anything to that, but at least he nodded. I guess you were right about the 'pride' thing. I could see he couldn't let it go…like it was beneath him to do so. Anyway, he said I might as well have some lunch and then told Mom to fix me some.

"Then after lunch, he did ask me about the football scholarship and when I'd be leaving for school. It was pretty much small talk after that and then he left the house. I guess that was a start. We both had to swallow a little pride."

"Small steps," Jake said.

"Well, I'll take a few clothes with me tonight, but if you don't mind, Jake, I'd like to leave the rest of my stuff. No sense of moving it out now and then again when I leave for camp."

"No problem, Blaise. Will you need a ride to Tuscaloosa?"

"Actually, yes. My old man said he would've taken me, but he has an important business meeting that day. I think he feels he gave too much up in our conversation and taking me to the university would make him lose too much of his pride. His ego can only take so much."

"Okay, then. I'll take you. I guess you also need a ride back home this evening, unless you plan on running back."

"If it's no trouble. I hate taking advantage of you, though. You've given so much."

"I had nothing else going this evening. By the way, I meant to ask you. Is Janet also going to Alabama this fall?"

Blaise dropped his eyes and shoved his hands into the pockets of his sweat pants. "She applied there, like she did several other schools, but her parents decided for her. She's going to Notre Dame. It's a Catholic thing in their family."

"Umm, sorry to hear that. But I'm sure it'll work out. It wouldn't be the first time young lovers went to different colleges, only to keep their relationship going."

"Somewhere along the line I've become a realist, Jake. I can see us writing one another, talking on the phone a few times, seeing each other at Christmas. But people change…people grow apart with the distance. I don't have a good feeling about it."

Jake placed a firm hand on Blaise's shoulder. "Your world will go on with or without her. If at the end of your first year, you still cling to one another, I have a feeling you'll make it just fine. Just don't let it distract you."

Blaise nodded. "Don't worry. I know what my priorities are."

Jake patted Blaise's shoulder a couple of times and then said, "Let's get your clothes."

Jake's phone rang on Sunday morning, rudely interrupting not only his peace, but his full breakfast of flapjacks, bacon and eggs, the one luxury he afforded himself once a week. He was a bit miffed to say the least.

"Hello," he barked.

"Jake?" a woman's voice.

"Yes."

"It's Rosie. Wow, that didn't sound like you."

"It wasn't. It was a grumpy old bastard who was getting ready to sit down to breakfast and the Sunday paper."

"Oh, I'm sorry, sweetie. I'll just call back a little later."

"No, no. Not a problem. What's going on?"

"Well, guess what. I'm now the new head of the county library. I got a call out of the blue from the county supervisor and he said the lady who had that job for over thirty years died last week…God bless her…and he was looking for someone with experience to replace her. His cousin, Miss Prader, you know our Phys Ed teacher, told him about me. I met with him yesterday at the library and after our interview, he offered me the Head Librarian job. I'll actually be making more money, now."

"Great. That's great, Rosie."

"And you know what else? When the assistant librarian found out she wasn't getting the job, she quit. I hate that she felt that way, but she had only been there a couple of years…and I don't think the supervisor liked her anyway."

"I'm happy for you and sure you'll do fine there. I guess I need to get back to breakfast; it's getting cold."

"Wait. I want to tell you something else. He said I could hire anyone I choose for the assistant job. How would you like it?"

"Me?"

"Yes. You read everything and you know the Dewey Decimal System like the back of your hand. And you need a job."

"I don't know, Rosie. Thanks for thinking of me, but I'll have to mull it over."

"What's to mull over."

Jake readily couldn't think of a reason, except that it might be a bit boring to him. But he didn't want to tell her that. "What say we have dinner tonight to talk about it?"

206

"That would be nice. Do you want me to cook something?"

"No. It was my suggestion. Let's go to that new steakhouse over in Christiansburg."

"The Laredo House?"

"That's the one. Pick you up at five, okay?"

"I'll be ready."

No sooner had they sat down in the booth and began breaking up their shelled peanuts from the metal container that lay between them, a hard rain began to tattoo the tin roof. Streaks poured down the window by their table like melting crystal.

"I hope we're getting some of this rain back in town. We're barely into summer and we're already dry," said Jake.

"My daisies and daylilies sure could use it. And my grass…it's already turning brown. Summer can be like that in Alabama with hit and miss thunderstorms."

"Okay, Rosie. Enough about the weather and daylilies. I did think about the offer and believe I'll take you up on it."

"Oh, dandy!" she squealed, grabbing both of Jake's hands which were still breaking up peanuts. She was as bubbly and blithesome as a tenth grade majorette. He studied her as she went on about how much fun they would have and that they would make a good team. Her face was flawless, cameo-like even. Her violet eyes danced as she talked and he suddenly found that her beauty was actually drowning out her voice.

Jake wasn't sure why he was drawn to her, although any man would be without hesitation. She wasn't even his type. He preferred a woman with less flurry about her and more grace...like Emily, who had reminded him so much of Allesandra. But they were both dead. Tragically so. And with them were buried their images. He had suffered so deeply inside while he was in prison for several reasons, but mostly because he could not fully remember their faces. At least he managed to hold onto their photographs, which sometimes helped him remember.

The storm was clearing out and gradually Rosie's voice was fading back in. As for some reason his past had returned to his mind, blotting out her voice, he hadn't heard much of Rosie's chatter.

"...and I start work on Monday. You'll have to go through the formality of the application and I'll take it to the supervisor. You'll have to be very specific about your work history."

What she was saying was that she was looking forward to learning something...anything...about the man of mystery. And that would be a problem for him. He had two years under his belt as the school custodian, but before that, nine years in a machine shop at Folsom. He would have to fabricate his history...perhaps some small business in California that had since gone out of business. Maybe no one would check it out. How important would an assistant librarian position be where a background check would be required?

Rosie was still going on and on, which was perhaps one of her qualities that kept Jake from getting more deeply into her. "...you'll probably end up starting the next Monday after the county has you in their system."

"Right," he replied, nodding.

"Well, Mr. Dumas, are we going dancing again anytime soon? I had fun that night. And like I said before, you're really not that bad on your feet for a guy who swing-dances to country music. Maybe we should go over to a club in Birmingham where they play all the forties music. I may be a country and rock 'n roll gal, but I like the Big Band stuff, too."

Her incessant dribble was suddenly giving Jake a headache. He was slowly convincing himself that they could never be an item, knock-out gorgeous as she was. But…she was female companionship and for now, it felt pretty good.

They sat for another hour after their dinner sipping on margueritas, him knowing how Tequila made him feel the next morning. But for another week, he had no job. However, he did have some business to conduct the next day that would involve a clear head and some shrewd bargaining.

Jake was already out of the house, sitting on the front porch when Blaise and his mother arrived.

Blaise exited the car on the passenger's side while his mom slid out from behind the wheel of her Buick. He stopped short before stepping onto the sidewalk and let out a low whistle. "Hey, Jake. Who's bike?"

"It's mine…good morning, Mrs. Honeycutt."

"And good morning to you, Mr. Dumas. I'm Deborah. You know, actually I believe this is the first time I met you. Blaise has gone on so much about you, it's like I already know you. It was good of you to offer to drive him to Tuscaloosa."

Jake stepped down from the porch and extended his hand. She was a handsomely attractive and stately woman in her late forties, not to mention refined, gracious and Southern. He had seen her at a distance in the auditorium at Blaise's graduation, but had not gotten a good look at her.

"It's a Harley!" exclaimed Blaise. "When did you get it?"

"A couple of days ago. I bought it off a guy who had only ridden it a dozen times or so. He took a spill and his wife made him sell it. There're some scratches on the right side pipe and the seat has a rip in it, but I can live with that."

"I didn't figure you for a biker."

"Blaise, my boy, a dozen years ago I spent a good number of weekends riding an old Triumph up and down the Pacific Coast Highway. And then I too was one of those husbands whose wives made him give it up." Jake stood looking at the Harley for a moment, conjuring up again all those regrets of whiling away those valuable Saturdays he should have been spending with his wife and baby. But then he shook off the nostalgia and said, "So, are you ready to roll out?"

Blaise nodded. "Guess I'll load up my things. Gotta be at school by four."

Mrs. Honeycutt was already teary-eyed, and Jake, noticing her moist cheeks, pulled a crisp, clean handkerchief from his jean pocket. Once he had escorted her inside, he offered her his sofa chair and a cup of coffee. Blaise went on to his bedroom of six months, bringing out first his stereo which he took directly to the Valiant to lay carefully in the back seat. While he was outside, Mrs. Honeycutt reached up from where she was sitting and took Jake by the hand.

"Thank you, Mr. Dumas, for being there for my Blaise. You helped get him through school and then you encouraged him to come back home to make peace with his father. I don't know why you did all this, but I'll never forget it."

Jake sat down opposite her and replied. "I just saw in your son a potential that had every chance of being wasted. I…don't have a son of my own, ma'am, and I saw he needed someone to be there for him, to kick him in the butt, and embolden him to excel, in spite of himself."

She smiled. "And he told me you wrote that letter that got him the scholarship. If there is anything…and I mean anything…you ever need, Mr. Dumas, you don't hesitate to call me."

"You just continue to love and support that boy, Mrs. Honeycutt, and that will be enough for me."

Blaise had made a half-dozen trips back and forth, carrying the remainder of his boxes and clothes to the car while Jake and his mother were talking.

"Got everything?" Jake asked.

"I think so. Anything else you find, you can take to the Salvation Army. Now you've got your bedroom back."

"You didn't get everything, Blaise."

"Mmm, yes, I'm sure I did."

"You forgot this." He handed Blaise an envelope. "I didn't get you a graduation gift."

"Yes, you did, Jake. Getting me to the point where I *did graduate and arranging the scholarship...*" "Well, there's still one more thing. Open it."

Blaise pulled from the envelope a pale yellow document which read The State of Alabama, Department of Motor Vehicles. "What...?"

"The Valiant, Blaise. She's yours. You're going to need a car around campus. You do have a license don't you? You said you did."

"Yes, but..."

"No buts. You're her new owner."

"No. You love this old car."

"I think it's as tired of me as I am of it. It needs some new blood behind the wheel."

"I...I don't know what to say, except I will take care of it."

"You won't exactly be the most sporty guy on campus, but you'll have something dependable."

Blaise dropped his sports bag on the floor and held out his hand. Instead, Jake embraced him. "You're a good friend, Jake, and..."

Jake slapped him on the back and pushed him away. "Yeah. Yeah. Now get the hell out of here and go start your life. If you flunk out over there in Tuscaloosa, I'm jumping on that Harley and coming to kick your butt." "I won't let you down." Then Blaise turned to his mom. "I won't let anybody down."

With that, he took his mom's hand and led her to her car. He hugged her and after she slid onto the driver's seat, closed the door after her. After she backed out, he went to the Valiant which was parked behind the Harley. Taking note that it needed some paint and a few dents pulled out, he smiled. She would do just fine. The engine turned over and purred as quickly as he turned the key. He then patted the steering wheel and pushed the 'reverse' button on the dash. As he backed down the gravel driveway to the road, he threw up his hand to wave to Jake. But he had already gone back in.

CHAPTER 17

Jake awoke early on the morning of the 29th, brewed some coffee and dropped a piece of dry toast onto a saucer. Finishing neither the toast nor coffee, he took the shed keys off the nail by the door, grabbed his flashlight and popped open the lock on the shed door. Once inside, he opened the memorabilia trunk and rummaged around until he found the large manila envelope he was looking for. After relocking the shed, he returned to the kitchen table where he emptied the envelope's contents. He sorted through a dozen or so snapshots until he put his fingers on his one favorite photo…the one of Emily and their two year old son on a blanket at Malibu Beach. Jake had taken the photo. Emily was holding Johnny and smiling that bright, beautiful smile that he so remembered. He folded his hands under his nose and studied their faces for the longest time, then closed his eyes to see if they were still there in his mind. After several moments, he carefully and lovingly returned the other photos to the envelope as though they were delicate pieces of crystal, keeping out his favorite.

At just after seven, he called Rosie, rousting her from a deep sleep. She seemed considerably more put out than he did the previous Sunday morning…the morning she told him about the county library job.

"Why are you calling me at this ungodly hour?" she said in a raspy voice.

"I needed to ask you something. Is it possible for me to delay my start date at the library, say for another week?"

"Well, yes, I suppose. Couldn't you have called me a couple of hours from now on this?"

"No. I have to go out of town and am going to leave shortly so that I can get a good start."

"Where are you going? More mystery from the mystery man?"

"It's personal, Rosie. I'll be leaving the state, but will be back for work the next Monday."

He heard her sigh. "Can I really depend on that? How do I know you won't just leave me high and dry?"

"Because I'm telling you I won't. You have my word."

"All right, Jake. Have it your way. I'll see you next week. But I do need your application from you before you leave. Did you complete it?"

"Yes, I did. I'll drop it in your mailbox on the way out of town."

There was a long pause. "Okay. Goodbye, Jake."

Jake threw together his toiletry kit, a couple of shirts and an extra pair of jeans to put in one of the Harley's saddlebags, donned his mirrored sunglasses and helmet, and roared out of the driveway, violating the quiet peace of the morning. From her bedroom window, Rosie watched as Jake pulled up to her mailbox, dropped in the application and then sped away. Who was Jake Dumas, why was he on that motorcycle and where was he going, she wondered.

By mid-morning he was crossing the Mississippi and by nine that night he was deep in the heart of Texas. In Abilene he finally pulled off at a truck stop for a sandwich and after filling his tank, he retired for the night across the road at the Prairie Wheel Motel. Sailing the rest of the way through West Texas consumed the entire next morning and at one o'clock in the afternoon he found himself seeking shelter under an overpass in New Mexico until a blinding rainstorm moved on. At seven that evening, the merciless Mohave sun which had scorched his face and neck like a branding iron finally disappeared over the horizon, forming a stunning purple and pink masterpiece. The second night on the road he spent in a fleabag just outside of Palm Springs and by eleven the next morning, he made Los Angeles.

The last time he had entered the gate at Restlawn was just over two years ago, the day he started east. It was not even a consideration for him to stay in California. There were just too many bad memories. And anyway, after he was arrested, the bank foreclosed on his beautiful home in Malibu Canyon. They took everything…except his box of memorabilia. The three hundred dollars he had on him at his arrest, which was placed in the envelope along with his watch, wedding ring and favorite pictures, was returned to him at his release. He became Jake Dumas the day he bought the Valiant, filled its tank and set out for nowhere particular. The real Jake Dumas, his boyhood friend who was killed in 1944, had lain in his grave under a cross in Southern Italy for over seventeen years. He no longer needed his name.

Jake put down the kickstand on the Harley which he had parked off the cemetery lane and made his way through symmetrically-aligned rows of tombstones until stopping at a monument that read:

Emily Jane Roberts Caruso

Beloved Wife and Mother

At the foot of the grave was a smaller marker with the image of an angel in the upper left corner and the engraved name of his child:

John Angelo Caruso, Jr

Our Son

The dates of their births and deaths were indicated beneath their names. Although Jake's name, which then was John Angelo Caruso, was not inscribed alongside Emily's, he had been buried there with her more than twelve years before.

The lilies Jake purchased from the flower shop earlier in the morning had been beaten by the wind on the way to the cemetery. But they were still beautiful. They were Emily's favorite. Above the flowers he placed the beach photo of Emily and Johnny and then sat cross-legged for nearly an hour. When his eyes were not fixed on the photo, he closed them to recall in his mind those wonderful, happy days in their lives…their wedding, Johnny's birth, his first birthday, their days at the beach. But then the image of the day his heart broke in a thousand pieces invaded his brain. Tears streaked down his cheeks. The photo he had placed at the base of the tombstone soon became blurred. It was time for him to go.

Jake leaned forward one last time and touched his forehead to the cool marble. It was at that moment he realized he would never again return to their graves. Coming back only served to perpetuate his grief. And for some reason, the pain had started up again in his leg the very moment he positioned himself on Emily's grave. Psychosomatic? Perhaps. But his pain was very real just the same. And so was the pain in his heart…the pain which he had hoped his trip to the cemetery would quell.

He would be on the road, coming and going, the better part of six days only to spend merely an hour at their graves. Upon retrieving the photo and placing it gingerly into his breast pocket, Jake stood over Emily's stone to recite aloud an excerpt from Pushkin which he had burned into his mind along with his other readings in his cell at Folsom:

Time passed-a rebel storm blast-shattered

The reveries that once were mine

And I forgot your soothing accents,

Your features gracefully divine.

In dark days of enforced retirement

I gazed upon gray skies above

With no ideals to inspire me,

No one to cry for, live for, love.

And came a moment of Renaissance;

I looked up and you again are there.

A fleeting vision, the quintessence

Of all that's beautiful and rare.

Taking a white handkerchief from his pocket, Jake wiped his eyes. "Goodbye," he whispered. "I will always love you. I will always love you both." He then turned away to face a sudden, stirring breeze…and the long road home to Alabama.

Jake was grateful to Rosie that she had thought of him first for the library assistant position. There had been no problem with his fabricated application and apparently there was neither a background check done nor any questions. He could still go on being Jake Dumas. And just as he had used the real Jake Dumas' Social Security card for his job at the school, he continued to do so for the new job at his personal, not to mention legal, risk.

He would also feel at home among the books he loved and have access to them anytime he wanted. To him, it was like an ice cream addict getting a job at the Tastee Freeze with the perk of sampling all he wanted.

The county library sat in the geographical center of New Hope between the courthouse and Department of Social Services building. A rather ancient gray block building that needed a good cleaning on the outside complemented the other government structures with its tall, stately columns and ornate accents. Many of the books dated back into the early 1900s and were in sad disrepair; however, Mrs. Bostwick, the county's long- time librarian, had kept up with the world by ordering the latest in fiction, non-fiction and reference material. It was a considerably more sizable operation than Rosie Green was used to managing.

Jake did start up the Monday after the weekend that he returned from California. Rosie did not press him about where he had been; on the contrary, she was just happy that he had actually returned for work. As they now saw one another every day, there would be a great deal more opportunity to get to learn more about him, to include his mysterious past. She would merely have to be patient.

Jake could see that the work would be mindless for him; but certainly not so mindless as his last job was. Most of the day, he retrieved books from the bin that had been returned by patrons and placed them in proper numerical order within the Dewey system. He also had to learn Rosie's job, part of which entailed updating the system by making new cards for the books. And their hours overlapped. Rosie opened the doors at ten o'clock and left at six. Jake came in at one and left at nine when he closed up. Two summer interns worked staggered hours as well, but they would be returning to classes at school in scantly two weeks.

It was all about smiles, being helpful to the customers who had no clue where to look for anything, and lots of shushing with the index finger touching the lips. And speaking of smiles, Rosie had a lot of them for Jake. She watched him often. She watched him move, bend, reach and stoop as though she were making love to every part of his body with her eyes. He would catch her. And there were the little touches of the hand to his. It was actually a little embarrassing for him, if not unnerving. She was used to seeing him coming and going in a janitor's work clothes; but now that he wore a nice pair of slacks, a crisp white shirt and a tie, he was a different-looking Jake. She told him so.

But because of their staggered hours and working six days a week, they had little opportunity to socialize off site. That left Saturday night and Sundays. Being the social butterfly that she was and hungry for the companionship of a man, she was forward with asking him over for dinner or to go out for a movie. And he did go. Not often, but enough to suit the both of them.

There was also that lovely September Sunday where they took a walk along the Summerwoods Trail at Crystal Lake, where they spread out their blanket at water's edge and sipped wine from Dixie cups. Drinking wine from paper cups seemed to Jake like showing up at a gala in a tuxedo and tennis shoes. But she said it was a Southern thing. Something to laugh about. And her laughter was indeed infectious. She leaned into him a few times when she laughed, allowing her blonde hair to lay on his chest. Because she was in no hurry to righten her body, it made it easy for him to kiss her. The afternoon was filled with tender moments as they acted out the parts of lovers with the sounds of nature as their supporting cast. Their kisses went from delicate to ravenous in a matter of seconds; but the moment she pulled him down to the blanket, he disengaged and sat up.

She was quiet for a moment and there was a kind of rejected hurt in her eyes. "What's wrong?" she asked softly.

"There's nothing really wrong, Rosie. It's…just territory I can't enter at this point in my life."

"What does that mean? What point of your life are you talking about?"

Jake shook his head without reply and stared emotionless out over the water.

A frown formed along Rosie's eyebrows. "I've done everything I know except throw myself at you. Why don't you let me in?"

"With me, it's just a matter of getting too close. You live your life as an open book, Rosie, and I never have. Just trust me. There are things in my past you would not want to know about…that would make you run far away from me. You may not even want me to work with you, if I told you."

"Then try me, Jake. What could be so terrible about you that would matter? I can't imagine you, Jake Dumas, having any horrible deviances that would change how I feel about you. You're not a sadistic rapist or axe murderer, are you?"

221

Jake smiled and then let out a chuckle. "No, nothing like that. Just a lot of cobwebs and a lot of pain in my past, and I'm still trying to deal with it all."

Rosie latched onto his hand. "And you think it's enough to draw a demarcation line in our relationship that I can't cross over."

"I'm not sure what our relationship is."

"I know what I'd like it to be."

Jake turned full-face to her. "There's a part of me that would like that, too. Maybe we just need more time for that to cultivate."

"Okay," she replied softly. "I won't press you, Jake. But remember, I'm a great listener, and you can always trust me to be discreet."

"Thank you, Rosie."

They sat quietly holding hands after that. And then there was that mellow call of the loon again. Jake listened and watched for his mate. She never responded.

On the Tuesday afternoon of the second week in October, Jake came into work with an envelope in hand, smiling. He held it up to Rosie.

"A letter from Blaise. I had been keeping up on him through his mother, but it's actually the first time he's written."

Rosie thought to herself how much Jake was acting like a father and it looked good on him. But after all, from what she had gathered from tutoring and fine-tuning the boy, Jake had been more of a father to him than John Honeycutt, a man she clearly despised.

"Can you read it to me?" she asked.

"Sure. Here goes."

"Dear Jake,

Sorry I haven't written before now to let you know how I'm doing, but as you can imagine, I'm trying to juggle football and an eighteen hour semester. Bear made us hit the ground running that very first day of practice. I stay so whipped that by the end of the day in this heat, all I want to do is guzzle liquids and hit the bed. He treats us well, but the coaches are all disciplinarians. If we break even one rule, there is no second chance.

"I think I've lost ten or twelve pounds, but laying off a year like I did, I needed to. Gordo and Paulie drove over last week and said I looked like I had been pulverized and simonized, whatever that means. I could see they've got nothing going in their lives. I'm too tired after school and practice for any social life, but who wants to go out with a guy who owns an old Valiant. Ha! Ha! By the way, it's purring fine."

Rosie interrupted. "I wondered what you did with that car. Did you sell it to Blaise or just let him have it?"

Jake didn't answer, but continued reading.

"I haven't heard from Janet. I did write her, but I guess she's either too busy or like I said she would do, forgot all about me.

"The varsity won its first game, 36-6 over Tulane. That Joe Namath is amazing. Everybody says we'll go undefeated this year. I actually got to dress, even though I'm just a freshman, but sat on the bench. The Bear says all he wants me to do is study Namath and the play book. I can do that.

"Well, I guess that's about all I have to say. Again, Jake, I want to tell you...yawdy, yawdy."

Rosie smiled. "You should be proud of what you did to get that boy there, Jake. You..."

"Yeah, okay." He folded the letter and placed it back into the envelope. "I'd better get started. That stack of books is not going to jump on the shelves by themselves."

Throughout the entire season, Blaise dressed every game, but sat on the bench. The Tide went on to roll over all of its opponents to include a 21-14 defeat of cross- state rival Auburn on Thanksgiving Day. Jake sat with Rosie watching the game on her TV while gulping down a piece of her delightful pecan pie and a cup of coffee. They kept looking for Number 8 on the field and figured they might have missed Blaise since her picture tube was small. But anyway, the cameras mostly stayed zoomed in on the future Hall of Famer, the guy who would soon be referred to as Broadway Joe.

Blaise came home four days before Christmas, stopping on the way to see Gordo and Paulie, still at the garage, and still floundering. After dropping his bags and giving his mom a quick peck on the cheek, he found Jake at the library helping eighty-six year old Miss Julia Hanson Pryor, the oldest living former schoolteacher at New Hope High. She was trying to locate the biography of Woodrow Wilson, having learned from her sister's daughter, the family genealogist, that Woodrow may actually have been a cousin.

Jake turned around and nearly bowled Blaise over. "Holy cow! Blaise. When did you get back?"

"About an hour ago. You look good, Jake. But what's with the shirt and tie? You look…corporate."

"Well, it's not my idea. And good grief, boy, you must be down twenty pounds."

"Twenty-two to be exact. Coach Bryant works our tails off."

"I looked for you on the tube Thanksgiving Day, but wasn't able to pick out the famous number eight."

"Well, I was there…benched like all the other neophytes. There's always next season. Say, I was just on my way out to see Janet. She's supposed to be home from Notre Dame. But first I wanted to drop this off to you. Merry Christmas." Blaise handed Jake a fairly large package, perhaps 11X14, haphazardly wrapped in green paper with a gold bow.

Jake stood looking at the gift and remembered that he failed to remind himself to pick up the autographed Johnny Unitas football for Blaise that he had laid away at the new Sports and Hobby Shop at the strip mall in Waterford.

"You shouldn't spend your money like this, Blaise. I'm sure you've had a lot of expenses, scholarship or not."

"Hey, this didn't cost much. Go ahead. Open it, now."

Jake smiled and began running his hand under the paper, finding beneath it the slickness of glass surrounded by wood. A picture frame. But when the final strips of paper came off, the images under the glass caused a choking lump to form in his throat. The tears swelled immediately.

Rosie, who had seen Blaise with Jake, joined the men about the time old Miss Pryor became impatient. "Are you going to get that book down for me or not!" she barked in her scratchy little voice.

"Oh, yes, ma'am," Rosie said. "Which one was it?"

"That one there on the top shelf. The one about my cousin, Mr. Wilson."

Rosie went ahead and brought it down and said, "Here you go. Woodrow Wilson: the Man and the President." Miss Pryor snatched it from her hand. "I'm glad somebody works here." She then paraded off toward the checkout desk.

"I'll be there in a moment, ma'am," Rosie said. Then she turned to Jake. "What on earth are you doing, Jake? Oh, hi, Blaise. You're home." Then she turned back to Jake. "We can't let our customers wait around while you socialize." She then looked down at the picture Jake was holding. "Who's that?"

Jake, still trying hard to keep his tears from spilling out of his sockets, replied, "It's a photograph…of my wife and son."

Rosie looked as though all the blood in her face had drained away. Her mouth fell open, but for a moment she had no words. Finally, she said, "Do I assume they are part of that troubled past you told me about…or the present?"

Miss Pryor's voice then rang through the library from check-out. "In my day, librarians spent time helping their customers, not carrying on idle chit chat."

Rosie gave Jake a venomous parting glare and in an icy tone said "When you get off work this evening, Mr. Dumas, we will have a talk." She then turned abruptly and with a plastic smile on her face she called back to her customer, "Coming, Miss Pryor."

And when she had turned heel, Blaise explained all about his gift. "Jake, remember the day you closed down the school after graduation? Well, while you were at work I went back into the shed. I know, I know. You told me to stay out of your personal life. But I remembered that wallet-size picture of your wife and son and thought I'd get it blown up and framed for you. They even touched up a couple of scratches on the 11X14. I returned it to the foot locker a couple of days later. I hope you don't mind me taking it, but I wanted to do something nice for you this Christmas."

Jake was quiet for a while and then he nodded. He could not be angry with Blaise. Not for doing this. Holding the picture up toward the fluorescent light, Emily's smile was even more radiant than he remembered. The details of her and Johnny's faces were sharper, more discernible than on the well-worn wallet photo. Jake smiled at Blaise and fought back his tears. "Thanks," he said in a low voice. That was all that would come out.

"Well," said Blaise, checking his watch. "Gotta go.

I'll see you some time before I go back to school."

When both Blaise and Julia Pryor were out the door, Rosie was quick to get in Jake's face. "Do you want to explain yourself, Mr. Dumas?" she said snidely. "You seem to have a wife and child."

"Not anymore, Rosie."

"What do you mean by that?"

"Can we talk about this another time? It's...not something I can easily discuss."

She placed her hands on her hips and sighed, looking every bit put out. "Suit yourself, Jake. But I think it's time we talked about a lot of things. Especially why it is I don't know anymore about you than the first time I laid eyes on you...unlike your young friend Blaise."

"All right. After I close down tonight, I'll stop by.

Will you still be up?"

"I'll be up."

The remainder of the afternoon she was cool to him, having formulated in her mind that somewhere in the country or perhaps even close by, there was an ex-wife out there. It wasn't just that such a woman existed, but Jake had chosen to be secretive about her. And about having a son.

At twenty minutes past nine, Jake killed the engine to the Harley and sat for a moment looking at the big, yellow house on the corner. He wasn't all that sure he even owed Rosie an explanation about his wife and son. The relationship between them, whatever he had allowed it to become, did not warrant any dialogue beyond who the present Jake Dumas was. If they were lovers...intimate lovers who were planning a future together, she would certainly be entitled to know all his truths. But as they were little more than friends who enjoyed an occasional dinner and some light, impromptu smooching at the lake, she did not have any reason to 'get her back up' about anything in his past. And the fact that they worked together mattered even less.

But then again, he knew that whatever their relationship was, it had been one-sided. She had been open with him…at least he believed so…and there were things in his past he could actually discuss with her. Maybe he wasn't being fair with Rosie. And since she now knew that there was an Emily and John, Jr., perhaps he did owe her that explanation. He could still maintain his anonymity by not getting too specific about things.

When she opened the door, she had on a new face. It no longer had that look of exasperation and injury. She also had on fresh make-up and was wearing a smile. "Everything good at work, this evening?"

"Everything's fine," he replied.

"I have some hot coffee cake on the table if you'd like some. Fresh from the oven."

"Smells great."

"Well, have a seat on the couch in the parlor and I'll bring you some with a cup of coffee. You're okay with caffeine this late, aren't you?"

"No problem."

After a long minute, she returned to the parlor with a tray on which were two saucers containing squares of decadent cinnamon cake and steaming cups of coffee. She removed the coffee and set them atop coasters, one on each end table.

"Wow. Good," Jake said after savoring the first bite.

"My grandmother's recipe. It goes way back in our family. My ex-husband was a diabetic and so I never made this even one time the couple of years we were together."

Jake sensed that the mention of her 'ex' was her way of jump-starting the talk she had been waiting for all afternoon.

"Okay," he began. "About my wife and son…it's not what you may think, Rosie. Emily and I met in college…"

"That's a good start," she said. "Now I know you went to college.

Jake appeared annoyed at her interruption, but continued on. "We were at USC. I was majoring in History and she was in one of my classes. We fell in love and got married, staying in Southern California to start our lives. We had a kid, Johnny, pretty much right away. It was the perfect little family living in a small house in the canyon with a white picket fence and a dog in the yard. But it ended all too soon."

"How so?" she asked, nibbling on a piece of the cake.

"They were killed."

She dropped her fork. "Oh, my God. How?"

"On the street in L.A. Somebody shot them."

Rosie placed a hand on her breasts, looking as though she couldn't get her breath. "Why?" she gasped.

Jake laid his saucer on the coffee table. "A question that I have asked God countless times. Somebody was shooting at a gang member and my family got in the way. It was…senseless. It's like one moment I had a life…a beautiful wife and a little boy I adored…and the next, they were gone. My life as I knew it…that perfect, All-American life, was gone in an instant. Stolen. Needlessly."

As he was talking, Jake had been staring at his hands that he had unconsciously been wringing. When he looked up, Rosie was crying. She then placed her moist hands onto his.

"I am so sorry, Jake. I feel so awful for the way I acted today after seeing the picture Blaise gave you. I know this is painful for you to talk about."

"Well, some days are worse than others, but I get through them."

Rosie dabbed at her eyes with a napkin and smiled. The kind of smile that was something between love and sympathy.

"Did they find out who shot them?"

"Yes," he replied. "And the man paid for it with his life." Jake said that in a way that she would think the man received the death penalty. Which he did. "Then after that all happened, I just fell out of society. I had no desire for a career or to seek out another relationship."

"I guess I can understand why. I don't know what I'd do if I lost a child." She touched the tissue to her eyes again. "I wish you had been able to share this with me early on."

"Would it have made any difference?"

"I wouldn't have been the bitch I was in pressing you like I did. I guess you felt more comfortable about sharing this with Blaise. Maybe a man thing."

Jake could still sense some angst in her voice about 'why Blaise and not her.' After all, they had gotten rather close. But he didn't respond.

"From what I saw of the photo, she was pretty…and your little boy was adorable."

"Yes." He took another sip of his coffee. "Can we talk about something else, now? Or maybe I should call it a night."

"No," she replied. "Please stay a while longer. I think I need you to. Maybe neither of us needs to be alone tonight."

"You're feeling sorry for me, now."

"No, no. That's not it at all. I just thought you'd like…"

"…to stay the night?"

"Well, would that be such a bad thing?"

"I don't know. Is our relationship close enough for that?"

"You tell me," she said.

"Maybe it's not such a good thing for us to be working together…especially you being my boss. If we're going to get friendlier, it could get complicated."

"We can't be close and work together?"

"Not the kind of closeness I think you'd like to have," Jake replied.

"Well, I don't see a problem with it. But then again, I'm not sure after what's happened in your life you're actually ready for real companionship. I don't think you could get into me like I would get into you. And when I do get into a guy, I admit I'm pretty possessive. Brutally possessive."

"Well, I guess you're not any different from most women."

She laughed. "And you're some kind of expert on women?"

"Not really; but then I do read a lot."

"Reading and doing are two different things, Mr. Dumas. You know, I can't believe it's been a year since you were here for Christmas dinner. Are you coming back again?"

"Is that an invitation?"

"I'm not asking anyone else."

"Then I accept."

There was a bit more small talk and then Jake announced that the hour was late…and he would not be spending the night. She put her arms around him at the door and kissed him, saying 'maybe another night,' and then he left. As he stood by his bike under the streetlight, putting on his helmet and riding gloves, she watched from the parlor window. She figured she could now sleep the night peacefully, having been satisfied that Jake Dumas did not have a wife and child out there somewhere to whom he just might return at any time. But she would still be lonely tonight

CHAPTER 18

Jake found the perfect spot for the framed enlargement of Emily and Johnny…in his bedroom directly across from his bed. It would be the first thing he saw in the morning and the last before he turned off his lamp at night. It was simply the most treasured of all gifts he ever received, except for the Seiko watch Emily had given him the Christmas before she died. He had never taken the watch out of the box, except to read the inscription from time to time, "To the Love of my Life." He had found the watch under the tree on Christmas Day, four days after he buried her.

The sales clerk at Ogletree's had talked Jake into the bracelet the week before Christmas, telling him that because it was made of both yellow and white gold, it would go with anything. It also had a small safety chain, that should the clasp come apart, it would not be lost. And it was a bargain at fifty-five dollars. This was the first money he had spent on a woman since Emily.

When Rosie opened the box, she reacted as though the bracelet had cost a thousand. "Oh, Jake, that's too extravagant. You shouldn't have. But I love it. Thank you." She then placed her gift in Jake's hands and gave him a peck on the lips. "Merry Christmas," she said.

Jake opened the present quickly, finding in a box a First Edition of Hemingway's For Whom the Bell Tolls. She could tell he was thrilled. His eyes lit up brighter than the lights on her tree. "It's very thoughtful, Rosie. And here I was expecting a tie."

"Well, I thought about it, and decided that since you already have one...one...I asked myself 'Why would he need another?' The narrow black one he wears every day...every day, I said...looks so nice with that white shirt."

Jake laughed. "I actually bought another one the other day and planned to wear it to work tomorrow. A striped one."

Then she laughed. "You're just getting too crazy these days."

After they had had fun with the 'tie' subject, she said, "Are you ready for dinner?"

"Starved. I didn't eat a thing all day in anticipation of your meat loaf."

"Well, let's go to the dining room...wait." She paused at the door. "We can't go in there yet."

"Why not?"

Rosie pointed to the mistletoe over the door. Jake looked up and said, "Now, I wonder how that got there?"

"Traditions must be followed, you know." She raised up on her toes and swept his tongue with hers, then planted a kiss that felt to him like a suction cup.

"Wow!" Jake exclaimed, taking a deep breath after she had held onto the kiss for over ten seconds. "Nothing like getting a tonsillectomy for Christmas."

She laughed and then followed up with a quick peck on the lips. "Let's eat."

After they ate, they sat drinking an after dinner wine and watching the lights on her tree blink and twinkle through the needles. Only moments before, Jake had placed another oak log on the fire and it was just now catching, sending a sudden, emanating warmth into the room. Lounging close together, they sipped the wine and talked over a number of subjects…stories from the school, where some of the teachers had gone, and happenings at the library during the previous week. Just before five, when the wine had added weights to his eyelids, Jake said he'd better be going.

"Hmm," she replied. "So you're not taking me up on my offer to spend the night."

"That, my dear, would be dangerous for the both of us. Anyway, I feel like I won't be long for the bed."

"That's what I hoping." Her eyes twinkled like the Christmas lights with romantic folly.

"To sleep," he said, smiling.

"But it's Christmas…a time for giving. And I don't think I'm through giving."

Jake put his arm around her and drew her into his chest. "It's been a long time since I had a woman in my life. And would I be ready for anything beyond who we are right now? I don't know. I've been haunted by what happened to Emily for so long, I just haven't been able to even think about being with another woman. To do without, has become a lifestyle for me. I think I may even be afraid to sail into the 'physical' waters right now. I care a lot about you, Rosie, but sex would not come easy for me at this time. My heart wouldn't be in it. I guess my hurts are stronger than my urges."

"I can help you with that."

"I know, but let's let things be the way they are for a while. Maybe one day, I'll surprise the both of us."

236

"Well, hopefully, Jake Dumas, I'll still be available when you get to that point…if you know what I mean."

"Yeah. I know what you mean. But just be patient."

He rose and started for the door. "Thanks for the wonderful day. The meatloaf was splendid and the company, superb."

"What are you doing New Year's eve?" Then she giggled. "Hey, that's a song, isn't it?"

"Spending it with you, I guess."

"Let's do something special…like go to some gala in Birmingham, then climb the Vulcan and watch the fireworks over the city."

"Sounds like a plan." He then began pulling on his leather jacket.

And then the phone rang. Rosie went to the end table and picked up the receiver. "Oh, hi, Mom. Merry Christmas."

Jake pointed to the door which signaled that he was leaving.

"Wait a minute, Mom…Oh, Jake. Before you go, I forgot to give you your Christmas card. It's…" She looked toward her study. "It's in one of those pigeon holes on my desk in there," she said, pointing.

"Okay," he whispered. "I'll get it."

Rosie nodded and went back to her phone conversation.

The study was a small room off the parlor and it looked to have at one time been a guest bedroom. On the right was a large shelving unit full of books, brass book ends, vases and the like. A quaint secretary sat beside it against the adjacent wall. A window on the left was covered by a handsome set of white, louvered shutters which cut out much of the light coming in from the outside. Seeing the white envelope protruding from one of the cubby holes, he pulled it out and shoved it into his inside breast pocket on the jacket. As Rosie was still engaged in a draining conversation with her mother about why she hadn't found someone to be a part of her life as yet, Jake smiled and waved as he slipped quietly out the door.

As soon as Jake arrived home, he tossed his jacket on the couch, turned on a local radio station which was currently playing A Midnight Clear, and slumped into his sofa chair. He knew if he dozed off, he would wake up some time in the early morning hours and then not be able to get back to sleep. After the heavy meal, the wine and a head full of Rosie's jabber, he just needed to relax. Mostly, to relax alone with his memories. He hadn't observed Christmas since the year before Emily and Johnny had been murdered. And it was only these past two years that he had even had a good Christmas dinner.

Jake closed his eyes to drink in what he believed was the music of Montavani's orchestra and images of his first Christmas with Emily. It was a traditional scene right out of a Rockwell print...two young people in love, stringing lights on a tree with cups of egg nog on the table and a baby in the crib. And then the image went forward to the next year when Johnny was barely two years old, scampering all over with out-stretched arms, getting into the tree and knocking bulbs off, then finding the prettiest of packages to get into. And then there was that next Christmas when Angelo Caruso sat on the carpet by the tree, holding Johnny's huge stuffed bear, crying and rocking back and forth, thinking at that moment that he would never be able to survive his grief. He remembered that he placed the bear tenderly under the tree, then stood and walked to his bedroom wardrobe to retrieve his Army .45 and stuck it in his mouth. He sat on the same bed where only a week before he lay cuddling with his wife, and squeezed, released, squeezed and released again the trigger. And then he thought…if he did this thing… if he blew his brains onto the very bed where they had made love to one another and where Johnny, who was sometimes afraid of the night thunderstorms, slithered in between them…he would disrespect them. And that thought was all that saved him.

It was also at that very moment that he vowed to use the gun in another way. To send the monster, Joe "the Piranha" Romine, to Hell.

Jake opened his eyes to find them no longer heavy. It was anger that always awakened him or caused him not to sleep at all. Anger had taken a toll on him through the years, tearing him down, ageing him. And still, long after he had killed the bastard on the courthouse steps…long after his nine years of imprisonment…he was still angry. It was the holidays…sentimental days such as this…that he allowed himself to be haunted by his memories. And each time he went there, he ended up angry. In retrospect, Jake thought perhaps he should have spent the night with Rosie. That is, if he could survive the guilt after he had awakened the next morning. And guilt was that other emotion that wouldn't let go.

The card that Jake had snatched from Rosie's secretary had fallen out of his jacket pocket to the floor. After leaning over to pick it up, he saw immediately that it was not Rosie's Christmas card to him after all. He had picked up the wrong card. It was simply addressed to 'Rosie.' When he pulled the card from the envelope, he was surprised to see that it was not a card at all, but a handwritten letter, probably from her mother. He didn't want to read it, but his curiosity got the better of him after reading the greeting. He immediately reminded himself of a nosy old woman.

"My Darling Rosie,

It pains me to have to write this letter to you and I admit that it is a coward's approach to a difficult situation. I didn't intend to do this right at your birthday, but I do wish you to have a happy one, anyway.

I have decided that I cannot go on with our secretive relationship. When we last talked, you as much gave me an ultimatum to divorce my wife or let you go. I don't want to let you go, simply because I love you, and have loved you since I first laid eyes on you. The ties we have had together, secret as they were, I will cherish as long as I live. That wonderful trip to the Bahamas, where I told Doris I was going on a fishing trip, was the best time ever.

I know you're angry with me and I hate that little tiff we had the other day; but, Rosie, I have a status in this community, and me getting a divorce and marrying the beautiful school librarian would be the end of my career, not to mention the trauma it would bring to Doris.

We're getting ready to start up a new school year and if you still want to talk about it, please come by my office to see me. On Tuesday, the first day of school, after everyone has gone from the building would be good for me. Around 5:30 or 6? That way, a letter such as this would not be construed as impersonal or uncaring. I'm putting this in your mailbox at home so that only you will find it. I couldn't fathom anyone else getting their hands on it as it would not be a good result for either of us. We'd both lose our jobs and you certainly wouldn't want that.

If there is any way we can continue what we have, I ask you to consider it. But I cannot deal with ultimatums and I certainly can't marry you. But as you have made it clear you will not share me with anyone, including Doris, then I must end this now. I hope you will find it in your heart to forgive me.

My eternal love,

H.E.S"

Jake was stunned. He read the initials again: "H.E.S." Horatio Edward Sharpe. But he did not even need to read the initials. The letter mentioned 'Doris.' And the content of the letter itself gave Sharpe away. Rosie was his mistress. According to the letter, she was the person who would have been in his office between five and six on the first day of school...the day he was murdered. It was all too difficult for Jake to believe. Was this the same woman who had just fixed him a wonderful holiday dinner, who he had picnicked with and who he could easily have gone to bed with? Certainly a woman scorned, but a murderer...? But then Jake suddenly remembered what she had said a few nights before: "I admit I'm possessive. Brutally possessive." Brutal being the operative word.

Jake laid the letter on the coffee table with the envelope. It was an absolute dilemma for him. He had slowly begun developing feelings for Rosie. Now, he found that she could have and probably did kill New Hope High's principal out of rage. She and Sharpe had argued and then he 'once and for all' shut her out. She then picked up the letter opener, and in anger, plunged it into his neck. Likely, she didn't mean to kill him...just wound him, thinking it would never be fatal. She had killed a man out of passion, Jake thought. Then again, so did he. But it was a different kind of passion. His was justifiable. Maybe Sharpe deserved a slap in the face or kick in the groin...but not a letter opener in the jugular. Jake settled back in his chair and folded his hands under his chin. He knew what he had to do. The situation had to be dealt with right away. And he would have to be the one to confront her...to convince her to turn herself in.

A hard rain began to beat on the gutters, sounding almost like ice pellets. It was certainly cold enough. Jake was not cold, but a sudden chill cut through his spine, the very thing a cup of hot tea would cure. He went into the kitchen and pulled from the cupboard the Lipton box, and then ignited one of the gas burners on the stove to bring a kettle of water to a boil. After about ten minutes, he lifted the kettle and poured the steaming liquid into his coffee mug. After dunking a tea bag several times to turn the water a deep mahogany, he pulled it out and stirred in two sugar cubes. Jake stepped back into the living room with his tea, suddenly catching out of the corner of his eye a smallish figure standing by the door. It startled him enough to where he allowed the cup to slip from his hand and shatter into a dozen pieces on the hardwood floor.

Slowly, she walked from the shadows into the dim light of the table lamp. Her blonde hair was matted and dripping to a point where Jake did not immediately recognize her. She wore a tan trench-style raincoat with the collar pulled up on the back of her neck, all of which gave her a sinister look. Her eyes were piercing, crazy- like.

"I should remember to lock my doors," he said.

Rosie continued walking one or two steps at a time toward him. She saw the opened letter and envelope with her name on it lying on the table. "I guess you and I need to have a talk, huh Jake? Why did you pick up the wrong envelope?"

"It was dark in the room and it was the only one I saw."

"Well, obviously you looked in the wrong pigeon hole."

"You killed him, didn't you, Rosie?"

Her head jerked a little as though the reality of someone actually saying the words stunned her.

"I didn't go to his office with the intention of killing him. I tried to reason with him and even told him I'd give him until the first of the year, so that his precious little wife's Christmas wouldn't be ruined. And then he said the wrong thing. He said there was no way he would leave a good woman like her for a common whore. I was good enough for him in the bedroom and the Bahamas, but then he flushed me down the toilet so that he could keep on being Mr. Big. You know the funny part about it? I don't even remember stabbing him. Somewhere between the school and my house, I noticed my blouse sleeve was covered with blood. But then when I heard later that he was dead, I knew I must have done it."

Jake moved toward his end table and the telephone. "You know what has to happen now."

"If you mean giving myself up, forget it. I will not do that. I will not go to jail, Jake. You'd better think of another solution, like forgetting what's in that letter."

"No, Rosie. Either you go to the police or I will." Rosie's eyes narrowed and bore into him like lasers.

"Don't make me do this." She then pulled from the pocket of her trench coat a .22 caliber revolver and aimed it at Jake's chest.

"Put it down, Rosie. You're not going to shoot anybody." He reached for the phone.

"Stop right there, Jake. I swear to God I will shoot you if you pick up that receiver."

"Look, Rosie. They might just charge you with manslaughter. Maybe he threatened you and you had to defend yourself. You might just get a couple of years, that's all. But if you shoot me, that will be premeditated murder."

She cocked the hammer on the .22 with her gloved thumb. "Call it what you want, Jake, but I'm not going to jail…and you're not picking up that phone."

Jake studied Rosie's eyes to see if it was really in her to pull the trigger. He took a chance and placed his hand on the receiver.

It was a high-pitched, deafening crack. The bullet entered his abdomen causing immediate excruciating pain that took his breath away. The last thing he saw on Christmas Day night was the fading face of Rosie Green.

He collapsed and fell against the couch, then to the floor.

Rosie took off her left glove and laid her hand on his chest. She felt nothing. She figured no one would have a clue who killed him. It was probably a home invasion. There had been reports of gypsies in town and they were burglarizing homes. Jake must have surprised one of them.

She stood over Jake and sobbed. "I really liked you, Jake. I really did." Rosie then slipped the gun into her pocket and wiped her eyes with her gloved hands. "Why did you make me do this? You could have let it go. We could have been good together. You bastard," she cried.

Rosie then moved hurriedly out the front door and down the sidewalk. Looking at each house, she wondered if anyone had heard the shot. No one appeared at any of the windows or doors. After pulling the collar of her trench coat close to her face, she put her head down and walked quickly in the cold rain toward the next block where she had parked her car. When she had cleared the last street light, she then disappeared like a ghost into the night.

Jake lay on the hardwood floor with his life's blood seeping into the cracks. Suddenly, he gasped and took a full, deep breath. "Not dead yet, Rosie," he whispered coarsely. He knew he didn't have much time and pulled the phone off the table by its cord. After dialing zero, the operator's voice came on the line.

Jake took another breath and spit the words out the best he could. "My name is Jake Dumas at…168 Carriage Lane in…New Hope. I've been…shot. Send police and ambul…" And then he lost consciousness.

CHAPTER 19

When he opened his eyes, he knew immediately where he was. He could smell it. The combination of disinfectant, ether and hospital food. The odors alone made him nauseas, but the pain and tightness in his abdomen combined with the medication Jake tasted in his throat sent him into dry heaves. After burying his face in the bed pan, he righted himself and lay back on the pillow exhausted. And then when he reopened his eyes, he found the face of Lieutenant Wade.

"Well, my friend," Wade said. "We meet again. So, tell me...who put you here."

"Ah, Lieutenant. What are you doing in my dream?"

Wade smiled. "He lies near death and still manages a sense of humor."

"I'm about to die?"

"The doc says you'll live." He paused and moved in a little closer toward the bed. "You've had an extraordinary life...Mr. Caruso."

Jake winced and turned his head away. "And how did you find out?"

"I took the liberty of liftin' your fingerprints. Well, let's see...war hero, Medal of Honor winner, teacher, killer...quite a resume. You had me fooled, janitor. You had us all fooled." And then he wagged his finger. "But... remember that first day I met you? I knew there was somethin' unusual about you. You came across too smart for a janitor."

Jake didn't respond.

"So, Mr. Caruso, let me ask you again. Who shot you?"

"What day is this?"

"Wednesday. Eleven-thirty in the morning. You've been away a while."

Jake took a coughing spell and his face showed the pain. He put a hand on his stomach, thinking his guts would surely fall out. When he had caught his breath, he wheezed and then let out a long sigh. "All right, Lieutenant. You should find my assassin down at the county library. One Rosie Green."

"A woman shot you? So, what did you do to piss her off?"

Jake grunted as a sudden pain shot through his abdomen and into his back. "I found out something about her."

"What?"

"That she…" He winced again. "…killed Principal Sharpe."

Wade's mouth fell open. "Explain."

"You'll probably remember…she was the high school's librarian. I'm sure you interviewed her."

"Oh, yes. How could I forget that face?"

"Well, we became friends. By accident, a letter fell into my hands that Sharpe had written to her. It would have been written a few days before he was murdered. He had invited her to come by his office the first day of school. They were having an affair and he was going to dump her. She didn't handle it well and stuck the letter opener in his neck. And because I was going to turn her in, she put a bullet in me."

"A black widow, eh? I suppose she's long gone by now."

"If she thought I was dead, maybe she didn't take off."

"Where is that letter now?"

"I had it at my house and when she came by to put a hole in me, I'm sure she took it back."

Wade signaled to a trooper standing outside the door. "Okay, Ben…take Charlie and go pick up a Rosie Green at the county library. She's a petite little blonde in her thirties. Pretty woman, but deadly. So watch yourself."

When the trooper had departed, Wade fidgeted with the water pitcher and cup on the rolling table at the foot of Jake's bed. Jake knew he wanted a cigarette…and badly. "So, John Caruso, what are we to do with you?"

"Have I done anything wrong?"

"Not that I can tell. You are living under an assumed name, which sets a person to wonder."

"Is that against the law?" Jake replied.

"It depends. If you took somebody's name and identity for profit…then yeah, that's against the law. Otherwise, I reckon not. But why don't you think of me as a friend and confidant and tell me about yourself? Why're you here in Alabama?"

"I just wanted to get away from California and all the bad memories. Being an ex-con, nobody is going to hire me at the professional level…especially as a teacher. The lower the profile for me, the better."

"You've lived an unusual life in your forty or so young years. I've never seen anyone experience all you have. You're quite a fella."

"Just an ordinary person caught up in extraordinary circumstances."

Wade nodded slowly. "I actually admire you, you know. I know you killed a guy, and broke the law. About the worst law you can break. But I'd prob'ly done the same thing…or at least thought about it. So, what are you…"

Suddenly another head popped in the door. "Jake. What the hell happened?" Blaise asked. "I didn't hear from you, so I went by your house and found yellow tape all over the yard. There was a cop there who said you had been shot."

Wade approached Blaise. "You're that kid… Honeycutt, the Golden Boy, aren't ya? I actually saw you play a couple seasons ago. My boy played for the Wildcats opposite you. You and that Echols boy killed us. 56-10." He extended his hand. "I hear you're now off to Alabama and the Bear."

"Yes, sir," replied Blaise, accepting the handshake. "I don't think I know you."

"Lieutenant Jerrod Wade, State Police."

"Good to meet you, sir." Blaise then turned his attention back to Jake. "Is it true? You were shot?"

"Yeah. Somebody came in the front door and let me have it."

"Who?"

Wade spoke up. "Now, son, we can't let anything out at this time until we complete our investigation and arrest the suspect. I expect you'll hear about it in due time."

Blaise then went over to Jake's bedside and clamped onto his hand. "Where were you hit?"

Jake pointed to his stomach. "You okay?"

"I'll make it. When are you going back to school?" "On December 29th? I have to be back for practice.

Remember, the Orange Bowl is New Years Day. When are you getting out of here?"

"I'm not sure. I haven't talked with any doctor yet. As a matter of fact, I've only been back in the world just a few minutes."

"Jeez Louise. I can't believe all this."

At that moment, Dr. Paul King came into the room. Gentlemen, this man is not supposed to have visitors. Would you all please leave so that I can check him over?"

Wade threw up his hand. "I'm going, Jake, but I'll see you again."

"Good luck on finding my killer, Lieutenant." Jake replied.

"See you, Jake," Blaise said. "I'll come back tomorrow."

Wade pulled the doctor off to the side and whispered. "I'm positioning another officer at the door, Doc. No one comes in here unless I say so. No one...male or female, okay?"

"Fine, Lieutenant. Now you fellows get on out of here."

Rosie was not at the library when the officers arrived. A young new-hire who appeared to be struggling with grasping the responsibilities of her job had worked her second back to back twelve hour day. Rosie had called in on Monday telling her she was taking a few days off for family reasons. The officers made a sweep of the library anyway, then went by the big yellow house to look for her. It was closed up tight as a drum. When they looked in the windows, they saw that she had covered the furniture with bed sheets.

On Thursday, the County District Attorney obtained a court order to open and search Rosie's house. After rifling her desk and turning other drawers upside down, investigators found several letters addressed to 'Rosie' by someone with the initials 'H.E.S.' But the incriminating letter that Jake had erroneously and fatefully taken from the secretary could not be found. The officers also found a white silk blouse in her closet that had a faint, dark stain on the right sleeve. It appeared she had tried to remove it to no avail. The State Police lab would be able to determine whether or not it was blood. Would there be enough evidence to charge Rosie with Sharpe's murder? Whether or not there was, they would still have her for the attempted murder of Angelo Caruso, alias Jake Dumas.

The word was already out about Rosie. And wherever she was, she probably read where Jake was still alive. Obviously she was not going to materialize anytime soon. An APB went out for her arrest for the murder of Horatio Sharpe and Assault with a Deadly Weapon on Jake.

The bullet had traveled into Jake's stomach and lodged into his right kidney. His stomach was repaired, but the kidney could not be saved. Nonetheless, on the fourth day of his hospitalization he was up and around, walking down the hallways, gown open in the back and showing his bottom to nurses and visitors. He did manage to make it home on New Years Day. It was Paulie and Gordo who helped him ambulate from the car to the house. After they had settled him in on the couch, Gordo said, "Well now you take it easy, Jake. We'll be comin' by to check on you."

"Not necessary, fellows. I'll be fine."

"Well, don't expect Rosie Green to come by and play nurse," said Paulie, laughing. "Gawd, I still can't believe a good lookin' chick like her would do a thing like this… not to mention stick a knife in old Horatio."

"You just never know what anyone is capable of… even people you think you know," Jake said.

As Gordo slipped his jacket back on, he said, "Well, what if Rosie does come back here to finish you off?"

"There are supposed to be roving patrols out there and they're looking for her car. She won't be back here. She's running."

"Well, call either one of us at the garage if you need anything," Paulie said, shaking Jake's hand.

"Thanks, boys. You know, you both turned out all right after all…in spite of yourselves. Of course, I wonder about my self. Maybe I am a 'dumb ass,' considering I allowed one Rosie Green to get the drop on me."

Paulie and Gordo both broke out in laughter. Then Gordo shook Jake's hand. "Guess we'd better shove off, Jake. Keep your doors locked. There are gun-totin' broads out there, you know." They laughed again and then closed the front door behind them.

It was a long two weeks of recuperation for Jake. Lieutenant Wade came by twice to let him know there was still no sign of Rosie Green. How she could throw away a good job and abandon her big home was beyond him. But one or two bad decisions could cause anyone to end up like her, he said. "You buck the Good Lord and He will for sure bring havoc down on ya."

Nights were not all that restful. Rosie invaded Jake's dreams a couple of times. After one dream where they were sitting by the water at Crystal Lake, he opened his eyes in the dark to see her standing over him again, gun in hand. Only this time, it was a higher caliber weapon. He rose up suddenly to find that she was only a figment of his unconscious mind. When he rubbed his eyes and opened them wider, she was gone. And that was the morning he tore open one of his stitches.

As he slowly recovered his strength, he set out on short walks in his small neighborhood. Occasionally, he saw a patrol car; then he would give the officer the 'all is well' sign. However, he did remain vigilant, checking out every parked and passing car to see if there happened to be a pretty, blonde woman behind the wheel.

On the 17th, Mrs. Honeycutt came by to take Jake back to the hospital for a checkup. It was the first time he had seen her since Blaise went off to the university. She was, of course, aghast that this had happened to Jake, and although she really didn't know Rosie, she couldn't believe 'a woman like that would commit such crimes.' It was unheard of in her community. The doctor released Jake that day and on the 20th he returned to his job at the library. After meeting with the county supervisor there, he was appointed as the interim librarian. The board would then meet in March to decide on Rosie's permanent replacement. Jake would not be considered.

The head librarian had to have experience and the required certification. He was okay with that.

Rosie remained underground. It was for sure that unless she was apprehended, no one would ever see her again. Of course, if Jake had died from his wound, she would have assumed the role of the grieving, but outraged friend. Why would anyone break in and murder such a gentle, harmless man like Jake Dumas. And then she would have gone on with her life.

Jake remained ambivalent about Rosie. It was true that she had shot him and left him for dead; but he actually missed her. He not only missed her at work, but he missed the good times they had at her house...and when they went to that first dance...and the sweet days they spent at the lake. It was difficult for him to rationalize these feelings. If for some reason she just showed up at his door, would she be all apologetic or would she put another bullet in him? This time, making sure he was dead. Rage had driven this beautiful woman to commit a heinous crime to salvage her pride and self-respect. But then she committed that second crime to cover up the first...and to salvage her life. She would never again enjoy her stately home nor her life-long accumulation of cherished heirlooms.

Jake just could not stop wondering where she was and whether she was all right. He almost hated himself for his worry. It made him wonder what kind of man he really was to let someone who tried to kill him get inside him.

It was on February 9th that Rosie's car was found on a bridge over the Mississippi just south of Vicksburg. The driver's side door was open and a note was taped to the instrument panel:

"I can no longer live with my guilt. I have taken a life and was sure I had taken another. Now, I take a third—my own. Forgive me, Mother, and forgive me Jake. I loved you both."

The day Jake learned of her suicide, he did not go into work. He called his young library apprentice and told her to contact him if there was a problem; he was just not feeling well. It was not a lie. He felt awful. He sat in his sofa chair for nearly five hours reading Rosie's Christmas present to him. One passage that Hemingway had so wonderfully penned, he read a second and even a third time:

"If people bring so much courage to this world, the world has to kill them to break them, so of course it kills them. The world breaks everyone and afterward, many are strong at the broken places. But those that will not break, it kills. It kills the very good and the very gentle and the very brave impartially. If you are none of these, you can be sure it will kill you too, but there will be no special hurry."

It made him think again of Emily and Johnny. Their faces miraculously appeared in his mind when he closed his eyes. It was the first time their faces came back to him voluntarily without him having to look at photos. And then he saw Rosie's face. It was happy and she was laughing. Her eyes dazzled like lustrous diamonds.

Rosie's body was never found. The swirling waters of the mighty Mississippi had likely taken her down deep and carried her as far as the Delta or buried her in slime under a network of fallen branches.

Her house was boarded up for several months and then sold in public auction in the first week of July. Jake was there. He was the high bidder on two items: a set of bone Fostoria dinnerware on which he had eaten two Christmas dinners, and a painting of a beautiful, thirty- something blonde woman with deep violet eyes and red red lips…smiling.

CHAPTER 20

The Bear allowed sophomore quarterback Blaise Honeycutt a few plays in the first two games of the '65- 66 season. Jake was in the stadium with Paulie and Gordo in that second game where Blaise threw three straight bullets to receivers down-field to put the team in scoring position. Jake hooted and hollered until his abdomen hurt, which forced him to sit down the remainder of the game. It would be Blaise's last performance. At a practice the following Wednesday, he sprained his ankle when a 285 pound defensive tackle came down on his leg. It would put him out the rest of the season.

Blaise's grades after a semester and a half were mediocre…all C's except one B. He wrote Jake in March that not being able to play out the rest of the season with the National Champs was an emotional let-down for him. And he admitted because of that, he hadn't applied himself. But Jake wrote back that he needed to shake his funk and buckle down in his classes. He certainly didn't want to risk losing that scholarship. Anyway, he had the '66 season to look forward to. And already, the radio jocks were talking about that kid from New Hope having a shot at becoming the Tide's first string quarterback next fall.

At the end of the school year in June, Blaise only managed to bring up one of his C's to a B. And for his Uncle Sam, that was not good enough. After receiving his draft notice on the 16th of that month, which also provided him the alarming news that he had lost his II-S student deferment status, he sought help from the Dean's office. The Dean himself took the matter up with the Selective Service Board. "You don't understand how valuable this boy is to the

Alabama football program. He could win us another National Title," he said. Unfortunately, his pleas fell on deaf ears. Even Big John Honeycutt did battle with the board well into July, which surprised Blaise. But the board was unrelenting. Finally, the Bear got into the fray; but even he couldn't save his rising star. Blaise was going into the Army.

Blaise sat opposite Jake on the couch the last Sunday afternoon in July moping and brooding about his dilemma. "I guess I blew it again, Jake. I didn't see this coming. My grades slipped away before I realized it. The worst part of it is, I let you down. You put so much work in me to get my sorry ass motivated…got me that shot at the best football program in the country…"

"Don't beat yourself up. It's easy for a young athlete like yourself to lose focus on the academics when his whole world is football. Especially when you're a star that suffered a season-ending injury. All I can say is that you'll have to accept what's facing you in your life. You can be out of the Army in a couple of years and back in college on the GI Bill playing football again. I know this is a bump in the road for you; but if you have the patience and tenacity to get through this, it will be in your rear view mirror before you know it."

"Unless I get killed in Vietnam. What's this damn war all about, anyway?"

"It appears to be our country's idea of stopping the flow of Communism in Southeast Asia. I wouldn't doubt it's deeper than that, though. A political war, mostly… between hawks and doves in the Congress."

"Whatever. Looks like I'm doomed to be a part of it."

"Maybe you'll get lucky and land an assignment in Germany. Go down and talk with the recruiters. Maybe you can write yourself a ticket."

But after working all angles and coming up with nothing, Blaise succumbed to the fact that his education and football stardom would be put on hiatus for a while. On July 5th, he received orders to report for induction at Ft. Bragg, NC, for Basic Training.

The Saturday before the Thursday he was to report, Jake and Blaise drove to Crystal Lake in the old Valiant where they sat on the same large rock as before, casting hooks baited with bloodworms into the water.

"Strange how in just a matter of a few months your life can turn around," Blaise reflected. "All my dreams and aspirations are down the rabbit hole."

"Put on hold, remember?"

"Okay, put on hold. I've been reading up on this place called Vietnam. I can see myself six months from now hacking my way through the jungle. I never knew it was even a country, much less having to fight in a war there."

"You're not there yet, Blaise. Don't give up on the idea that you could be assigned somewhere else. And if not, then God will guide the winds."

"They told me my branch will be Infantry. So that says to me…combat."

"Perhaps," agreed Jake. "I heard Gordo got drafted back in June."

"Yeah. He's already been through Basic and is now an M.P. out in San Francisco…the Presidio, I think. Can you imagine that? A guy who was always finding a way to dance around the law…now a military cop?"

Jake smiled and shook his head. "It's probably the best thing that will ever happen to him. But, see? If he gets an assignment like that, it could definitely happen to you."

"With my luck? Yeah, sure thing," Blaise replied sarcastically.

"What about Paulie? I haven't seen him all summer." "His number was higher than mine and he hasn't heard a word from anyone. It's all a bit ironic, isn't it?"

Jake didn't reply. He was watching Blaise's bob about twenty yards out. He pointed just about the time Blaise yanked his pole back. Reeling in his line, he found a flopping three pound bass on the other end. Ripping the fish off the hook, he said, "Naw. Go back home and gain some weight." After tossing it back in, he baited another hook and cast out again.

"Will you continue on at the library, Jake?"

"For a while. The new librarian is a lady, kind of what you'd expect…older, plump, white hair and a bit of a battleaxe. But we get along okay."

Jake then stared off into the tree line and the trail that led to the high plateau on the distant horizon. "You know, I brought Rosie out here a couple of times. We walked along that trail over there and up that hill to have a picnic. It was a nice day…" And then his voice trailed off.

"You gotta hate her, now. She left you for dead."

Jake shook his head. "No. I don't hate her. She was mixed up in the head, that's all. She did what she did for self-preservation. And I was standing in her way."

"Well, you're a hell of a lot forgiving man than I would ever be."

"The thing is, she's gone now. I can't hate her. I prefer to remember the sweetness and goodness she had in her."

Blaise frowned. His eyes had a confused expression in them. But then he realized that he had not lived the life that Jake had. He had not experienced the horror of war, an unbearable grief, and spent nearly a decade in prison. They sat on the rock for another hour, talking about other things, laughing and drinking the cold, bottled beer Jake brought in his ice chest. It was a day that Blaise recalled on many occasions as he hacked his way through banana grass, exhausted, emotionally spent and miserable from the endless days of monsoon rain.

The new owners of Rosie's house were from New Jersey, Jake learned. The couple, in their late fifties, had bought the place as a retirement home, but would not take up residence for probably another three or four years. Jake passed by the house every day. And every day it set him to remember the times he sat with Rosie Green on her couch in the parlor, talking, drinking coffee and looking into her eyes, wondering if he would ever bring himself to go all the way with her. The few pieces of Rosie's furniture that did not sell in auction remained with the house. Jake further learned that the sale price of the large Victorian came in at just over $20,000.

"13 September, 1967

Dear Jake,

I know I haven't written very much since I've been over here. Actually, I've only written Mom a half dozen times these entire ten months. I don't know if it's because I don't take the opportunity or I just don't have any words left in me. There seems to be a lull in the action and I'm actually in the bunker on radio watch, but my brain dry as a bone.

I remember so vividly your stories about World War II, not necessarily your experiences, but about the experiences of soldiers in combat in general. The stories have stayed with me all this time, which goes to show you how good a teacher you are. I never learned more from anyone else in all my years of education.

This is a difficult war, Jake, but I'm not so sure it's an honorable one or even a valid one. My country called, and well, I'm not in Canada, am I? Right or wrong, I'm here. You taught me book stuff, but you also taught me what honor and duty are, and that we must love this country, even when we don't always agree with its policies. I am doing and will continue to do my job and keep my mouth shut to my superiors.

It's rained for a week solid. My poncho doesn't do me any good and I stay soaked. I look like one big, white prune. The officers keep checking to see that we don't get trench foot, which I remember you telling me was a common thing in your war.

Sometimes I lay in my foxhole that is filled with water, waiting for the enemy to come. They aren't on the move when the moon is out bright; but on a night like this, we can expect it. Fortunately, this is not my night on the perimeter. We hear these birds out there we call the 'f--- you birds,' because their call sounds like Charlie trying to spook us by yelling "f--- you, f---." You see that I didn't write the word out. My mom always said that was the one word that if she ever heard me say it, she would just up and die. So, I've never in my life said it or wrote it.

I got a letter from Paulie the other day and he said that Gordo was now in Germany…lucky stiff. He's probably over there drinking a ton of Bavarian beer and doing it with some pig-tailed blonde named Helga or Gretchen. Paulie also said he thought Janet was going with some guy in South Bend and might be getting married. I guess that's why she didn't answer my letter.

I've got just another month to go here. The last couple of weeks they bring us back to the base camp to reduce the chance of us getting zapped. I've been wounded by shrapnel twice, but it's no big deal. Just spent a couple of days at the MASH.

Okay, you might think I'm nuts, but I re-upped the other day and will be going to Ft. Benning, GA, for OCS. Can you imagine me an officer? If I can make it through the 23 weeks, I'll be commissioned as a second-lieutenant. I know we talked about me going back to school and football when I got out, but football's over for me now, thanks to that knee shrapnel. Okay, okay. Maybe it was a little more than a flesh wound. I can always go back to the university any time.

Well, that's all I can think of to write. I hope you're well and not having any problems from your wound. I'll be back home in a month and will see you then.

Your protégé,

Blaise Honeycutt

Sergeant, U.S. Army"

Jake sat in the library reading room on a late Saturday afternoon digesting the letter and his supper, a PB&J sandwich. Coincidentally, Paulie stuck his head in the room. "Hey, Jake. Got a minute?"

"Yeah, Paulie, what's up?"

"Bad news. I heard Blaise's dad had a heart attack down at the bar. He's...dead, Jake."

Jake dropped his head and exhaled an audible sigh. "How did you find out?"

"I saw Mrs. Honeycutt getting out of her sister's car as I drove past the funeral home. She was crying, so I stopped to ask if everything was all right. Then she told me. Happened only a couple hours ago. She said that Mr. Neptune is calling the post locator office at Ft. Benning to get a message to Blaise."

"Ironically, I was just reading a letter from him," Jake said. "He's supposed to be home in December. I reckon it'll be sooner now."

Jake had kept Blaise's Valiant while he was in Vietnam, driving it just enough to keep the battery up and the oil flowing through its veins. Today, he drove it to Birmingham where he stood by the car in the parking lot at the airport, looking into the western sky for the Delta jet that finally appeared, descending from out of the setting sun and then disappearing behind the terminal. He then stepped away from the car and walked to the gate where he watched passengers through the plate glass window deplane and make their way into the lower breezeway. Blaise was the last passenger down the steps of the plane. Looking ten years older, thin and gaunt, and wearing khakis, Jake hardly recognized him. After Blaise came through the door, Jake moved toward him with out- stretched hand. The boy's hand was stronger and firmer than Jake remembered. His eyes were tired and reddened, and Jake surmised that Blaise had captured little sleep on his seventeen hour jaunt across the Pacific and the U.S.

"You look good, Jake."

"You look…older, Blaise."

"Combat does that to you."

"Sorry about your dad."

"It happens," replied Blaise.

"Do you need anything to eat before we get back?" Jake said, walking slightly ahead of Blaise toward Baggage Claim.

"No. I had a burger on my layover in Houston. How's Mom doing?"

"I think she's managing okay. I swung by the house to see her for a few minutes before I came over here."

"Thanks for doing that."

"I knew she was in no condition to pick you up."

"Yeah."

Stopping at the turnstile, Jake said, "Green duffle bag there. Obviously yours."

Blaise picked it up and slung it over his shoulder. As they were walking toward the car, Jake noticed Blaise's slight limp. Blaise caught his eye and said, "Yeah, that's from the shrapnel. We're a matching set of cripples now, aren't we?"

There was little said that evening, that hour it took to get from the airport to New Hope. There were no war stories, no talk about Alabama football, no talk of past days. Jake was not good with consolation and felt to a degree uncomfortable when he noticed half-way home that Blaise's cheeks were glistening from his fallen tears. Then Blaise, sensing Jake's occasional eyes on him, turned his face toward the passenger side window.

"I don't know how I'm supposed to feel, Jake."

There was a long moment before Jake replied. "What do you want to feel?"

"Like I have to feel a sense of loss, but there's a part of me that feels a sense of relief. Maybe it's for my mom. I have harbored so many ill feelings about him over the past few years that pretty much killed any love I may have had. Mom's letters said he brought me up in conversation every day, but somehow, I think she just wrote that without it being true. You know, there were days I wished he was dead…and now he is. I'm sad, but I don't know why. I thought that if he did die, I'd feel that sense of relief. But you know what? I feel like he's still got a grip on me. What am I feeling Jake? Is it right or wrong?"

"You're just sorting it all out in your head, Blaise, that's all. You have such a conglomeration of memories, both good and bad, shooting through your mind right now, you're trying to rationalize it all with your feelings… all that guilt, blame and even anger. Here's the thing. He may not have been the easiest person to live with; but, every father loves his son. Some fathers are incapable of showing it. As a matter of fact, they sometimes do destructive things to their kids to keep from showing it. It is one of the most difficult of paradoxes to comprehend. Don't blame yourself for any guilt pangs you might be having. Just go home and comfort your mother. You'll work through your feelings in due time."

Big John "Bigger Than Life" Honeycutt was indeed an icon in New Hope. On the day of his funeral, the town turned out in mass. Stores even closed at noon in advance of his two o'clock service, posting signs that read, We'll miss you, Big John and R.I.P. Big John. Guy changed the words on his marquis outside of the bar to read, Big John Honeycutt. Gone to that big watering hole in the sky.

Jake did not attend the funeral because he wanted all of Blaise's focus and feelings to be on his father. He knew how Blaise felt about him. Blaise had written him from Vietnam like a son would write his father. And Blaise had not even mentioned his father in his letters to his mom. Jake would be nothing but a distraction that would keep Blaise from going through the catharsis he needed.

He did ride the Harley out to the cemetery in advance of the funeral procession and then stood off under a large Mimosa during the graveside service. Blaise stood in uniform beside his mom with his arm locked in hers. His eyes searched about the gathering of mourners for the face he did not see at the funeral, finally spotting Jake standing in the distance, further up the hill. He lifted his hand slightly and Jake acknowledged him with a nod.

When all of Big John's friends had finally departed the gravesite, Jake finally walked down the hill to pay his respects. "Mrs. Honeycutt," he said. "I'm very sorry for your loss."

"Mr. Dumas," she replied. "It's very kind of you to be here. Thank you for coming. Would you come by the house for something to eat?"

"Oh, I think not, but thank you. You'll have a lot of people there and I'm just not very good with crowds. But I do want you to know that when Blaise leaves again for his new assignment and you ever need anything done around the house, please call me."

"Thank you again for your kindness and the wonderful support you've given my Blaise here," she replied.

Blaise finally spoke. "I'll see you in a couple of days, Jake. I'm on thirty days leave before I start Officer Candidate School, so we'll have some time to kick around. For now, I guess I need to get the cobwebs out of my head...about a lot of things."

"Relax and take your time with all this, son. We'll catch up."

Blaise's mom invited Jake for Thanksgiving dinner, but Jake respectfully declined. He felt she needed to spend the day of food and family with Blaise, although she said her sister and brother would be there with their spouses and kids. All the more reason Jake felt compelled to decline her invitation. He would spend yet another holiday alone.

On Christmas Day it was a high of 49 degrees and after Jake had digested a late Christmas brunch of steak and eggs he had whipped together, Blaise, who had temporarily repossessed his old Valiant, went by to pick him up for a brisk day of bass fishing at the lake. It did give the men opportunity to at last talk about topics they had danced around over the past month...such as how Blaise was dealing with the loss of his father and stories from the war. It seemed easier now for Blaise to talk about things.

Although it was obvious that Blaise had adopted the same sense of humility about his actions on the battlefield as Jake, never once boasting, Jake had learned by happenstance of his young protégé's heroism. Mrs. Honeycutt, who had also invited Jake for dinner on Christmas Day, and again receiving his regrets, spent an extra moment telling Jake she had found in a box a number of medals Blaise had been awarded. "Did you know that he carried several wounded men to an awaiting helicopter even though enemy soldiers were still shooting at them? There's a paragraph on some kind of certificate that said something like, "ignoring his own wounds, he killed several of the enemy while evacuating members of his squad…" and a bunch of other things. He got a Distinguished Service Cross along with a Bronze Star for his valor. I had no idea he was even in danger much of the time, because he kept writing me about his boredom sitting in a base camp away from the action."

"So, I hear you lied like a rug to your mom about what you were doing in Vietnam."

Blaise smiled and slowly reeled in his line, finding not the eight pound bass that he expected, but a branch he had been dragging through the water. "It's not a soldier's job to make mothers and wives worry about things."

"Quite the hero, were you?"

"Naw. Things sometimes get embellished when superiors write up awards on their people."

"Sometimes," replied Jake. 'But not in this case,' he thought to himself. However, he didn't argue the point with Blaise. DSCs and other medals of valor are not given out like candy. He knew beyond any doubt that Blaise had indeed distinguished himself on the battlefield, regardless of how much he played it down. And Jake was certainly proud of the mature, modest and caring young man Blaise had become.

Sitting for the remainder of that cool Christmas afternoon on the series of craggily rocks, casting, reeling in and throwing back out, two valiant men, a generation and two wars apart, shared a moment in time that drew them even closer.

CHAPTER 21

On May 11th, 1968, it had been warm in the morning, but cooling rapidly, thanks to a cold front that had pushed out Friday's rain. Officer Candidate Class 01- 68 was brought to attention by its cadre commander on the parade field adjacent to Infantry Hall just a moment before the rolling snare drums introduced The Star Spangled Banner. Blaise always smiled when he heard the first bars of the National Anthem. It reminded him of school mornings at New Hope High, especially that day when Louie, Louie sent the school into cheering pandemonium, thanks to Paulie, Gordo and him. But this day, his day of graduation from OCS, he was forced to fight off that smile. Simultaneously, Jake and Paulie, who stood in the stands beside Deborah Honeycutt, also smiled, remembering the exact same event. It seemed like eons ago.

Nine hundred fifteen candidates in dress greens, gleaming helmet liners and jump boots would be commissioned Army second lieutenants. After a few remarks by the school commandant and post commander, the first candidate to be commissioned was called forward. "Second Lieutenant Blaise Carter Honeycutt. Ladies and gentlemen, I present to you the Outstanding Graduate of Class 01-68 who was selected by unanimous decision by the cadre for his leadership skills and that he scored the highest in OCS history on his battery of proficiency tests. Lieutenant Honeycutt is commissioned into the Army's Intelligence Branch and will be assigned to the Office of Defense Attaché as an assistant attaché to the U.S. Ambassador to the Republic of Italy. He will initially be assigned to Camp Darby at USAG, Vivorno. He has also been selected for the Operation Bootstrap program where he will attend at the University of Rome to complete his Bachelor degree. Please join me in congratulating Second Lieutenant Honeycutt."

A grinning Jake turned to hug Blaise's mom as both the corps of candidates and guests in the grandstand erupted in cheers and applause. Only a half-smile appeared on Deborah Honeycutt's face as she applauded. "I thought the Army would assign him to a post somewhere here in the United States."

Jake understood her disappointment. It is what a mother would say. But as the applause waned and the list of candidates were called forward now alphabetically to receive their butter bars, Jake turned to her and in a low voice said, "Blaise has been given the opportunity of a lifetime, Mrs. Honeycutt. He has excelled far beyond what any of us could have imagined and he will go nowhere but up. I know you want to have him close, especially now that you are alone; but feel good for him about this assignment. Just be proud of him. This is not only his moment, but the beginning of opportunity."

She turned her head to Jake and replied, "You are right as always, Mr. Dumas. This old mother is only thinking of herself. I am proud of him."

Blaise had one week's leave before he left for Europe, which he would primarily spend at home with his mother. Janet Lullwater, who had basically abandoned Blaise his sophomore year at Alabama as well as his two years in the Army, had graduated from Notre Dame and was back in New Hope for the summer. She had heard Blaise was coming back home and felt that considering they had been sweethearts throughout high school, she at least owed him a face-to-face explanation over why she had never written him. He had no sooner set his bags down when she materialized on the Honeycutt front porch.

"Well, hello," he said coolly after opening the front door. "Long time no hear."

"Can I come in?"

Blaise held out his arm toward the parlor, but didn't reply. Once in the room, he didn't offer her a chair, which was a clue to her she wasn't to stay long. Her hair was different. Still dark, but pulled back away from her face, which made her look older. She had on a sleeveless white top and a mini-skirt that broadcast her shapely legs.

"You look absolutely marvelous," she began. "Army life must be good for you. I've never seen you in hair that short. Might not have recognized you if we passed on the street."

"And you're as beautiful as ever. Getting engaged must be good for you."

"Well…that didn't last. We broke up in February. I thought we were getting married after we graduated, but he wouldn't set a date with me."

"You must've gotten into the guy your first week at Notre Dame. One day we were an item and the next…"

She looked embarrassed, flushing a little. "I am so sorry, Blaise. I know I didn't handle us very well. I should have written you about Mike, but I just couldn't find the words."

"No need to apologize. I understand how things happen. Sometimes, absence doesn't make the heart grow fonder…sometimes it makes it forget. But I got over it… and you…in a few days. Life goes on."

Janet looked down at the floor and shuffled her feet. "Well, anyway, I'm back home for a while looking for a job. Will you be around long? I hear you're going to Italy soon."

"Next week."

She threw her head back and sighed. "I've always wanted to see Italy. Maybe I could arrange to go there some time after you're settled."

"Maybe that would be nice."

"Does that mean you're forgiving me?" she asked. "Nothing to forgive, Janet. We're still friends, I guess.

But friends and lovers? I can't see that happening again." "Oh," she replied, appearing a bit uncomfortable.

They both were with the moment.

"A milkshake at Mabel's for old time's sake?" Blaise posed.

"Sure," she said softly, smiling. There was a slight crack in her voice. "I'd love to."

They stood for a moment looking at one another, both remembering what their relationship once was, but also thinking about what could have been. Blaise smiled and nodded, then ushered her to the door. "After you."

Jake was still at the county library working for Myrtle Barnes-Grayson, a 63 year old lady with hair the color of a steel-gray pistol that had been blued. And as he found out more than two years before, she was actually not a 'battleaxe.' In fact, to him, she was one of the sweetest ladies he had ever known. She reminded him in looks and ways of his maternal grandmother, which is probably why he not only stayed on in the job, but became endeared to her. Over the weekend, she would bake up batches of chocolate chip and molasses cookies just to bring in to him on Monday morning. It didn't take long for a noticeable pouch to form above his belt. So as not to hurt Mrs. Grayson's feelings, he would eat a couple and then sneak cookies here and there to children via their mothers. He would tell them not to mention it to Mrs. Grayson and why.

After a while, Jake was doing most of the work and even working longer hours, which allowed Mrs. Grayson to socialize more with her friends in the Garden Club, the Ladies Tea Society, the Ladies Bridge Club, and the New Hope Women's Society, all of which she was a long-time member. If the ladies were not coming in each day off and on to gossip, she was zipping out to one of the meetings. But even though he was not getting paid for his over-time work and was performing most of Mrs. Grayson's responsibilities, he didn't mind. The job gave him purpose: he was allowing a nice, older lady to enjoy her friends and interests, and he was surrounded by his literature, which to him was as precious as gold and gems.

Meanwhile, Blaise was learning the gamut of his military, social and diplomatic responsibilities, fast becoming the entrusted uniformed aide to the ambassador. He would be in his assignment more than six months before his first leave was granted. He would come home for Thanksgiving.

This time, Jake accepted Deborah Honeycutt's invitation for Thanksgiving dinner. The invitees would be the same, except that her younger sister had recently been dumped by her husband; so there would be one less outlaw. For the second time in just over a year, Jake picked up Blaise at the Birmingham Airport. Only this time, it was under happier circumstances.

It was the biggest spread Jake had seen since he was a kid, except when his Uncle Leonardo Caruso died and there were over a hundred people at his wake. His father, mother and Mr. Gottuso, the deli owner, had gone all out with a smorgasbord. So it was over-kill at the Honeycutt house: traditional turkey and dressing, cranberry relish, country ham, roast chicken, a dozen side dishes, and the desserts…pumpkin, apple, peach and good old Southern pecan pie. A great much of it would go home with Jake and Sarah Jane Kirkheimer, Deborah's poor, divorced little sister. She was there with her two kids, nine and twelve.

Debbie Honeycutt was a bit weepy, since the first anniversary of Big John's passing had just gone by. Blaise's uncle Bob, his mom's brother, was an ordained part-time lay minister and full time mill worker. Somewhere in his blessing was a ten minute long sermon, interrupted twice by the gurgling of his wife's stomach which set everyone to laughing…except of course Uncle Bob. After Esther's second indiscretion, he gave her the evil eye, then abruptly ended his eloquent prayer.

Deborah Honeycutt's sister, Sarah Jane, was a 'plant.' A rather rotund, happy sort, in spite of her recent divorce, she was intentionally placed at the table beside Jake. Whenever anyone would say anything remotely funny, she would cackle chafingly and touch Jake's hand. He could readily feel what was going on and so could Blaise who was sitting across the table. When Deborah Honeycutt went to the kitchen to bring out the tray of pies, Blaise followed her.

"What are you doing, Mom?" "Getting the dessert, why?"

"I don't mean that. You're shameless, Mom, pushing Sarah Jane onto Jake like that. And don't try to deny it." "Well, what of it. Both are unattached and need someone in their lives."

"Jake doesn't want anyone in his life. Now go out there and stop her from making a fool of herself and embarrassing Jake."

"Oh just let her be. She's enjoying herself. And if Jake is not interested, she'll take the hint."

"The woman's a piranha, Mom."

Deborah smacked Blaise on his rear with a hand towel. "Don't talk about your aunt like that. She's always been good to you and loves you like one of her own."

And then they heard more cackling from the dining room. Blaise gave his mother a look of disgust. "I'm going in there now to rescue that man."

After Blaise had pushed through the double doors, he came to a stop behind Jake's chair. Sarah was still pawing and Jake seemed to be inching his chair away from her.

"Hey, Jake. What say we go sit on the front porch and let our dinner digest? Mom will bring us some pie later. I think we both need some fresh air."

Jake was quick to take him up on the offer. "Excuse me, everyone," he said politely.

Once out on the huge wrap-around porch, they placed their behinds on the banister.

"How do you like Rome, Blaise?"

"It's marvelous. I just toured the Vatican the week before I came home. Last month I went to the Sistine Chapel. My boss is a Bird Colonel, although the real boss is the ambassador. I work about ten or eleven hours a day, but I'm generally off on the weekends. There's an area called the Piazza Navona that has a neat shopping area with magnificent fountains and what they call Roman Baroque art. Great place to pick up girls…beautiful Italian girls with dark hair and captivating eyes."

"Wow. Blaise Honeycutt. Hopeless romantic and a man of culture as well. Look who the Golden Boy is now. And it seems like it was no time at all you were showing your ass, literally, and breaking and entering."

Blaise laughed and punched Jake lightly in the bicep. "You're bad, Jake. Hey, you ought to come over sometime next year and I'll show you around."

Jake ran his fingers over some lattice work through which a vine of clematis still hung on in the advance of winter. "It's been over twenty years, maybe twenty five since I was in Rome. When I got out of the hospital after rehab, I found my unit was occupying the city. A beautiful place to get my body and mind back in shape. With my leg all bummed up, they wouldn't put me back on the line. I was reassigned till mid-1944 as a radio operator in Mark Clark's headquarters."

"I heard the stories from English-speaking Italians about when the Fifth Army came through. And you were there. Damn."

"We rolled in on June 5th, forcing the Germans out without a shot being fired. There were at least a hundred thousand people in St. Peter's Square and the adjacent streets, cheering and waving. I was on the back of a deuce-and-a-half tossing Vienna Sausages, Hershey Bars and packs of Chesterfields to the people. It was nothing short of spectacular. I had never seen anything like it."

Jake then became a bit somber. Blaise's vivid Roman 'postcard in words' was conjuring up other, haunting memories that had long been buried in the Italian countryside as well as in the deep abyss of his mind. He stood looking out across the front lawn and down the street where four children played whiffle ball in a yard. It caused him to recall another time when two boys, one of Italian and the other of Puerto Rican descent, played stick ball with their friends also on a Thanksgiving Day in 1938. The two would be inseparable…until Italy.

Jake shook off his memories and turned back to Blaise. "Good to see you back here, buddy."

"I've actually missed this town," Blaise replied. "I don't know why. Maybe it's because I spent my life here. I see an awfully lot of places run down. The town seems to be dying right along with our old school."

Jake nodded. "A lot of people are looking for jobs around here. Property values are down, people are moving away and more stores have closed."

"Mom said the Rosie Green house is back up for sale."

"Yeah. The guy from up north who bought it, died before he could retire, and I heard his wife has no desire to move down here. I don't know the asking price, but it probably could be bought for a very reasonable amount."

"Are you considering buying it?" asked Blaise.

"No way. I wouldn't have the capital to put down and what would I do with a place that big, anyway? Even so, I've been thinking about moving on."

"Really? Moving on where? I thought you were pretty well ingrained in the area now."

"I don't think I ever told you this, but had the old Valiant not quit here, I actually had planned to end up on the Carolina Coast."

"I didn't know that. What were you going to do?" "Live at the beach. Maybe operate one of those boardwalk bars or even set up a beach umbrella and chair business."

Blaise laughed. "What kind of business is that?"

"It would be for hotel guests and even walk-on sun bathers. I'd buy up a dozen umbrellas and twice as many chairs, set them up in the morning at some hotel on the beach, and rake in five dollars a pop."

"You'd starve in the winter, you know."

"Oh, I'd supplement it in the off season doing something. But can you imagine making fifty or sixty bucks a day doing nothing all day long?"

Blaise laughed again. "No, not you."

The door then swung open and Blaise's mom came out with two pieces of pecan pie and steaming cups of coffee. "Everyone else is inside looking for you all. Sarah Jane asked, 'Where is that good-looking Jake, anyway?'"

"Give it up, Mom," Blaise chided.

"We'll be back in directly, Mrs. Honeycutt. Thanks again for the splendid dinner. You don't know how much I appreciate it."

"You're very welcome, Mr. Dumas...and it's still high time you called me 'Debbie.'"

"Then Debbie it is, but you have to start calling me 'Jake.'"

"Okay then, Jake. Don't forget to take home the leftovers I promised you."

Jake nodded and said, "Thank you again."

When Blaise's mom had gone back in, he spoke in a low voice. "So, when will we ever get to meet Angelo Caruso?"

"You never will around here. It would be too confusing for people, which would manufacture a lot of suspicion about me. Maybe when I finally get to the beach, eh?"

Jake and Blaise then took their pie and coffee to two high back rockers. After he had stalled all he could, eating small bites of the desserts and savoring the last drop of the Maxwell House, Jake checked his watch. It was going on three. "I guess I'd better go in and say 'goodbye.' About time to saddle up. By the way, do you need a ride to the airport, Sunday?"

"Mom said she'd take me."

Okay, then, I guess I won't see you till your next leave."

"Probably not. Saturday, Janet and I might go to a movie. I think we're seeing The Graduate which is still playing at the Plaza over in Clanton."

"Then good luck to you, son. Say hello to the Pope for me."

"And good luck to you. Take good care of my Valiant, old man."

"As though it were my own. Still purrs like a kitten." With the amount of calories and carbohydrates Jake had taken in, the biting air flowing through the open windows felt good. On his way home, he turned onto the street that would take him by Rosie Green's old house. He wondered if the For Sale sign was still in the yard. Or had it sold? As he began passing the house on the left, he noticed an Oldsmobile Vista Cruiser parked on the street across the way. Perhaps an interested buyer or a real estate agent, he thought. Then on the porch, standing with a small briefcase in hand, he caught sight of a woman with short black hair and black-rimmed glasses fiddling with the front door. Jake passed on by the house, but then in his side mirror he saw her leave the porch and walk around to the right side of the house to try the cellar door.

After getting through the intersection, Jake made a u-turn and pulled off to the curb within seventy-five feet of the house. The woman was gone, but her car was still sitting in front of the house. He then wondered if she was in fact not an agent, but a burglar who had already gotten inside the house. No one would consider a woman in a nice coat to be a burglar. Jake wondered if he should go to one of the neighboring houses to call the town police or just forget about it and go home.

After sitting in the Valiant for another ten minutes, he saw that the woman had still not materialized. She was either in the house or in the back yard. After exiting the car, he slowly walked along the sidewalk past the Olds to see that it bore a Virginia license plate. Looking into the rear compartment glass, he saw two suitcases, some articles of clothing, a couple of lamps and two framed paintings. Either she was the daughter of the owner and checking out the house, or she went about the country targeting unoccupied homes to burglarize. He suspected the latter.

Jake then noticed there was something strange about the windows. And finally it dawned on him what it was. In passing the house nearly every day, the blinds had always been up. Now they were all pulled down… obviously so that no one could see her at work. Jake then walked to the right side of the house and observed that the basement door where the woman had likely entered was ajar. Quietly, he pushed open the door and stepped into the cellar, closing the door behind him. It was as though he had suddenly found himself in a cave. The darkest of all darks. After taking another step, his weak right leg suddenly gave way and he fell into what appeared to be some furniture. He had knocked something off a table.

Jake held his position to not only gain his purple vision, but to see if the clatter had alarmed the other intruder. After waiting more than a minute, he heard nothing overhead that would indicate anyone else was in the house. That is, unless the woman had heard the commotion he made and stopped what she was doing. His vision getting better by the second, he was able to pick up images of boxes and other objects in the basement by way of a slim ribbon of light from around the painted- over glass of a window. Jake still waited several moments, continuing to listen for any footfalls coming from the first level of the house. Hearing none, he eased his way to the base of a staircase that led to the upper floor. Step by step, he planted his feet softly on the stairs so that only small creaks sounded from where the boards gave way to his weight.

At the top of the stairs, Jake put his hand in front of him to find the doorknob. But he didn't have to turn it. The intruder had left the door open just a crack, where as he peered in, he was able to see that it led to the kitchen. Satisfied that no one was in the room, he slowly pushed the door open, stepped inside and pulled the door back to the same position he had found it. Pausing to listen again, he then heard a noise directly above the kitchen. And then a commode flushed. Water from the toilet above trickled audibly through the pipe that ran through the kitchen wall, carrying the waste water further down into the basement lines. Jake listened to hear the woman's footsteps creak and pop on the floor in what he thought was a bedroom above his head and to his right.

In small steps, he moved from the kitchen into the dining room to where it ended in the hallway that led to the staircase. Looking around, he saw that the table and chairs were gone from the room, as was Rosie's huge china hutch, all of which he had watched being sold at auction. Peering into the living room and parlor, he found them bare as well, except for a sofa and the old upright piano which she had said her mother gave her.

Suddenly, Jake heard the woman's footsteps at the top of the staircase. Moving quickly behind the dining room wall, he peered around the corner as the woman's slight form appeared on the bottom step. She was carrying a half dozen books and a small lamp that had probably sat on a nightstand. She was pretty in a sort of natural way, but wearing no make up…which is why it took Jake several seconds to fully realize who she was. His bones chilled to the marrow. The woman was Rosie Green. Either her or her ghost. Jake was as stunned as if he had just suffered an electric shock. At first he reasoned with himself that perhaps she was Rosie's sister; but Rosie had told him that she was an only child. Of course, any woman who would shoot him and leave him for dead could also as easily lie to him. But it was her all right.

Jake wondered if she had a gun on her. She had already shot him on a Christmas Day, so he wouldn't take a chance catching a second, perhaps fatal bullet, on yet another holiday, three years later. He allowed her to take a couple more steps and then quickly moved onto her. Grabbing her by the arms and causing her to drop the articles, he then said, "Hello, Rosie. Back from the grave?"

She was so startled her knees buckled, pulling him to the floor on top of her. When she dropped her hand inside her coat pocket, Jake clamped down on it with his, forcing her to release her grip on the gun. "Oh no you don't, sweetheart," he said, fishing the .25 automatic out of her pocket and jerking her to her feet.

She glared at him in arctic silence. Finally finding her voice, she said, "What do you want from me?"

"Well, certainly not what you gave me the last time I saw you. Why did you come back?"

"To pick up the remnants of my life. I see there's not much left."

"So, you went to Virginia."

"How did you…oh, you must have seen my license plate," she said softly.

"Pretty slick, Rosie. You leave your car on a bridge with a suicide note and everybody believes you jumped. Poor little Rosie. Couldn't live with her shame and guilt. Do I assume you're not Rosemary Green anymore?"

"Sally Persinger, library assistant, Spotsylvania County."

Jake smiled sardonically. She was still attractive behind her glasses. But the black hair made her look pale. Tiny crow's feet had formed around her eyes...eyes that didn't seem to have the same fire in them the last time they bore down on him.

"Well," he said. "You and I seem to have the same jobs." And then the smile dissipated. "Get over by the dining window and put your face against the wall."

"Are you going to kill me?" "Not unless you try to escape."

"So you're not going to let me go."

"You're either kidding or delusional. Why would I allow a murderer and someone who tried to kill me go free?"

"What would it take for you to just casually let me walk away?"

"The conversation's over, Rosie." Jake then yanked a tie-back cord from the dining room drape. "Put your hands behind your back."

She did as ordered and he wrapped her wrists together tightly, punctuating the binding with a double knot.

"You're hurting me," she whimpered.

"You know what, Rosie? I hurt every day where they had to remove one of my kidneys."

"I'm...sorry."

"I think you're more sorry you didn't check to see that I was dead. All right, now move to the door."

"So you're really going to do this?"

"Would you rather I take you over to Mississippi and drop you off that same bridge where you faked your suicide? To the law, you're dead anyway. So what would it matter?"

"You couldn't live with yourself."

"I've lived with a lot worse things, Rosie. Now move."

Jake opened the front door and shoved her out onto the porch where they came face-to-face with uniformed officer, Kevin Rockne. Placing his hand on his still- holstered pistol, the officer shouted, "All right, hold it right there! What do you people think you're doing?"

"Officer, my name is Jake Dumas. You've been looking for this woman for murder. I give you one Rosie Green."

"Rosie Green? Damn!" he said. "I heard about her when I joined the force last year."

"How did you happen to be here, Officer?" asked Jake.

"A neighbor lady reported seeing a woman nosing around the house and then a man going in after her. I guess the old lady never thought she'd be turning in the notorious Rosie Green. Hey, aren't you supposed to be dead?"

Rosie scoffed. "Obviously, it was old Mrs. Morris across the street who called. I thought she would be dead by now."

"Let's go, Miss Green," said Rockne, grabbing her at the bicep.

"Officer, can you also put a call in to Lieutenant Wade at the State Police?" Jake asked. "He'll be interested to know about this."

"Will do. Follow me to the station, Mr. Dumas. I know somebody will need to get your statement."

Rosie looked down the street at the Valiant. "So you still have that old piece of junk, huh Jake?"

"It's never disappointed me, unlike former girlfriends."

After they arrived at the New Hope Police Headquarters, Officer Rockne took Rosie to have her booked. Jake sat in a chair near the reception cage, ready to give his statement. As Rosie was leaving the room, Jake gave her a parting half-smile. "Nice seeing you again, Miss Green. Maybe they'll let you go to work in the penitentiary library."

She neither looked back nor otherwise responded.

Blaise called Jake around eight-thirty on Friday morning, having heard from his friend Sam Kelly, a confidant of Officer Rockne, that Rosie Green had materialized. He was shocked not only to learn that she was not dead after all, but that it was Jake who captured her at her old house. Realizing that Jake did not seem all that eager to talk about the incident, he cut the conversation short, telling him that he hoped to see him a few minutes on Saturday, considering he would be returning to Italy on Sunday and would not be back for Christmas.

Friday afternoon, Jake sat at the checkout desk at the library trying to absorb in his head the events of the day before. Operating on no more than three hours sleep, the combination of too much food at Deborah Honeycutt's Thanksgiving table and the shocking reappearance of the dead Rosie Green had no doubt made him sick at his stomach during the night. Twice he had left his bed to retch and hug the commode. And now he was left to revisit and reassess his long reconciled feelings he had about Rosie after she had been declared dead. His preoccupation with the matter put him into a stupor much of the day to a point where he failed on two occasions to hear questions directed to him by patrons.

"Mr. Dumas," a rather impatient-sounding young lady called. "Did you hear me? I have a paper due on Monday on the recognition of insects indigenous to the South? Can you show me where to look?"

"I'm sorry. Yes. First check the card catalogue for any related titles and then if you can't find what you're looking for there, go to 500 where you'll see titles on Biology."

When the teen turned away toward the catalogue table, Jake rubbed his eyes and called over one of the two library assistants to take over for him while he went into the office for some coffee. Once inside, he poured the still steaming black liquid from his thermos into a cup. Sitting over the cup, he first inhaled the aroma into his sinus passages and then took a sip.

The ten minutes he sat at the desk without interference of work allowed him to further process the myriad of thoughts and feelings that were bouncing through his brain like a pinball. First, Rosie was alive… and back. She was also not the same Rosie that he knew… or thought he knew. And beyond any doubt, she was an authentic enigma…sweet but deadly…compassionate but manipulating. Jake had to get past these paradoxes before he could resolve the matter of Rosie Green once and for all.

And then he revisited the same thoughts he had had more than three years before. Were he and Rosie, after all, cut from the same mold? They lived secret lives, took on assumed names and ran out on life. And both had committed murder. But again, Jake had killed for vengeance. Rosie, out of scorn. Furthermore, she intended to kill Jake for no other reason than her own self-preservation. The ultimate battle between the self and the super-ego.

Now that all pieces of the Rosie Green puzzle were in place and she had been behind bars a full twenty-four hours, could there be closure? In his mind, there was still a dialogue between them that had to take place to bring about that closure. He didn't know why, but it was like putting the period at the end of the sentence. Maybe once and for all, it would help untangle his network of twisted feelings and a satisfying peace would then come into his mind.

It was in all the papers. The Rosie Green story was front page news on the Birmingham Star as well as the Atlanta Journal. It was also on pages two and three in the Chicago Tribune and the San Francisco Chronicle, respectively. In essence, the accounts read that the female suspect in the murder of a high school principal and attempted murder of a co-worker had surfaced from her watery grave in the Mighty Mississippi three years later. The story had also been in the Lincoln Journal Star which both shocked and elated Rosie's mother. The daughter who had admitted in a suicide note that she in fact committed such atrocities had betrayed her mother's love yet one more time…by causing her three years of unbearable grief that had aged her ten.

But as a mother's love is unconditional and all-forgiving, she wrote Rosie the fourteen page letter that told her that her Lord Jesus Christ would also forgive her if she would just humble herself to Him. She really wanted to fly in from Nebraska to see Rosie at the county jail, but unfortunately she had suffered a stroke that left her paralyzed on the right side the same day she learned of her daughter's suicide. As her husband, Rosie's step- father, had left her, she had basically become an invalid and was living in assisted care. It would yet be one more pang of guilt for Rosie to endure.

As it seemed there were a great number of significant events that occurred in Jake's life on or around the holidays, especially at Christmas, he figured there may as well be one more. He would for the second time in a month face off with the woman who had tried to kill him on Christmas Day three years before. He needed her to look him in the eye and tell him who Rosie Green really was. It would hopefully end with that closure he needed.

Jake sat for more than five minutes at the visitor's table that was separated from the inmate's table by a piece of Plexiglas. When the door finally opened, he thought the matron had escorted the wrong prisoner into the room. But it was Rosie all right…thinner, wanly and hair disheveled. No longer wearing her disguise, the glasses with the clear lenses, she appeared as even a different woman from the burglar he had caught in the big yellow house. She slid into her chair, however, with all the grace that she carried some five years before at the school library.

Rosie forced a weak smile. "Do I say Merry Christmas?"

Jake did not return the smile or immediately respond. But then after a few seconds, he replied, "You know, Rosie, I'm not even sure why I'm here."

"For old time's sake?" "Hardly."

"Then why, Jake?"

"Maybe to set things straight between us or at least in my mind."

"What's to set straight?" she asked. "We were once friends who were having a lot of fun and then I shot you?"

"A cavalier statement, if I ever heard one. You don't see an absurdity in what you just said?"

She dropped her eyes to her interlocked fingers resting on the table. "I don't consider myself a murderer as I think about who murderers are. I guess I just acted out of anger with Horatio."

"And me?"

"I was afraid you'd turn me in. And I know you would have. You went for the phone and I panicked."

"You know what, Rosie? I wasn't absolutely convinced it was you who killed the principal. The letter was incriminating, because it said you were to be in his office around six that day. But that wouldn't have meant you killed him. You would have probably been a suspect along with Conroy. But it was when you showed up at my place…it was then I knew. And then the gun was the cherry on the sundae. You gave yourself away, Rosie."

"You know they'll have a hard time pinning the murder on me, considering the letter is only circumstantial evidence. So I admit to the affair. That won't make me a murderer in the eyes of a jury."

"Obviously, you've been talking to a lawyer." She didn't respond.

"You knowwhat I think, Rosie? You're apsychopath…a conniving, manipulating psychopath."

Her face then lit up with fire and Jake could see a hint of the old Rosie coming back in her eyes. "Don't call me that!" she snapped. She then stood up and walked to the barred window which was high up on the wall. She gazed up and out through the opening into the white sky for a long, uncomfortable moment.

"It's dreary out today," she said softly. "Christmas Day should be bright and pretty with a blue sky or even a day of heavy snowfall with large flakes."

Jake shook his head. What he was feeling now was pity. Yet another emotion that he did not want to have.

Rosie leaned her forehead into the cool concrete below the window and became silent. After a minute she walked back and sat down in the metal frame chair at her table. Her eyes were now soft and reddened. Her cheeks were also flushed and moist from her tears. Jake tried to conjure up the image of her once beautiful face. He remembered another day that she cried…the day they learned of JFK's assassination. But even in her sadness, her face was almost angelic-like, sweet and kissable.

"I've really made a mess of my life, haven't I? And yours as well, Jake."

"My life was already a mess by the time I came to New Hope."

If things had been different, this would have been her opportunity to press him to open up about his past life; but it didn't really matter anymore. A faint smile returned. "Do you remember that spring day when we had that picnic up on that knoll by the lake? It was a perfect day. The sun was warm on our faces and the wildflowers were out blooming in all their glory. I thought for a moment that day that I could actually be in love with you. But then it dawned on me. You were merely a breath of fresh air in my life…unpretentious, chivalrous and handsome. And I think that somewhere in my mind you became one of those rake, romantic characters in the classics that you always read. Maybe one of them had lain in you all those years and I saw it come out. I thought about that day only a few months ago when I was out walking in the Virginia countryside. It was a perfect day, you and I sitting on that hill with all the clover around us…" Her voice then trailed off and she turned her head so that Jake would not see the tears come again.

And then without further word, she stood, kissed her hand and placed it gently on the glass that separated them. After nodding to the matron behind her, she quickly left the room.

Jake sat for a moment staring at her empty chair. It would be difficult for him to sit on the witness stand and point an accusing finger at the woman that he could have loved so easily. But reality checked in again when a pain suddenly shot through his abdomen where her bullet had gone in. Perhaps it was his brain sending a message through the peripheral pathway to his gut that said, "Listen to me, not your heart."

He shook his head and gathered himself up to leave the room. But before he did, he stretched out his hand to touch the spot where Rosie had placed her fingers. The bright fluorescent light overhead enhanced the tear- dampened smudge on the opposite side of the glass.

CHAPTER 22

In April weather

when the meadow was bloomin'

we walked together

to the top of the hill.

Upon the clover

when the meadow was bloomin'

we dreamed together

just as true lovers will.

But summer flies on

far across the horizon,

and winter lies on

over the valleys and hills.

Do you remember

when the meadow was bloomin.'

In bleak December

do you think of me still.

Do you remember

just as I always will.

Johnny Mercer

Barry Manilow

Rosie was charged with manslaughter. The District Attorney was not sure he could win a case of murder, first or second degree, given the fact that the incriminating letter Jake said he had read was never found. At best, the D.A. had a case of circumstantial evidence and only inadmissible hearsay testimony from the witness to back it up.

On March 17, 1969, Sheriff's Deputy Linda Kelleher brought Rosie down the Federal courthouse hallway through the side door of Courtroom 3 and placed her in her seat at the defense table. Judge Quincy Newman, who was presiding over the case, had not yet arrived. Rosie's counsel, Jed Boatwright, leaned into her and whispered a few words, and then she slowly turned her head around to her left where Jake sat on the first pew behind Prosecuting Attorney Art Hamner.

Jake expected her eyes to be full of hate and venom, considering that he would be testifying against her. Instead, they were colored with weakness and helplessness, even submission. The four months in jail had apparently broken her down. She looked tired as though she hadn't slept; and although her hair was combed out nicely, it had returned to its original color which to Jake's surprise was actually a mousy shade of brown. There was neither a smile nor look of sadness in her eyes as she stared at Jake that moment. Instead, her face was stoic and expressionless.

Suddenly, the command "All rise" was given by the bailiff and Judge Newman entered the courtroom. After a few administrative words and admonishments to the court, he read the charges against the defendant, Rosemary Green: "Count One, ladies and gentlemen, is the charge of Manslaughter in the First Degree in the wrongful death of one Horatio Sharpe. Count Two, we have the charge of First Degree Assault with a deadly weapon with the intent to commit murder on the person of John Caruso."

Rosie then turned her head toward Jake again. Her expression was still the same. Obviously, her counsel had already informed her that Jake was not who he had claimed to be, and that he had taken an alias. Apparently, that didn't surprise her. She had known all along that there was something in his past that she could never uncover. Assistant D.A. Hamner was compelled to share this information with her attorney. When Hamner was gathering evidence against Rosie, he learned in a conversation with Lieutenant Wade and through medical records that it was in fact John Caruso whom Rosie had shot, not Jake Dumas. Before then, there had only been one other person who had known Jake's true identity.

Hamner's opening statement was articulate and eloquent. He took nearly an hour to tell the story of how "a woman scorned, while in a heated argument with Horatio Sharpe and in an act of passion, ended the life of a respected high school principal. And as regards the second count, having been found out by a friend and associate, Rosemary Green, with premeditation and malice, shot John Caruso, leaving him for dead and creating the impression that a Christmas Day home invasion had gone sour."

Boatwright's opening was laced with words such as "circumstantial, hearsay and speculation." It was clear he intended to put Rosie's second victim on trial, attacking his credibility not only as a liar, but a murderer himself who subsequently took the identity of another.

This prompted a series of gasps from the gallery, many of whom were former teachers, students and curious citizens of the New Hope community who had known Jake Dumas either from his position at the school or the county library. After the gavel came down twice, Judge Newman again admonished the court regarding any future outbursts.

The prosecution's star witness then took the stand. Hamner began a series of questions starting with when John Angelo Caruso first took the name of Jake Dumas. Hamner then asked Jake to explain his relationship with Rosie Green, specifically elaborating on what occurred on that Christmas Day evening, 1965. Jake told of the letter he had accidentally taken, his confrontation with her at his house, and ultimately, the shooting. During his testimony, the courtroom became spellbound. Not a sound could be heard throughout as everyone wanted to catch each carefully-delivered word.

The prosecution rested and then it was Rosie's attorney's turn. Boatwright, reminding Jake that he was still under oath, instructed him to bring out his entire past, to include his teaching history, his murder of a man who by the way was never convicted of a crime, his nine years behind bars, and the fact that he illegally assumed the name of another person. So Jake told everything. The total truth. But the truth about him had already gotten around in places anyway, so what did he have to lose? As his story unfolded, Rosie's eyes widened in disbelief.

But then when Jake began telling the court about Sharpe's letter, Boatwright stopped him, objecting to the information as hearsay. Judge Newman, however, over-ruled the objection and allowed Jake's testimony in.

"So, Mr. Caruso, why should we believe this story about you finding a letter allegedly written by Mr. Sharpe to Miss Green? I say the letter never existed except in your mind...the mind of a man with dark secrets who is himself living a lie."

"Objection, your honor," interjected Hamner. "Mr. Caruso is not on trial in this courtroom. His verification of the letter is important to the credibility of the People's case. It is the foundation to the evidence we found in her closet. Mr. Sharpe's blood was found on Miss Green's sleeve, even though she tried in vain to remove it. And then remember, she also admitted to killing the man in her 'suicide' note."

"Counsel is speculating on alleged evidence that has yet to be introduced, your honor," replied Boatwright. "And anyway, in Miss Green's statement, she explains the blood. It was hers where she cut her hand on a paring knife. Ironically, she and Mr. Sharpe had the same blood type...O+."

The bantering continued between the prosecution and defense for three more days after which they provided to the jury their summations. On March 21st the case was finally placed in the hands of the four men and eight women. After two days of deadlock, they emerged with the following verdict, read by the jury foreman:

"As to the charge of Manslaughter in the First Degree, we find the defendant Rosemary Green 'not guilty.' As to the second charge of Assault with a Deadly Weapon with Intent to Commit Murder, we find the defendant Rosie green 'guilty.'"

A deafening hush followed several groans from the gallery. Billy Conroy, who had sat through the entire proceeding, merely shrugged. Mrs. Horatio Sharpe, who had only learned of her husband's affair shortly before trial, sat emotionless. And so did the State's witness, John Caruso.

After a full day of mulling over the verdict, Judge Newman, who obviously had felt that Rosie had gotten away with murder, gave her the maximum sentence under the law for the second count…ten years in the State Penitentiary with eligibility for parole in six.

After the sentencing, Deputy Kelleher ushered Rosie to her feet and nudged her toward the side door. But Rosie stalled for a moment and turned toward her accuser who was standing within a few feet of her. "I'm sorry, Jake. I know you don't believe I am, but it's true. Can you forgive me?"

Jake searched her eyes, finding something he had apparently not seen in them before. Sincerity. So he nodded a couple of times and then turned away. It was the last time he would ever see her.

Once outside of the courthouse, he stood on the steps with flashbulbs going off in his face and reporters barking questions that ran together into something unintelligible. They all wanted the John Caruso story. It was then he said to himself, "It's time for me to go."

Jake left town the first week of May after his nearly seven year stop-over in New Hope, pulling the Harley behind him on a trailer. As he had set out from California with the intention of landing somewhere along the Grand Strand in either North or South Carolina, as far away from his troubles as he could get, he had now changed his mind. Slightly. Instead, he decided on the sugar-white sands of the gulf…Gulf Shores to be exact, where he rented a rather dilapidated beach house that had seen its share of tropical lows. After buying fifteen beach umbrellas and thirty Adirondack chairs from a furniture manufacturer in Kitty Hawk, NC, he signed a contract with a new hotel that had been built in Gulf Shores for exclusive rights to the beach front. At last, the dream that he had postponed since the day he left prison had become a reality.

He would work three seasons of the year making an average of seventy-five dollars a day. There would only be two hours, more or less, of labor involved in erecting and taking down the units, and only his lay-out costs. And he would get that back in a week. He had never had that kind of money. Even if he ever would have the opportunity to return to teaching, he would be fortunate to make merely half of what he took in as a beach bum tending to sun bathers. Janitoring and restocking library shelves would soon become a distant memory, although he already missed the smell and the feel of his books… the very essence of his sanity through the years.

To Jake it was working and retiring at the same time. His own slice of Heaven. What other job would allow him to sit all day inhaling the sultry, salt air, listening to the crash of blue-green waves upon the white sand, cooling down with an ice cold Rolling Rock, and enjoying a good book through the dark, sheltering lenses of his sun glasses…all the while, acquiring a healthy-looking tan.

Occasionally, as he lay back in his lounge chair in his usual spot just down the slope from the bank of sea oats, he would observe a young mother in a two-piece bathing suit, tanned and perfectly formed, standing at the shoreline watching her two year old running in and out of the lapping foam, his legs moving as fast as a sandpiper's. It always took him back to Malibu and that short time in his life when he was the happiest. Perhaps it was what drew him back to the beach…to a different beach far away from his past, but still where he could keep that memory alive.

On the last Saturday evening in July, after he had broken down his umbrellas, folded the chairs, and locked them up in his beach lean-to, he limped the ageing Valiant, its exhaust now beginning to spout audible farts, along the beach highway to his house at the end of Palmetto Key. Checking his mailbox, he found inside a single letter. The return address was from Captain Blaise Honeycutt, U.S. Army Europe, Rome, Italy. The letter had been addressed to Jake at his residence in New Hope, originally post-marked 18 June, and it had taken over a month to be forwarded by the post office. "And they want a two cent increase in their stamps," Jake muttered to himself. It was the first piece of correspondence he had received from Blaise since his Christmas card and a postcard in March which pictured a lovely Tuscany vineyard scene.

After pulling a cold beer from his refrigerator, Jake zipped open the envelope flap with the pocket knife Blaise had given him, and settled down in the old sofa chair to read the letter.

"Dear Jake,

Sorry I haven't written, and it will be no excuse at all to explain that my job as military attaché has been increasingly demanding, not to mention my classes at the university.

Surely I had a moment somewhere to sit down to write you at least a note and fill you in on what's happening with me. But as you know, I've never been faithful about writing anyone, including my mom. She writes me a lot, wondering if she 'still has a son.' After she shames me like she does, I write her back with a few lines to reassure her that not only am I still alive, but I still love her.

Well, I did make Captain on what they call the accelerated promotion program. I think the fact that they need company command officers for that lovely war called Vietnam has a lot to do with that. And that brings me to one of the points of my letter. I have orders which state that in mid-September,

I am to report to Travis in Oakland for an unaccompanied short tour…which means a second tour in Vietnam.

But the crux of my letter is to let you know that I'm getting married. I met this beautiful Italian girl at the piazza in January, who by the way speaks fluent English, and we fell in love almost at first sight. Her name is Elisabeth and we're planning to be married on September 3rd. I know this doesn't give you much time to prepare, but if you'll check the envelope, you'll find your round-trip ticket to Rome for the 1st. The thing is, Jake, I not only want you here for the wedding, but I want you to be my best man."

Jake let out a whoop that carried out his living room window to the beach which caused a couple of passers- by to look in the direction of his house. But Blaise was right; it didn't give him much time. Less than a week to be exact, thanks to the Postal Service. He would have to engage some trusty teenager to run his business a few days and buy some clothes. His ageing sport coat would not do, and for the past three months, his idea of dress clothes was a golf shirt and pair of khaki slacks.

So, his protégé, whom he had for years referred to as his best friend, Blaise Honeycutt, was taking the plunge. Good for him, Jake thought. Except…there was that nasty little war and Blaise's first year of marriage to Elisabeth would be spent apart.

The last time Jake had entered the coastline off the blue southern seas of Italy, his name was Angelo Caruso and he went ashore from an LCM via the U.S.S. Indomitable. And now from the air, he was able to take in not only the hills and buttresses of the Apennines, but the plains of the hinterland. The land, rich and green, climbed along imposing ridgelines to ancient, now inactive volcanoes. It was beauty that he had not remembered, considering that when he was on the ground, the countryside was war-scarred and covered with artillery smoke.

Soon, off the right wing of the Lufthansa jet loomed the Holy City of Rome showcased by the unmistakable architecture of the Cathedral of St. Peter, where he had passed through the throng of liberated revelers in 1944, and the Coliseum.

After landing at Fiumicino, Jake, dressed in a light blue oxford shirt and grey slacks, slung his travel bag over his shoulder and looked for Blaise at the gate. For a few moments he stood rotating his head and eyes, looking at every young man in uniform with a buzz cut. But then, behind him he heard, "Jake! Jake Dumas!" Turning around, there he was, walking toward him with an early twenties-something dark-haired beauty with flawless, olive skin and a captivating smile.

"Buono giorno. Come sta lei, my friend?" called Blaise.

"I think you just asked me how I was doing. Multa, multa."

They shook hands and then Blaise turned to his fiancée. "Elisabeth, my darling, this is the man I have told you about. Meet Jake."

"Hello, Jake," she said. "My goodness. Blaise did not tell me how handsome you are."

Jake laughed. "Thank you, Elisabeth. It's a pleasure to meet you."

"Well, let's get out of here," Blaise said. "I want to get you settled. I hope you don't mind, Jake, but I only have an efficiency apartment with one bedroom and a living room/kitchen combination. I'm putting you up in the Lugano, which is near the famous Trevi Fountain in the heat of the city. Actually, the hotel is where the wedding rehearsal dinner is tomorrow night."

"You don't have to take care of my hotel, Blaise. I…"

"Nonsense. Your trip here is all on me…and of course, Elisabeth."

"Okay, I won't argue with you this time. What's the plan tonight?"

"Well, Elisabeth is having the equivalent of what we call in the U.S. a bachelorette party. You and I are having dinner at the hotel."

"Sounds good. Do I have some time for a little shut-eye?"

Blaise laughed. "I guess old farts like you need your afternoon naps. But yes. I thought we could meet in the bar at eight."

"Perfect."

"Jake," began Elisabeth. "I do look forward to knowing you. I feel I already do." Her English was extremely good, but still there was that touch of Italian brogue in some of her pronunciations. It made her sound to Jake like a young Sophia Loren.

"You are everything I expected you'd be…and more.

My kid, Blaise here, did very well."

Blaise appeared to be taken aback for a moment. Although the "my kid" statement was probably a slip of the

307

tongue, Blaise had long thought of Jake as a surrogate father. Now apparently, so did he. But Blaise smiled and replied, "I have excellent taste in women."

By eight-thirty, Jake and Blaise were sitting opposite one another at the dinner table in the Lugano, splitting a carafe of Chianti and catching up on the past six months.

"So, your profession is now 'beach bum', eh?"

"Hey, wait a minute. I actually make pretty good money at being a bum. Don't knock it. I make people happy, read all day, work on my tan and eat gobs of seafood. Somebody has to do it, so it might as well be me."

"Life of Riley. But you know something, Jake? If anyone ever deserved it, it's you." He took a sip of the wine. "Say, how's my old car?"

"The Valiant? Well, it's finally showing its years. Smokes a little and the transmission is slipping a bit. But at almost 300,000 miles with only minimum maintenance, well, I'd be on my last leg, too."

"Speaking of…is your leg giving you much trouble these days?"

"Everything's good. Trudging through salt water a couple times a day for my exercise has helped keep it going. Is your mom good?"

"She is. Actually, she'll be flying in tomorrow afternoon before the rehearsal. She wrote and asked about you recently. Says she misses seeing you about."

Their dinner finally came and Blaise exchanged some words in Italian with the server. Jake smiled and remarked to himself how Blaise had matured, becoming not only a fine young officer and gentleman, but a man of culture and values.

"Elisabeth. She's a lovely girl, Blaise. Reminds me of someone I knew a long time ago."

"The girl in the picture."

Jake nodded. "I hope you'll be happy. How are you going to handle the separation...you know, Vietnam?"

"We'll be fine. We've talked it all out. She's staying here, and then after I get back, she'll join me wherever I'm reassigned."

"You stay out of harm's way, boy."

"I'm supposed to be assigned to MACV. That could mean anything from an advisor job deep in the jungle or a nice cushy desk job in Saigon."

"I hope the latter, although any place over there is not exactly safe."

"Have you been back to New Hope?" Blaise asked. "No. Nothing there anymore."

Blaise seemed to be chewing on his next sentence before he spit it out. "I was wondering if you had maybe visited Rosie."

"For what reason? The woman tried to kill me."

"I don't know. Maybe it's because I know your heart.

There's a forgiving nature about you."

Jake laid his fork down and pushed away his plate of escargot. "Snails. Why would anyone order something he would scrape off the bottom of his shoe?"

Blaise chuckled, but then Jake continued. "I did in fact go to see her last Christmas Day."

"What did she have to say?"

"Very little. She wondered why I was there if I was going to let her off the hook."

"Mom wrote me about the trial and that she skated on the murder portion of it."

"Actually, the D.A. charged her with First Degree Manslaughter. Not a very good case and it didn't surprise me she wasn't convicted."

"But you nailed her on the assault charge. I heard you were very convincing. But I also heard everything came out about Mr. Caruso."

"Yeah. Probably time it did." "But you still go by 'Jake.'"

"I've kind of gotten used to it. Hard to break old habits."

"I had wondered how Rosie reacted when she found out about you."

"She probably wasn't all that surprised." Jake finished the last drop of his Chianti and turned up his nose. "This stuff doesn't go too well with snails. Well, anyway, we had some good times, you know. We went to a couple of dances and movies. I remember we had a long, sweet afternoon together in the early summer back in '65 where we sat on her veranda taking in the perfume of gardenias that were blooming, drinking lemonade and eating sugar cookies she had prepared. And we spent two Christmas Days together. Of course, the second one didn't go so well." Jake then became very reflective. "The fact is, Blaise, she didn't know me and I didn't know her. Maybe we were two of a kind, I don't know."

"No way," replied Blaise. "Remember what you told me that day at school when you said I was not cut in the same mold as Paulie and Gordo? Well, you and Rosie... you're not the same either."

"Speaking of your two numbskull buddies...have you heard from either of them?"

"Gordo sent my mom a letter from Vietnam, wanting to know where I landed. That was a couple months ago. I guess he's still there. Paulie? I suppose he's still a grease monkey. He had hopes of one day buying the Phillips garage, but don't know that he could ever come up with the money."

An accordionist then began sweeping through the restaurant playing a medley of classic Italian ballads, stopping momentarily at their table to end his rendition of Innamorata. Jake dropped some lira onto the table in front of the serenader. The server then came back and refilled Jake's wine glass from the carafe.

Jake held up his glass to Blaise. "You turned out good, son. I'm really proud of who you've become."

"Whoever I have become, I can only thank you for it."

"No, you'd have made it fine. Maybe your life would have been a little different, but you've always had inside you what it takes to succeed."

Jake pointed to his heart. "Here's to you…and to Elisabeth." He clinked glasses with Blaise. "I wish you all the happiness. You take good care of that lass."

"You know I will."

Jake arrived at Santa Maria della Pace, the stunning Baroque church built in 1656, just before six for the rehearsal the next evening. At eight, the wedding party of twenty four would then return to the Lugano for dinner.

Elisabeth, who had been standing on the altar, saw Jake coming down the aisle and stepped down to greet him. "Oh, Jake," she called. "You made it. You look so nice in that sport coat. You will truly be Blaise's 'best man.'"

Jake lifted her hand to his lips and kissed it, something he hadn't done perhaps ever. "And you look beautiful, my dear. I can't wait to see how even more beautiful you will be tomorrow afternoon."

"You are a sweet man," she said, giving him a hug. "Hey!" a voice behind them rang out. "That's my fiancée you're pawing. Hands off."

"Then you'd better hurry up and marry this girl before I get designs on her," Jake replied.

Debbie Honeycutt then walked up. "Well hello, Jake. Good to see you again. My, what a nice tan. Have you been vacationing?"

He laughed. "Well, actually I'm on a permanent vacation."

"Whatever you're doing, it looks good on you."

"He has a business on the beach in Gulf Shores, Mom," interrupted Blaise.

"Well, that's nice. You know, my sister was just asking about you the other day. She told me to tell you 'hello' and come back to see her sometime."

Jake and Blaise flashed coy smiles to one another. Jake then turned to Elisabeth. "Are your parents here, yet?"

"My mother will be here in a while. My father died in the Great War."

"Oh...I'm sorry," he replied.

The priest then called for Blaise and Elisabeth to go over some preliminaries with him before the formal rehearsal. Jake and Deborah remained in place talking as other members of the wedding party straggled in.

Not long after the priest began his instructions, Elisabeth turned her head toward the aisle and called, "Mama."

Jake did not notice the woman immediately, but as she approached to where he was standing, it was as though his heart flipped upside down. Suddenly, he felt that he could not get his breath. Her face, though twenty five years older, looked much the same. For the second time in less than a year, he thought he had come face to face with a ghost. Their eyes met and her mouth then fell open. Tears formed in her eyes when he said her name.

"Allesandra."

She placed her hand over her breasts and tried to speak. Her voice came out in little more than a whisper. "Angelo."

His hand shaking, he reached out to take hers. "I thought…all this time…you had been killed," he stammered.

"And I heard you had died in the battle."

Elisabeth and Blaise then came up with looks of alarm on their faces. "Mama. What is the matter? You look so pale."

Blaise took Jake by the bicep and studied his face. "Jake?"

"Blaise. The Italian girl in the photo you found in the shed…"

"Yes."

Jake did not have to tell him.

"Her? Elisabeth's mother?" exclaimed Blaise. "Her."

"My God."

They all stood frozen for a few moments, resembling a group of manikins in a store front window. Finally, Jake said, "Blaise. Elisabeth. Before the rehearsal begins, may I have a few moments with Allesandra?"

"Yes. Yes, of course," Elisabeth replied.

Jake took Allesandra by the hand and led her off to the side by the baptismal, a beautiful font which had been lavishly carved from Carrera marble. The face of Mary in a replica of the Pieta at St. Peters looked down upon the two former lovers.

"Allesandra, I saw with my own eyes the destruction of your uncle's bakery only moments after I left you. The building completely caved in and no one could have made it out alive. Tell me how…"

"When you left me, Angelo, I followed you down the alley behind the bakery and watched from the front of another building when you led your men against the Nazis. I then saw you fall after you had blown up the tank and you did not get up. And then the firing continued and

I could not come to you. After the battle in Montevilla was over, I looked for you. They had taken you away and one of the soldiers said you had been killed."

Jake sank to the floor and leaned his back against the font. "All these years we both thought the other was dead. What a waste."

"Angelo, I do not think it is a waste any longer. We have found each other again."

"I understand you had a husband, and he was killed in the war."

"No, Angelo. I had no husband. I told that to Elisabeth so that she would not have to explain to her friends that she never had a father. I always understood that her father was killed in the war."

"I'm now confused. I don't understand what you mean."

Allesandra stretched out her hand in Elisabeth's direction. "Behold your daughter, Angelo."

Jake turned as pale as the marble in the Pieta. "My… daughter? Elisabeth is my daughter?"

"I have never been with a man before you or after you. You have been in my heart all these years." She sat down on the floor beside him and as he had done in that war-torn house

315

in 1943, he placed his arm around her shoulders. She trembled much as she did then and began to weep.

Blaise and Elisabeth seeing them holding one another, stood watching and smiling. Then Elisabeth also began to cry. "It's such a wonderful thing, Blaise. My mother spoke of this man…" Then a look of bewilderment came over her. "…but his name was not Jake."

"It's a long story, Elisabeth. I will tell it to you another day."

After a while, Jake helped Allesandra to her feet and placed her shoulders in his hands. Her eyes were the same…dark, beautiful, but older. She had not gained a pound over the last quarter of a century, and with the exception of a few faint wrinkles and some gray streaks in her black hair, she was the same twenty year old waif with whom he had fallen in love.

"Then do we tell her?" asked Allesandra.

"Perhaps we should first get them through their wedding so that there will be no distractions."

She smiled and her eyes glistened from the tears. "Now that we have found each other, what do we do?"

"We become very careful that we do not lose one another again."

After the send-off of the bride and groom in a horse-drawn carriage, Allesandra and Jake left Rome in her car for the hour-long trip beyond Anzio to a place called Nettuno. At the north edge of the town, she pulled the car off Highway 148 and into the Sicily-Rome American Cemetery where 7,861 white crosses lay in symmetry. They then left the car and walked uphill past the marble chapel where the names of another 3,000 American soldiers missing-in-action were carved on the walls. In the cemetery registry book, Jake found the name of the soldier and location of the grave he was looking for. Taking Allesandra by the hand, he led her through a grove of deep green cypress trees to an area of crosses in the center of the hill.

He then took from her hands a small cluster of lilies and placed them at the base of a cross on which was inscribed:

Jacobo Raul Dumas

Sergeant, 5th Army

1924-1944

New York

"Hello, Jake," he said. "It's Angelo. I'm giving you back your name, my valiant friend. I don't need it anymore. Thanks for the loan. Descanse en paz, amigo."

There are places I remember

All my life, though some have changed

Some forever not for better

Some have gone and some remain

All these places had their moments

With lovers and friends
I still can recall
Some are dead and some are living
In my life I've loved them all
But of all these friends and lovers
There is no one who compares with you.
And these memories lose their meaning
When I think of love as something new.
Though I know I'll never lose affection
For people and things that went before.
I know I'll often stop and think about them
In my life I love you more.

-The Beatles-

AFTERWORD

After I had written this novel in near entirety, I went back to do some research on the Salerno Campaign of 1943. Ironically, I came across a true story that to a degree paralleled The Valiant.

I had earlier acknowledged one William "Bill" Crawford, who had been found working as a janitor at the Air Force Academy, burying himself in his work and often averting the gaze of campus cadets. COL James Moschgat, Group Commander at the academy, gave in his address to the Class of 1977 a tribute to Bill Crawford. It was also published in his article entitled "10 Things a Janitor Can Teach You about Leadership." He said that "for many years, few of us gave him notice, rendering little more than a passing nod or throwing a curt "G'morning" in his direction… Perhaps it was because of the way he did his job. He always kept the squadron area spotlessly clean; even the toilets and showers gleamed. After all, cleaning the toilets was his job, not ours.

"Maybe it was because it was his physical appearance that made him disappear into the background. Bill didn't move very quickly. In fact, you could say he even shuffled a bit, as if he suffered some sort of injury. Face it. Bill was an old man working in a young person's world."

One day COL Moschgat was reading a book on World War II and was stunned to find out that a Private William Crawford from Colorado, assigned to the 36th Infantry Division, had been involved in a bloody battle for the town of Altavilla, Italy. He said the words in the article leapt out at him: "in the face of intense and overwhelming hostile fire…with no regard for personal safety on his own initiative, Private Crawford single- handedly attacked fortified enemy positions…" For his "conspicuous gallantry and intrepidity at risk of life above and beyond the call of duty," the president of the United States awarded to him the Medal of Honor.

Moschgat said that when the faculty and cadet corps found out about it and engaged Mr. Crawford on the subject, with great humility he replied, "That was one day in my life and happened a long time ago." He then said he had to get back to his chores.

After that, cadets who had once passed by with hardly a glance, then greeted him with a respectful "Good morning, Mr. Crawford." And those who had before "left messes for the janitor to clean up started taking it upon themselves to put things in order."

Pulling a few tenets from COL Moschgat's article on leadership traits, we must always be cautious of labels. Everyone deserves respect. Smile and speak to those doing even the most trivial of jobs. Not only are they and their jobs also important, but you never know when one will turn up a hero.

ABOUT THE AUTHOR

Lee Martin is a native West Virginian, now living in the Atlanta, Georgia area. After a career in the United States Army, which included a Vietnam combat tour and for which he was awarded the Bronze Star and Vietnamese Gallantry Cross, he retired with the rank of Colonel. He has a Masters and Doctorate in Counseling, is an adjunct professor at a Georgia university teaching a battery of Psychology courses, and works part-time as a Marriage and Family Therapist.

Kindle Customer

5.0 out of 5 stars **A great story.**

Reviewed in the United States on November 27, 2016

Verified Purchase

A fiction story that parallels a true story. I have read several books by Colonel Martin and found them to be good reads. This book had interesting characters and the ending of this book was outstanding.

Bill Deck

5.0 out of 5 stars **Great Book**

Reviewed in the United States on April 2, 2012

I could not put the book down. You'll keep trying to anticipate the next twist. If you're my age, it might even conger up some memories from the past.

Richard D. Parmenter
5.0 out of 5 stars **Five Stars**

Reviewed in the United States on December 20, 2017

Great Book enjoyed very much!

Roy Stanley Fuller

5.0 out of 5 stars **The Valiant**

Reviewed in the United States on December 9, 2011

"The Valiant". The novel is the work of a mature author, well in control of plot and structure. Clues are distributed carefully to keep the reader alert and interested throughout. In terms of characterization, the main protagonist is well-defined and believable. The "crime story" aspect is particularly successful, keeping the reader guessing until late in the work regarding the identity of the culprit. The "happy ending" is pleasing and emotionally satisfying. It was nice to encounter what many Europeans would consider a "positive minded" American finish! Such a dénouement is rarer here. Dr. Sharon Fuller & Dr. Roy Fuller

William M. Morris

5.0 out of 5 stars The Valiant by Lee Martin is a Must Read!

Reviewed in the United States on January 31, 2010

Mystery novelist COL Lee Martin continues to excite his audience with his latest release of "The Valiant". I have read most of his books, but "The Valiant" is by far my favorite. In baseball terms, COL Lee Martin has hit a standup homerun. "The Valiant" is an intriguing mystery novel that includes a silent hero, a HOT Blonde Liberian, and a cop that doesn't quit until he gets answers to his questions. The Valiant will keep you on the edge of your seat to the very end. This is a book you'll find hard to put down. You might also want to review

Jim Puckett

5.0 out of 5 stars Great Book

Reviewed in the United States on July 23, 2010

The Valiant is a great book, and a must read. I have read all of Lee Martin's books, and this is one of the best. Once you start reading you will not want to put it down.

linda lo

5.0 out of 5 stars **good read**

Reviewed in the United Kingdom on April 17, 2013

lee always astounds me with his versatility no one book is the same good read did enjoy this book very much

5.0 out of 5 stars **A great story.**

Reviewed in the United States on November 27, 2016

A fiction story that parallels a true story. I have read several books by Colonel Martin and found them to be good reads. This book had interesting characters and the ending of this book was outstanding.

Bill Deck

5.0 out of 5 stars **Great Book**

Reviewed in the United States on April 2, 2012

I could not put the book down. You'll keep trying to anticipate the next twist. If you're my age, it might even conger up some memories from the past.

Richard D. Parmenter

5.0 out of 5 stars **Five Stars**

Reviewed in the United States on December 20, 2017

Great Book enjoyed very much!

The Valiant

5.0 out of 5 stars **The Valiant**

Reviewed in the United States on December 9, 2011

"The Valiant". The novel is the work of a mature author, well in control of plot and structure. Clues are distributed carefully to keep the reader alert and interested throughout. In terms of characterization, the main protagonist is well-defined and believable. The "crime story" aspect is particularly successful, keeping the reader guessing until late in the work regarding the identity of the culprit. The "happy ending" is pleasing and emotionally satisfying. It was nice to encounter what many Europeans would consider a "positive-minded" American finish! Such a dénouement is rarer here. Dr. Sharon Fuller & Dr. Roy Fuller

William M. Morris

5.0 out of 5 stars **The Valiant by Lee Martin is a Must Read!**

Reviewed in the United States on January 31, 2010

Mystery novelist COL Lee Martin continues to excite his audience with his latest release of "The Valiant". I have read most of his books, but "The Valiant" is by far my favorite. In baseball terms, COL Lee Martin has hit a standup homerun. "The Valiant" is an intriguing mystery novel that includes a silent hero, a HOT Blonde Liberian, and a cop that doesn't quit until he gets answers to his questions. The Valiant will keep you on the edge of your seat to the very end. This is a book you'll find hard to put down. You might also want to review

[...].

Jim Puckett

Reviewed in the United States on July 23, 2010

The Valiant is a great book, and a must read. I have read all of Lee Martin's books, and this is one of the best. Once you start reading you will not want to put it down.

Top reviews from other countries

linda lo
5.0 out of 5 stars **good read**

Reviewed in the United Kingdom on April 17, 2013

Lee always astounds me with his versatility no one book is the same good read did enjoy this book very much

**View all novels from
Col. Lee Martin in our website:**

https://colonelleemartinbooks.com